PRAISE FOR DONNA GRANT
ROMANCE NOVELS

"Grant's ability to quickly convey complicated backstory makes this jam-packed love story accessible even to new or periodic readers." - *Publisher's Weekly*

"Donna Grant has given the paranormal genre a burst of fresh air…" – *San Francisco Book Review*

"The premise is dramatic and heartbreaking; the characters are colorful and engaging; the romance is spirited and seductive." – *The Reading Cafe*

"The central romance, fueled by a hostage drama, plays out in glorious detail against a backdrop of multiple ongoing issues in the "Dark Kings" books. This seemingly penultimate installment creates a nice segue to a climactic end." – *Library Journal*

"…intense romance amid the growing war between the Dragons and the Dark Fae is scorching hot." – *Booklist*

Dragonfire ~ Dragon Claimed ~ Ignite
Fever ~ Dragon Lost ~ Flame ~ Inferno
A Dragon's Tale (Whisky and Wishes: *A Holiday Novella*,
Heart of Gold: *A Valentine's Novella*, & Of Fire and Flame)
My Fiery Valentine ~ The Dragon King Coloring Book
Dragon King Special Edition Character Coloring Book: Rhi

DARK WARRIORS SERIES

Midnight's Master ~ Midnight's Lover ~ Midnight's Seduction
Midnight's Warrior ~ Midnight's Kiss ~ Midnight's Captive
Midnight's Temptation ~ Midnight's Promise
Midnight's Surrender

CHIASSON SERIES

Wild Fever ~ Wild Dream ~ Wild Need
Wild Flame ~ Wild Rapture

LARUE SERIES

Moon Kissed ~ Moon Thrall ~ Moon Struck ~ Moon Bound

WICKED TREASURES

Seized by Passion ~ Enticed by Ecstasy ~ Captured by Desire
Books 1-3: Wicked Treasures Box Set

HISTORICAL PARANORMAL

THE KINDRED SERIES

Everkin ~ Eversong ~ Everwylde ~ Everbound
Evernight ~ Everspell

KINDRED: THE FATED SERIES

Rage

DARK SWORD SERIES

Dangerous Highlander ~ Forbidden Highlander
Wicked Highlander ~ Untamed Highlander
Shadow Highlander ~ Darkest Highlander

ROGUES OF SCOTLAND SERIES

The Craving ~ The Hunger ~ The Tempted ~ The Seduced
Books 1-4: Rogues of Scotland Box Set

THE SHIELDS SERIES

A Dark Guardian ~ A Kind of Magic ~ A Dark Seduction
A Forbidden Temptation ~ A Warrior's Heart
Mystic Trinity (a series connecting novel)

DRUIDS GLEN SERIES

Highland Mist ~ Highland Nights ~ Highland Dawn
Highland Fires ~ Highland Magic
Mystic Trinity (a series connecting novel)

SISTERS OF MAGIC TRILOGY

Shadow Magic ~ Echoes of Magic ~ Dangerous Magic

Books 1-3: Sisters of Magic Box Set

THE ROYAL CHRONICLES NOVELLA SERIES

Prince of Desire ~ Prince of Seduction

Prince of Love ~ Prince of Passion

Books 1-4: The Royal Chronicles Box Set

Mystic Trinity (a series connecting novel)

DARK BEGINNINGS: A FIRST IN SERIES BOXSET

Chiasson Series, Book 1: Wild Fever

LaRue Series, Book 1: Moon Kissed

The Royal Chronicles Series, Book 1: Prince of Desire

<u>MILITARY ROMANCE / ROMANTIC SUSPENSE</u>

SONS OF TEXAS SERIES

The Hero ~ The Protector ~ The Legend

The Defender ~ The Guardian

COWBOY / CONTEMPORARY

HEART OF TEXAS SERIES

The Christmas Cowboy Hero ~ Cowboy, Cross My Heart
My Favorite Cowboy ~ A Cowboy Like You
Looking for a Cowboy ~ A Cowboy Kind of Love

STAND ALONE BOOKS

That Cowboy of Mine
Home for a Cowboy Christmas
Mutual Desire
Forever Mine
Savage Moon

**Check out Donna Grant's Online Store at
www.DonnaGrant.com/shop
for autographed books, character
themed goodies, and more!**

This is a work of fiction. All of the characters, organizations, and events portrayed in this novel are either products of the author's imagination or are used fictitiously.

www.DonnaGrant.com
www.MotherofDragonsBooks.com

This is a work of fiction. All of the characters, organizations, and events portrayed in this novel are either products of the author's imagination or are used fictitiously.

DRAGON MINE
© 2021 by DLC Craft, LLC
Cover Design © 2021 by Charity Heady
Formatting © 2021 by Charity Heady
ISBN 13: 978-1-958353-04-2
Available in ebook, audio, and print editions.
All rights reserved.

Excerpt from DARK ALPHA'S NEED
© 2021 DL Craft, LLC
Cover Design © 2021 by Charity Heady

Blurb from DRAGON UNBOUND
© 2021 DL Craft, LLC
© 2021 by 1001 Dark Nights

www.DonnaGrant.com
www.MotherOfDragonsBooks.com

A DRAGON KINGS® NOVEL

DRAGON MINE

CHAPTER ONE

Dreagan
February

"Vaughn."

He turned to the seductive voice, seeking the supple body, the undeniable pleasure he knew awaited them both. His arms wound around her as his lips descended upon hers. The kiss was fire and flame, consuming and devouring.

Desire and lust collided in a beautiful, timeless dance.

They were skin to skin, their limbs tangled as they sought to get closer, ever closer. The passion had begun as a spark, but that had soon turned into a raging inferno. The intensity of what he felt, the force of his need, his *hunger*, left him shaking. Completely addicted.

And she was his only cure.

Her skin was as soft as silk. Her lips decadent and utterly erotic. Her long hair brushed against his body, teasing him. He couldn't stop running his hands over her sensual form. There wasn't another soul like her in the entire universe.

She sighed as he kissed down her neck and cupped her full breast. Her breath hitched when his tongue flicked over her nipple. He could feel the heat of her body, hear the soft cries falling from her lips, and taste the sweat and desire on her skin.

He groaned when her fingers wrapped around his arousal. She moved her hand up and down his length, bringing him closer and closer to orgasm. He didn't know how many times they had shared their bodies. Whenever he was with her, time ceased, and he forgot everything else. There was nothing but her.

His breathing hitched. He wanted to stop her, to wait to take his pleasure until he'd made her climax at least twice. Her lips traveled down his neck and lower to his chest across his tattoo. The skin beneath the tat warmed from her touch. Her lips wrapped around his nipple, and she flicked her tongue over the hard bud. He was powerless to resist her. Wherever she touched, he *burned*. Eager.

Aching for more.

With every pump of her hand, he felt his orgasm approaching. He tried to open his eyes and see her face, but he couldn't. Then, it didn't matter because his body flooded with ecstasy. He reached for her, needing to hold her, to feel her against him.

Only she was gone.

Vaughn wrenched open his eyes to find himself alone, his harsh breaths filling his bedroom. He glanced down at his stomach to see evidence of his dream.

"Fuck," he murmured and rolled out of bed to clean himself off.

He tossed aside the towel and stood in the doorway of the bathroom, looking at his bed. The sheets were in disarray, the pillows on the floor. If he didn't know better, he'd say he'd had a fun romp with someone. Only, there hadn't been anyone but *her*.

And, unfortunately, he hadn't seen her anywhere but in his dreams in a very long time.

When would this end? Vaughn wasn't sure how much more he could take. It had been thousands of years since she had come into his life. One night. One beautiful, incredible night. Then, she vanished like smoke. No matter how far and wide he looked, he had yet to find her. He didn't even know her name.

Hell, he barely remembered her face. No matter how hard he tried to recall details of her, he came up empty. And the harder he tried, the more what little he did recall faded.

Vaughn shook his head as he dropped his chin to his chest. He could remember every detail of her body. He knew her sighs, her soft moans of pleasure. He knew the smell of her skin, the feel of her against him.

It was the other details he couldn't recollect that made him want to bellow to the heavens in frustration.

That night, so long ago, had been clear and sultry. Something had drawn him out. The full moon hung large and low in the sky as billions of stars watched from above. And the magic had been heavy and intoxicating.

He had left Dreagan with no particular destination in mind, flying for miles until he spotted the fires. He'd landed unseen far from the village and walked there in his human form. The Celtic tribe's cheers had been boisterous and infectious. They danced and celebrated their victory against an enemy around huge fires with flames that attempted to reach the moon.

They welcomed him, shoving a horn of mead into his hand. Vaughn had always had a particular interest in the Celts. They were attuned to the Earth in a way that others weren't. He'd been content to watch them despite their attempts to get him to join them.

Vaughn had moved away from the group and leaned against an ancient, gnarled oak with limbs that twisted and reached outward. He watched the festivities with a smile, content to witness the celebration. The mead was particularly good. Or perhaps it was the magic in the air.

The British Isle thrummed with magic. It was why the Dragon Kings had made their home in Scotland, where the heart of the planet's magic sprang forth. Dragon Kings were especially in tune with magic in all beings and creatures. Many times, mortals had no idea that magic was there, sometimes even changing events. That was because the humans couldn't feel it. But Vaughn did. It was thick, hanging heavily in the air like an invisible mist. Even if he had wanted to walk away, he wouldn't have been able to.

Then, he'd seen her across one of the great fires. She had stood staring at him. He'd immediately felt her pull, the attraction instant and irresistible. That's when he realized that she was the reason he had been drawn from Dreagan. The firelight gave her blond locks a red-orange tint. They said nothing as they started toward each other in unison, weaving through others and around the fires.

Until they were face-to-face.

For the first time in his life, he couldn't find words. He didn't know what to say. And yet, there was so much he wanted to say to her. She took his hand and, with a smile, led him to a cottage. The red-orange glow from a fire in the hearth coated the inside of the home. She faced him, and before he could speak, her mouth was on his.

Everything he'd ever felt, *ever would feel* had been in her kiss.

The emotions had been crushing and exhilarating at first. But it didn't take long for them to consume him. Just as his desire did.

He forgot about hiding who he was from the mortals, forgot about not showing his magic in front of them—because he had needed to feel her skin against his. Without hesitation, he used magic to remove their clothes.

Vaughn had no idea how many times they shared their bodies that night. Passion had never overtaken him in such a way before. Not before then. And not since. It wasn't until the sun woke him and he found himself alone in the bed that he realized he didn't know her name. He hadn't been too worried, at first. He'd assumed the cottage was hers.

But as the hours passed, and she didn't return, he decided to look for her. No one in the village knew of who he spoke. Worry crept in, but he didn't give up. He spent over a week with the tribe, hoping to see her again. With each day that passed without her, Vaughn began to wonder if she had been real at all.

He returned to Dreagan and tried to forget that night—and her. But it was impossible. That's when his search began. He'd looked far and wide, combing through the tiniest villages to the biggest cities, to no avail. Even when he realized that she was most likely dead, he still looked. Hoping against hope that he would somehow find her one day.

Perhaps that's why he discovered her in his dreams.

Vaughn blew out a breath and lifted his head, gently shaking the memories back into their corners. He couldn't go on like this much longer. He didn't know if this unknown woman he'd searched for through thousands of years was his mate or not. Maybe not knowing who she was had caused him to latch onto her and dream about her.

"Then why are my dreams different each time?" he asked aloud.

Vaughn made his bed, carefully pulling the covers taut and smoothing out any wrinkles in the tan tweed comforter. He meticulously placed the two black and tan windowpane-patterned euro shams in place. Next were the two copper suede shams, followed by an accent pillow in faux fur.

He strode into his closet and looked at the rows of suits, dress shirts, and ties. It was rare that he went a day without wearing *his uniform*, as Rhys called it. Vaughn quite liked his suits, as was evident in the number of them he owned. Today, however, he couldn't decide on one. Ever since he'd woken from the dream, he'd felt…off.

To put off making a decision, he showered and shaved. After he put on underwear, he found himself back in his closet, still unable to pick out a suit. A knock on his door pulled his attention.

"Enter," he called.

The door opened, and Kendrick came up behind him a

moment later. "You look like shite."

"Thanks," Vaughn replied without looking at him. Kendrick was silent for so long, Vaughn turned to him.

Kendrick quirked a dark brow. "What's going on?"

"Nothing."

Kendrick's green eyes regarded him solemnly.

Vaughn sighed. "I had a rough night."

"That, I can believe." Kendrick relaxed and leaned a shoulder against the doorway. "Since you are no' dressed, I guess you've no' heard."

"Heard what?"

"Rhi found a Fae doorway on Dreagan."

Vaughn instantly went on alert. "Where?" he demanded.

Kendrick's lips curved into a smile. "You sure are in a hurry to get to the other realm."

"Because of our dragons."

"Others might buy that, but I doona." Kendrick glanced at the floor. "The doorway is in the Dragonwood."

Vaughn watched Kendrick closely. "Why do you no' believe me?"

"We all want our dragons again, but these are no longer ours. There willna be any of ours left after so long. Who's to say we're no' challenged when we get there?"

"You think I'm ready to die?"

Kendrick shook his head slowly. "I think there's something else driving you."

"What?"

"I'm no' sure. Are you?"

Vaughn stared at him before looking away. "I can no' explain my need to get to the other realm."

"To look for the mystery woman you've searched for all these years, perhaps?"

Vaughn's gaze jerked to his friend. "How did you know about that?"

"You got drunk one night long, long ago and spoke about her."

That was one of the reasons Vaughn didn't like to drink in excess. Because everything always came back to her.

"Is she your mate?"

Vaughn shrugged. "I'm no' sure. It could be nothing more than me wanting to find her."

"If she's mortal, she's long passed, brother."

"I know."

Kendrick's brows drew together as he pushed away from the doorjamb and dropped his arms to his sides. "You think she's more?"

"I didna feel any magic, but then again, I wasna looking for it."

"Even if she was a Druid, her life span would still be that of a mortal."

Vaughn stopped him with a look. "I have no answers for you or me. You're asking the same questions I've asked for far too long. I wish I knew why I couldna forget about this woman."

"If you want to go to the other realm, you'd better get dressed. Con and Rhi are headed there shortly."

Vaughn spun around and reached for a shirt and jeans, yanking them on. He was halfway down the hall before he realized that he didn't have shoes. He used magic to call boots to him without breaking his stride.

"Are you coming to the other realm," he asked Kendrick.

When silence met his words, he looked around to find Kendrick gone. Vaughn rushed down the stairs to look for Constantine. When he couldn't find the King of Dragon Kings, Vaughn took the stairs three at a time to get to Con's office on the third floor. The door was open when he arrived, so Vaughn walked in to find Con sitting at his desk, sorting through a file of papers.

Con glanced up, then did a double-take and lifted his blond head. "Vaughn."

"I heard about the doorway."

Con set the papers and his Montblanc pen aside. "I can no' remember the last time I saw you in jeans."

"What does my attire have to do with anything?" Vaughn heard the anger in his words, but he wouldn't be refused. He was going to the other realm. One way or another.

Con sat back in his chair and laced his fingers together over his stomach. "You do understand there's a real possibility the twins may challenge any Dragon Kings who go through the doorway? My children might rule the dragons, but individual Kings going to their realm may shift the hierarchy."

"If I'm challenged, then I'm challenged."

"Every King wants to see their dragons again. Believe me, Vaughn, I und–"

"It's more than that," he said over Con.

The look in Con's black eyes grew intense, though his calm expression never changed. "Explain."

It wasn't a request, and Vaughn didn't treat it as one. "I'm looking for someone."

"Your mate?"

"I wish I knew. An eon ago, I happened across a celebrating Celtic tribe. I stayed to observe. The magic that night was…" He paused, searching for the right word. "Piercing. Its power felt by even the humans, though they had no idea what it was. We are made of magic, so you can imagine what it felt like."

"Euphoria."

Vaughn nodded and ran a hand down his face. "Across one of the fires, I saw a woman. I've never felt such instant attraction and recognition before. It was a night I've never forgotten. In the morning, she was gone. Like she never existed."

Con said nothing as he stood and walked to the sideboard, pouring a dram of whisky. He turned to Vaughn and handed him the glass. "It's early, but you look like you need it."

Vaughn accepted it and drank.

Con poured another and took it back to his desk, setting it down. "I suppose you looked for this woman?"

"Everywhere. I stayed a week with the tribe, hoping she would return. No one knew her. I continued my search, extending outward, bit by bit, thinking she might be in the next tribe. Years turned into decades. Decades to centuries. Centuries to millennia. I know if she was human, that she's long dead."

"But you keep hoping."

Vaughn looked into Con's eyes. "I know she's out there. I feel it. Here," he said and pointed at his chest.

"You want to check another realm."

"Would you no'?"

Con grinned. "You know I would've."

"I'm going to this new realm. You can try to stop me, but I'll find a way."

"I never intended to stop you."

Relief poured through Vaughn.

"Doona get too happy yet," Con cautioned. "Only three of us are going. I doona want to overwhelm the twins or the occupants of that realm. I also doona expect we'll stay long. This is the first time Rhi and I will have met our children. We're hoping the doorway is their idea of a peace offering."

Vaughn frowned. "Why would it be anything else?"

"Need I remind you that Varek was taken from our world to Zora?"

"That worked out."

Con snorted. "Barely. The fact of the matter is that someone on that realm can reach through and take one of us."

"They've never done it before."

"That we know of."

Vaughn squared his shoulders. "I know the risks. So do you and Rhi. It isna stopping either of you, and it willna stop me."

"The woman you seek might no' be on Zora."

"She might no'. I doona even know if she's the reason I feel the overwhelming need to go. Right now, it doesna matter why."

Con reached for his whisky and tossed it back. "Who knows when we'll get a taste of our whisky again? Come. Zora awaits us."

Vaughn walked out with Con, a smile on his face. Whatever happened, whatever awaited him, this was his path.

His destiny.

CHAPTER TWO

Zora

Eurwen gasped as she sat up in bed, sweat covering her. Her breaths were ragged and loud to her ears. And her body pulsed with an unquenchable hunger.

She drew in a shaky breath as she held the sheet against her bare chest. With her lips parted, she stared at the wall across from her bed, but her mind drifted back to the dream. The beautiful, erotic reverie.

And Vaughn.

Just thinking about him made her skin flush with need. It didn't matter how much time had passed, or how many worlds away they were, she couldn't forget him. And she had tried. So many times.

Just when she thought she might be able to, he found her in her dreams. She knew it was him because she didn't have that power. She could block him, but her heart wouldn't let her. Neither would her body.

Eurwen lay down to stare at the ceiling, even as her eyes filled with tears. Soul-deep loneliness kept her reaching out to Vaughn time and again. It would be easy for her to return to Earth and seek him out, but she hadn't. Partly because of her twin, Brandr, but also because she feared the intense feelings Vaughn stirred within her.

A violent pounding sounded on the door, jerking her gaze to it. Then her brother shouted her name.

"I'll be out in a moment," she called.

Thankfully, he walked away without saying more. There were many wonderful things about having a twin. However, others caused strife—especially when one twin tried to hide something from the other.

She and Brandr had ventured to Earth numerous times. Sometimes, it was to spy on their parents. Other times, it was to learn about the inhabitants of the realm. Eurwen kept the times she'd gone alone to herself. While she assumed that Brandr had likely done the same, she never brought it up in case he *hadn't* gone alone.

Her brother had very strong feelings about their parents. She had felt the same for a long time. Eurwen wasn't sure when things began to change for her, but once they had, she hadn't been able to turn them around. And she didn't want to.

What happened between their parents was between them and shouldn't involve her or Brandr. Especially since so much had been out of everyone's control. Erith had explained that to both of them dozens of times. The goddess and leader of a group of Fae called the Reapers had raised them. Erith, also known as Death, had done her best to convince Eurwen and

Brandr to get to know Constantine and Rhi. At the time, Eurwen had been just as adamant as her brother about refusing to let Con or Rhi know of their existence.

That secret had weighed heavily on Erith. The goddess could have ignored them and told Con and Rhi anyway, but she had respected their wishes. Though Eurwen knew that it was mostly because Erith had a difficult time accepting her role in things.

Eurwen drew in a deep breath and released it before sitting up and swinging her legs over the side of the bed. She rose and snapped her fingers, using magic to right the covers. She walked naked to her wardrobe and opened the doors to stare at the garments within.

Things on Zora were vastly different than on Earth. When she had secretly followed her mother on a shopping spree during one venture, Eurwen had picked up several items herself. She didn't particularly like shopping alone, though. It had been hard not to call out to Rhi and meet her mother for the first time.

It made her think of the doorway she had created for her parents—and any Dragon King who wanted to come through. A few days had passed since she'd opened the portal between their worlds. Eurwen had expected her parents to have already come through, and she was a little disappointed in their hesitation.

Then again, she and Brandr had kept them out for a long time. Maybe this was their way of getting back at her and her brother.

"No," she said aloud. "They aren't like that."

Eurwen carefully chose her outfit for the day as she had

for the past few. She wanted to look her best when her
parents arrived. She wasn't sure what she'd say to them. Or
even how to talk. She and Brandr had known of them for
eons, while Con and Rhi had only recently discovered their
existence.

Once dressed, Eurwen walked out of her dwelling atop the
mountain and breathed in the warm morning air. The sky was
clear around Cairnkeep. In the distance, she saw a group of
dragons flying. Birdsong mingled with dragons' roars. It was a
sound that always gave her peace.

Zora was a realm full of breathtaking scenery and beauty
unmatched in the universe. And Cairnkeep was an area that
she and Brandr had created for themselves. It was perfect.
Dragons were always near. It was similar to Dreagan, though
different in one key element. But it was her home, and she
loved it dearly.

While Zora offered a safe place for dragons, a species of
humans had unfortunately come once again. Eurwen didn't
want to think what could've happened had she and Brandr not
already been here.

She had seen firsthand what the mortals of Earth had done
to that realm and the dragons there. Neither she nor Brandr
would allow that to happen on Zora. It was why the realm was
divided. The humans had their space, and she and Brandr had
been generous in allotting them territory.

"I can no' believe you've jeopardized our peace."

She briefly closed her eyes at the sound of her brother's
angry voice behind her. Eurwen didn't turn to him as she said,
"I want to know Con and Rhi."

"Then visit them on Earth," Brandr stated.

"You do understand that everything that happened to us isn't their fault?"

He snorted in derision. "I beg to differ. I can pinpoint exactly where it all went wrong."

Eurwen blew out a breath. "You can't blame Con for everything."

"I bloody well can."

"You're acting like a petulant child."

Brandr moved to stand beside her. "I remember a time when you felt as I did."

"I matured."

He turned his head to her. "Something changed you."

"Change is constant. We all change every day." She looked at him, their gazes clashing. He had the same black eyes as their father and the same midnight hair as Rhi. Brandr wore his straight hair to his shoulders and pulled back in a queue. The smile that had always come so easily to him was gone. "For instance, you've become more bitter."

"Because my sister no longer thinks as I do."

"We're twins, Brandr. That doesn't mean we share a brain."

He narrowed his black eyes at her. "You never used to keep secrets from me."

"Everyone keeps secrets of some kind."

"Inviting Con and Rhi to Zora is a mistake, Eurwen. Mark my words," he replied and turned on his heel to walk away.

She looked down into the valley below, where the doorway she'd created stood. There was still no sign of her parents. Eurwen heard the beat of wings and looked up to see a flock of yellow dragons pass overhead. They roared in response to seeing her. She smiled and waved, but the grin dimmed when she thought about the Dragon Kings on Earth, having to live without their dragons. She couldn't imagine a day without them, much less eons of time.

As much as she'd like to discount her brother's words, she knew he had a point. If the Dragon Kings came to Zora, it could disrupt everything. They were Kings for a reason. The magic had chosen them as the strongest of their clan to lead. That wasn't how things worked on Zora, and the Kings might try to take advantage of that.

She and Brandr were powerful, but could they stand against all the Kings? The answer was no, and she was sure that's what Brandr worried about. To him, the Kings had lost their right to rule the dragons when they sent them away.

It was a discussion she and Brandr had had numerous times. While it was a real possibility that inviting Con and Rhi could result in a war, Eurwen didn't have a choice. Just as she and Brandr hadn't had an option for coming to Zora to lead the dragons, she'd had to form the doorway to Dreagan.

If that meant the end of her idyllic life, then so be it. Change was inevitable. Nothing stayed the same, and to try and force it put everything out of balance. Whatever force pushed her, she would listen. Come what may.

She walked to the edge of the cliff and stepped off, shifting into her dragon form and opening her wings to glide upon the wind.

CHAPTER THREE

Impatience burned hotly within Vaughn as he stood in the Dragonwood with Con. Only Fae could see the doorways they created. Vaughn had no idea where the door was, but Con had pointed to some rocks that Rhi had apparently marked.

"I doona know what's taking Rhi so long," Con stated, annoyance deepening his voice.

Vaughn didn't answer. His gaze was on the place where the doorway stood. He couldn't wait to walk through it. He wanted to go through it immediately, instead of waiting for Rhi.

"Is it my daughter?"

Vaughn's head jerked to Con as he frowned. "What?"

"The woman you search for. You saw her when Erith opened the small window between the realms."

"I got a glimpse of the twins. I didna see either's face. To answer your question, I'm no' sure."

Con nodded, his black gaze dropping to the ground for a moment. "Did the woman tell you her name?"

"We didna talk that night."

"But she knew yours?"

Vaughn shook his head. "No. At least, I didna tell her. As I said, we didna say much. At least, with words."

But he'd heard her say his name in his dream. Was it because he'd wanted to hear it? Or had she known it? The questions were eating him alive.

"What?" Con pressed.

Vaughn swallowed and shrugged. "It might be nothing."

"It's always something. What is it?"

"In my dreams, she says my name."

It was Con's turn to frown. "How often do you dream of her?"

"Frequently."

"Does she always say your name?"

"No."

"Do you see her face?"

Vaughn shook his head once more. "I try, but I'm unable to see her clearly. I feel her. I hear her, but that's all."

"You're the one with the power of dream manipulation. Are you using it?"

"I have to be near a person to use that gift."

Con quirked a blond brow. "Could it be just a dream?"

"It feels too real for that."

"I'm no' liking the sound of this. After someone on Zora took and imprisoned Varek, I'm no' sure you should go with us."

Vaughn crossed his arms over his chest and widened his

stance. "You're my King, and I've always obeyed you. But I willna on this. I'm going."

"Bloody hell," Con said as he ran a hand through his wavy blond hair. "We doona know what to expect when we get to Zora. No' with the twins, no' with the dragons, and certainly no' with the humans who live there."

"Varek came out fine in the end."

Con cut him a dark look. "Barely."

"We've lived for so many lifetimes. Both with our dragons and without. Varek will be there, as will the twins. If the humans try anything, we'll be ready."

"Rhi!" Con called, irritation tingeing his voice.

Vaughn waited for her to appear. A Fae always heard their name called, no matter where they were on a realm. Several minutes ticked by as Con paced, his agitation growing with each heartbeat. It was all Vaughn could do not to pace alongside him.

"Sorry," Rhi said in her Irish accent as she appeared beside Con.

Vaughn turned to Constantine's mate. Rhi's black hair and silver eyes identified her as a Light Fae. She wore her long tresses down with the sides pulled away from her face and gathered at the back of her head.

"What took you so long?" Con asked. "I thought you were ready half an hour ago."

She shrugged and glanced at Vaughn. "I didn't like what I was wearing."

Vaughn hid his smile. If Rhi knew one thing, it was fashion. The fact that she'd had a difficult time deciding on something to wear spoke of how deeply her anxiety ran at finally meeting her children. She typically wore all black, occasionally adding gold to match Con's dragon color. Today, Rhi wore a pale gold silk button-down blouse tucked into black leather pants, paired with her customary favorite shoe— Christian Louboutin—in a black mesh peep-toe bootie with snakeskin accents.

"My love," Con said in a soft voice as he ran his palms down her arms to take her hands in his. "You look beautiful, no matter what you wear."

She smiled softly. "We're meeting our children. I want to make a good impression."

"You will," he assured her.

Vaughn felt like an intruder as the two shared an intimate moment where they whispered words to each other. He turned his back on them, his mind returning to his dream. The sound of the woman's voice had been husky, seductive. He wished he knew if he had concocted her in his mind or not. She felt like the woman he'd spent that one amazing night with so long ago.

Their moment together had become branded in his mind and soul. Nothing, not even time, could make him forget her. He had to find her. Somehow. Some way. Whether she was a magical being and immortal as he was, or reincarnated. Until he held her in his arms again, he wouldn't stop looking.

Someone touched his arm, startling him. Vaughn swiveled his head to the side to see Rhi standing between him and Con. Rhi might be Fae royalty, but she was also his queen. She took her position as Con's mate seriously. Her love for the Dragon Kings and all those associated with them was beyond reproach. She had proven it time and again.

"Are we ready?" she asked, looking from Vaughn to
Constantine.

Con winked at her before meeting Vaughn's gaze. They
nodded at each other, then faced forward.

Rhi linked her arm with Con's and took a deep breath.
"I've been waiting for this day. Let it be everything we hope it
is," she whispered softly.

Vaughn held back as the couple walked through the
doorway together. He watched as they disappeared from the
realm. With one last look around at the Dragonwood, he
followed. The moment he stepped across the threshold, he
found himself in the other realm. The beauty was
indescribable.

Trees reached high into the vivid blue of the sky. There
were tall mountain peaks tipped with snow, deep valleys
awash in vibrant greens, and flowers running the gambit of
colors. Then he heard them.

Dragons.

His knees went weak to once again hear their many roars.
Vaughn closed his eyes as emotions crashed into him like a
tsunami, pummeling him one after another. For untold years,
he'd only heard the roars of the other Dragon Kings—and
only when there was a thunderstorm, so it hid the sound from
humans. He'd forgotten the different dragons' calls. Some
long and loud, others short and soft, and in every octave
imaginable.

The Kings had long feared that their dragons had perished.
Despite that, they held onto hope that the dragons were alive.
To finally find the realm and hear them was a dream come
true.

He opened his eyes and turned in a circle as he searched the sky. It didn't take him long to find a group of dragons flying nearby. More lay sunning in a valley. He saw Reds, Whites, Blacks, Golds, Silvers, Hunter Greens, and Yellows. There were Jades, Bronzes, Clarets, Ambers, Greys, Browns, and Ivories and even some mixed colors. When he saw his Teals, he dropped to his knees, emotion tightening his throat. His eyes watered as he watched a group of adolescents playing on the side of a mountain, taking turns seeing who could push the others off. It was the most beautiful sight that Vaughn had ever witnessed.

A hand clamped down on his shoulder. He knew it was Con without looking. Vaughn wasn't sure he ever wanted to leave this realm. Regardless of whatever negative things it held, the dragons were here. A Dragon King needed his dragons to fulfill his duties. Every King at Dreagan had suffered without their clan.

Vaughn finally looked up at Con. The King of Dragon Kings was just as moved at the sight of the dragons. They smiled through their tears, each understanding the Kings on Earth should witness the spectacular sight on Zora.

"Con," Rhi called.

Vaughn looked at Rhi to find her gaze directed up the slope of the mountain. He jumped to his feet at the same time Con turned and walked to his mate. Vaughn spotted the woman observing them. His stomach dropped to his feet as shock rippled through him.

He *knew* her.

He could barely draw breath as he stared at the woman he'd been searching eons for. The breeze teased the ends of her long, golden locks that hung to her waist. She stood tall, her bearing regal. Her gaze never wavered as she looked upon Con and Rhi. She was dressed in all white. Her sleeveless top molded to her breasts, stopping a few inches below, displaying the tight muscles of her stomach. The hem of her skirt brushed the grass, hiding her feet as the breeze moved the thin material, molding it to her legs.

Vaughn knew in an instant that this was one of Con and Rhi's twins. Nor did it go unnoticed that the doorway leading to Zora from Earth had been set in a valley, causing anyone who came through to look up.

"By the stars," Rhi whispered, her voice shaking with emotion.

Vaughn was thinking the same thing. Was the woman the reason he'd felt such a driving need to come to this realm? Would she recognize him? Would they share the same fiery attraction as the first time they met?

She didn't come to them. In the end, Con, his arm around Rhi, started toward her. Vaughn followed several paces behind the couple. The climb was steep and awe-inspiring. The more Vaughn saw of the realm, the more beautiful he thought it was. His heart sighed in contentment, knowing the dragons had found such a planet. No place was perfect, but this world came close. It reminded him so much of what their realm had once been before the humans arrived.

Before the war.

Vaughn put all of that out of his mind as they drew nearer to the woman. He didn't know what to say to her. Thankfully, he didn't have to since Con and Rhi were there and spoke first.

"We've been waiting a long time to meet you," Rhi told her daughter.

Con nodded, smiling. "Thank you for opening the doorway."

She didn't respond. Instead, her sharp gaze slid to Vaughn. It felt as if he'd been kicked by a dragon. He stared into her intelligent, spirited eyes, mesmerized by the various shades of silver. In that moment, in that very instant, he realized that she remembered him and their night together, as well.

Finally, she broke eye contact and returned her attention to her parents. She took a deep breath and said, "I'm Eurwen."

"Means gold and fair," Con said. "Which you certainly are."

Vaughn couldn't agree more. Now that he knew her name, something else bound them together. The more he stared at her, the more he suspected that his dreams hadn't been dreams at all. They had been real. Though he hadn't yet pieced together how that was possible. At least, he had her name now.

Rhi blinked as tears coursed down her face. "I don't know where to begin, Eurwen. You know more about us than we do about you. We have so much to catch up on."

"What are your intentions?" Eurwen demanded.

Con glanced at Vaughn over his shoulder. "Rhi and I have come to meet you and your brother. Obviously, we'd love to see the dragons while we're here."

"And him?" Eurwen asked as her gaze bored into Vaughn.

He moved a step closer. "You know why I'm here."

Con and Rhi wore identical frowns as they looked between the two of them. Eurwen broke eye contact with him first.

Vaughn felt the dragons before he saw then. They had moved closer as if sensing that Kings had arrived.

"Where is your brother?" Rhi asked. "We want to meet him."

Eurwen showed no emotion on her face, something she likely got from Con. "He isn't yet ready to meet either of you."

"In other words, he didna want us here," Con said, not bothering to hide his hurt. "I hope both of you understand that what happened was no' something Rhi nor I knew about until recently."

Eurwen nodded. "We do."

"What changed your mind about allowing us entry?" Rhi asked.

"By refusing, we acted like children when we are far from it." Eurwen jerked her chin and looked beyond them. "Even now, the dragons know who has arrived, without having to be told."

Vaughn glanced over his shoulder to see a mass of dragons approaching in the distance as more gathered around them—some on land and others in the air.

"I didna come to take over," Con told her. "Neither did Vaughn. None of the Kings who come from Earth will."

Eurwen's lips twisted. "Some things are out of your control. This is Cairnkeep. My home is over the next rise. Come when you've finished."

With that, she turned on her heel and walked away. Vaughn wanted to go after her. He was happy he'd finally found her but confused and disturbed to learn that she knew him. If so, why hadn't she come to him on Earth? Before he confronted her, he needed to get control of his raging emotions. Besides, Con and Rhi needed time with their daughter first.

Vaughn turned and searched for the Teals. The moment he found them, he shifted into his true form and jumped into the air, his wings catching a current. He flew above the other dragons. As he dipped his wing to turn back, he spotted his clan flying toward him.

A multitude of voices filled his head as the adolescents began talking at once. Then, suddenly, they grew quiet. Vaughn saw why a second later when a dozen adult Teals closed in around him in a defensive, aggressive manner. He took no offense. He would've done the same in their shoes.

He felt a push in his head before a female voice asked, *"Are you really the King of Teals?"*

"Aye. Before we had to send the dragons away to keep them alive," Vaughn answered.

"You should've wiped out those mortals," said a deep, male voice. *"Eurwen and Brandr have made it so the humans here willna try the same things."*

Vaughn understood their anger, which had most likely been handed down by past generations. Dragons lived a long time, but only Kings and their mates were immortal. And the only way a Dragon King could be killed was by another Dragon King or Queen. *"I'm happy to hear it."*

"Are you here to be our King?"

The young voice shocked him. Vaughn wasn't sure which of the dragons it was, but he heard the wariness in the tone. *"We've only recently discovered that you found a home. We've been trying to find you. I can no' begin to describe the ache of missing all of you on Earth. It's our home."*

"Your *home*," said another adult female, her anger palpable. *"This is* ours."

With that, the Teals flew off in a different direction. Vaughn watched them, wondering if he should follow. In the end, he decided against it. Hopefully, he'd have time to speak to his dragons again later.

For the moment, his thoughts were on a particular woman he'd believed he would never find.

CHAPTER FOUR

He was here.

He was really here.

Eurwen had hoped that Vaughn would come eventually, but she hadn't thought he would be one of the first. It had been everything she could do not to stare at him. Not to rush to him. She had forced herself to keep her attention on her parents.

Seeing Vaughn once more had caused her knees to go weak. Her blood had pounded in her ears, and her hands became clammy. Need, swift and powerful, coursed through her. The kind that only Vaughn could quench.

Her stomach had fluttered as if a thousand butterflies were in residence when she looked into his Persian blue eyes. No one had eyes that color. And his mouth. By the gods, his wide lips drove her wild. Her heart skipped a beat when she thought of the hard lines of his jaw. He moved with cat-like grace that belied the untamed, fierce dragon he was.

She both hoped he followed her to her cabin and prayed

that he didn't. He would no doubt demand information,
answers she wasn't sure she could give. Eurwen's legs shook
from anticipation and nervousness as she walked. Mixed with
her emotions about Vaughn were those concerning her parents.
It created a maelstrom of feelings that made her slightly
nauseous—and wondering if she could get through it all. This
was the time she would normally turn to Brandr. But he had
made his position clear.

Besides, he knew nothing about her time with Vaughn.

Eurwen reached her cottage and walked inside, leaving the
door open. Her curiosity was killing her. She desperately
wanted to know what Vaughn was doing. It became so
unbearable that she finally gave in and turned around. Her
gaze landed on her parents without any sign of Vaughn.

Her disappointment was swift and sharp. She tried to tell
herself it was for the best that Vaughn hadn't followed her, but
there was no getting around the hurt that opened like a
yawning void. Eurwen swallowed her wounded pride and
squared her shoulders as Con and Rhi reached the doorway.

"This is charming," Rhi said from the entryway as her
gaze swept the area.

Eurwen motioned them in. "Would either of you care for
anything to drink? Eat?"

"We're fine, thank you," Constantine replied.

His black eyes watched her thoughtfully, carefully. Eurwen
wondered what he thought of her and Brandr. The King of
Dragon Kings was someone she had studied for centuries. He
was pensive, brooding even, as well as astute and cunning.
There was a reason the magic had chosen him to lead the
Golds *and* be King of Dragon Kings.

As for her mother, Rhi was loyal, spirited, bold, and courageous. While Con thought things through, Rhi leapt before she looked more often than not. They complemented each other well.

"If this isna a good time, we can come back," Con offered. "Or, if it's better, you could come to Dreagan."

Eurwen drew in a breath and forced a smile. "My apologies. I wasn't expecting to see anyone with you."

"Every King wishes to see the dragons," Rhi said with a grin.

Eurwen motioned to the sofa as she walked to a chair and sat. "I'm sure you have many questions."

"Do you no'?" Con asked Eurwen as he led Rhi to the sofa and waited for her to sit before he lowered himself next to her.

Eurwen wasn't surprised by his words. "As you know from Erith, Brandr and I have visited Earth many times. We've seen both of you."

Rhi crossed one long leg over the other. "I hope that didn't cause you to form bad opinions of us."

"Of course, it did," Con said, though there was no heat in his words.

Eurwen looked from Con to Rhi, staring into eyes the exact shade of hers. She decided to choose her words carefully. "It's true that our feelings toward both of you were…not favorable for a considerable time."

Rhi blew out a breath and looked toward Con as the two locked gazes briefly. "There is much of our story you don't know."

"That's true. It's one of the reasons I created the doorway.

Although, I don't think any child should know everything
about their parents," Eurwen replied.

Con reached over and set his hand upon Rhi's. The instant
he did, Rhi twined her fingers with his. "We're verra glad you
did open the doorway for us," Con said.

Eurwen watched her parents. It was weird having them
together after seeing them apart for so long, but the one thing
nobody could deny was the love the two shared.

Rhi nervously licked her lips. "I'm probably going to
regret asking this, but why did you hate us? We knew nothing
of your existence. Otherwise, believe me, both of us would've
come for you and Brandr."

Eurwen glanced out the window to the mist-shrouded
mountaintop. "The first emotion I remember was desolation.
Coming close behind that was anger—before either Brandr or
I learned to speak. We weren't sure where those feelings came
from or why we had them. It wasn't until we were older that I
asked Erith. That's when she told me she believed the feelings
came from the day things ended between the two of you."

"And I went to the Fae Realm," Rhi said in a soft voice.
She looked down at her hand, a tear rolling down her face.

Con instantly turned to Rhi, a frown marring his face.
"Neither of us knew you were with child."

Rhi lifted her gaze and met Eurwen's. "You thought I
didn't want you. That we didn't want you."

"No," Eurwen said. "Erith made sure we knew the truth of
that."

"Then why wait so long to let us know you?" Con asked.

Eurwen leaned forward and looked between her
parents. "We all know everything happened for a reason.

Con, you broke things off with Rhi because of the other Kings. Rhi, had you remained with Con, you would've never become part of the Queen's Guard. You wouldn't have discovered Usaeil's deception—or your true parentage. Brandr and I wouldn't have known the dragons needed us here."

Rhi shook her head. "That still doesn't explain why you and Brandr had such strong feelings against getting to know us or letting us know of you."

Eurwen said nothing.

"You can no' possibly know how difficult it was to send the dragons away," Con said, his face lined with anguish.

Eurwen had known he would say something like that. And she couldn't hold back her words. "You had the power to keep the dragons on Earth."

"We made a vow to protect the humans."

"And look where that got you."

"We're no' murderers."

Eurwen shrugged. "You lost your own kind. You are Kings to nothing and no one."

Rhi swiped at the tears on her face, her eyes turning hard. "It's easy for someone to look back on another's life and pick apart every bad decision. I wonder, if you had been there during any of that, how would you have reacted? What decisions would you have made?"

"Do you no' think I regret all that's happened?" Con snapped to Eurwen.

She remained calm during all of it. She had replayed this entire scenario a million different ways, so she knew what to expect. "You forced your dragons to leave their home and sent them out into the universe in hopes they might find a place they could live in peace."

"Things turned out well," Rhi stated.

Eurwen glanced at the ground and huffed. "Do you think that was by chance?"

"What does that mean?" Con asked with narrowed eyes.

Rhi shrugged. "The universe has countless realms."

"That's right," Eurwen said. "What are the chances they arrived somewhere similar to their world? One that had only one sun and one moon?"

Con's shoulders rose as he drew in a breath and released it, all emotion wiped from his face. "How *did* they find this place?"

"They didn't find it. They were *directed* here," Eurwen answered.

Rhi nodded and looked at Con. "Erith."

Con's blond brows snapped together as he jerked his head to Eurwen. "Is that true?"

"Yes," she replied. "As both of you know, Erith spent a lot of time on Earth, watching the dragons and the Kings long before the humans or Fae arrived. She didn't want to leave anything to chance, especially since she knew it was wrong for the dragons to have been sent away."

"I was trying to save their lives," Con said in a low voice.

Eurwen shrugged. "And that's where we differ. Brandr and I protect the dragons above anything or anyone else. This was their home first. We won't allow the same mistakes you made to happen here. Your realm is overrun with humans who are slowly destroying it. How much longer until the magic fades? How much longer can the Dragon Kings remain hidden before you're hunted? Where will you go when that happens?"

"It's our realm," Con replied. "We willna allow any of that to happen."

"Just like you thought the humans and dragons could live together?"

Rhi got to her feet and looked from Eurwen to Con and back to Eurwen. "Enough. Both of you. Eurwen, you're an incredibly intelligent woman. You've watched things on Earth. You know how Con and the others at Dreagan have suffered. There is no need to rub salt in a wound that will never heal."

Eurwen slowly sat back in her seat. "Did you two think you could come here, and everything would be all smiles and roses? When Brandr and I finally convinced Erith to bring us to Zora, things were...horrible. The dragons fought each other to the death. So many died. There was no cohesion. No leaders. Some tried, but since they weren't Kings, no one listened. What we had to deal with—as children, no less—to restore order among the dragons was unspeakable."

Con got to his feet and bowed his head to her. "I'm grateful that you and your brother were able to get control and ensure order once again. I can no' express my joy at learning the dragons are thriving under my children's rule."

He met Rhi's gaze in a silent exchange before walking from the cottage.

Eurwen watched him go. She had hurt him. Once, long ago, she had wanted exactly that. She'd thought she was past all of that, but obviously that wasn't the case given her answers and tone.

"He's sacrificed everything for the Kings and the dragons,"

Rhi said, her gaze still on her mate. "He keeps it all inside, showing only me, but he's torn to pieces. He shoulders the blame for everything. Even when it's not his fault."

Eurwen blinked back sudden tears, swallowing past the knot of emotion in her throat. "We both know some things were out of his control. The Others, for one."

Rhi turned to look at her. "You know of them, then?"

"Of course."

"And you would still skewer your father as you did? Does it not go to show you his misery, his sorrow for all that has happened, that he didn't bother to name the cause of the arrival of the humans to our world?"

Eurwen was suitably put in her place. "I wasn't there to see the battle with the humans. I wasn't there to see him decide to send the dragons away. He wasn't here to see the state of this realm or the dragons when we arrived. He wasn't here to watch the utter destruction."

"And me?" Rhi asked, black brows raised. "You didn't hesitate to tell your father how you felt about him. Is it time for me to learn why you detest me so?"

Eurwen could only stare at her mother, unsure of what to say.

"Something had to keep you and your brother away from me. I'm far from perfect. Shall we look back on my life and point out all the things I've done wrong? Pick apart all the decisions I've made?"

Eurwen shook her head, tears threatening again.

"For months after we learned about you, I waited until the day I could finally meet you and your brother." Fresh tears fell down Rhi's face. "We knew something had kept both of you from us, but given the doorway, we were sure those things had been laid aside. Apparently, we were wrong."

The first tear fell down Eurwen's cheek as Rhi followed Con out of the house and then disappeared over the rise. Eurwen sank into the chair, confused and shaken by what had just happened. Con and Rhi were right. She shouldn't have hurled such things at them, not the first day. Certainly, not during their first conversation.

She blamed it on being discombobulated by Vaughn's arrival. But she wasn't sure that was the truth. She wanted to get to know her parents, but there were still a great many things from the past that she hadn't let go of yet. The only reason she had opened the doorway was because she'd thought she had released all her anger.

"Shite. Brandr," she mumbled, thinking about her brother.

If she had reacted this way when she *wanted* to meet her parents, she couldn't imagine how bad things could go with Brandr. She would have to keep her brother away from Con and Rhi. Or things might just turn into the war Brandr feared.

CHAPTER FIVE

Vaughn fought against wanting to talk to Eurwen and allowing Rhi and Con some time with their daughter. After the Teals left, Vaughn continued flying with no destination in mind. He took in the beauty of Zora and reveled in the ability to be his true self without worrying about humans seeing him. It wasn't long before he heard a familiar voice in his head.

"Vaughn? When did you arrive?" Varek asked.

Vaughn smiled. *"No' long ago. It's good to hear your voice, brother. Where are you?"*

"To your right. Come meet my mate."

Vaughn turned his head in Varek's direction and saw his friend standing in a glade. Vaughn swooped over the forest and landed in the opening before shifting to human form, being sure to clothe himself as he did.

"It's good to see you," Varek said as he rushed him, embracing Vaughn while pounding on his back.

Vaughn returned the hug before leaning back to get a good

look at Varek. "You've changed. I'm no' sure how, but you're different."

"It's this place," Varek said with a wide smile.

"Aye," Vaughn said, thinking of the Teals and how just the sight of them had lit up his soul.

Varek quirked a dark brow. "You saw the Teals?"

"I even got to fly with them for a short time. They doona seem too keen on me being here, however."

"Give them time," his friend cautioned. "The Lichens are the same."

Vaughn sensed movement to his left. "And your mate?"

"Here," said a woman, who walked from the forest.

Jeyra emerged with her head held high, her red hair pulled into a braid that fell over her shoulder. She wore a golden-brown sleeveless shirt and dark brown breeches, along with knee-high boots. Thick, silver armbands encircled both upper arms. Her amber eyes looked Vaughn up and down, but her lips held a smile.

"Varek has told me about each of the Dragon Kings," Jeyra said once she reached them. "Let me see if I can guess who you are."

Vaughn exchanged a glance with Varek as he grinned. "All right."

"Light brown hair and blue eyes. That narrows things down a bit."

Vaughn quirked a brow and looked at Varek again.

"She's got an amazing memory," Varek answered.

"Varek said that Merrill's eyes are dark blue. Yours are brighter, so I'm going with...Vaughn," Jeyra said.

Vaughn was completely taken aback. "Impressive."

"Not really," Jeyra said with a shrug. "Not too many Kings have your particular coloring."

"Your accent is different," Vaughn said, trying to place it.

Varek shook his head. "Doona even try. It drove me nuts for weeks. I've come to realize it's a combination of various accents from Earth."

Now that wasn't something Vaughn had expected. "How?"

"Those like Jeyra were brought here as bairns," Varek explained.

Jeyra moved closer to Varek. "Even today, babies continue showing up. We don't know how or why."

"How is the population here?" Vaughn asked, thinking of how quickly the mortals doubled their populations.

Jeyra's face was grim. "Mortals are unable to have children here."

Vaughn blinked in shock.

"There's a lot we need to catch you up on. I'd like to only tell the story once. Did any other Kings come with you?" Varek asked.

"Just Con and Rhi. They're with Eurwen now."

Varek's eyes widened. "Really? We've no' gotten to meet her. I've only spoken to Brandr."

"How was he?"

"Intense. He gets it honestly from Con, that's for sure."

They shared a smile before Vaughn said, "This place is incredible. I understand now why you didna want to leave."

"I willna lie, being near the dragons is something I'm no' quite willing to let go of yet, but I also wanted some time with Jeyra."

She playfully elbowed Varek. "I did tell him I would go

with him anywhere. My home is where he is. It isn't a place or a realm."

"You say that now. You might no' be so inclined once you see our world," Vaughn cautioned.

Jeyra shrugged and smiled adoringly at Varek. "I'm anxious to see the things he's told me about. The planes and such."

Varek put his arm around her before looking at Vaughn. "Go explore while you can. Though stay away from the barrier. You'll feel it as you get close. The twins erected it to keep the humans on their side. The dragons have the majority of the planet to themselves."

"I'll see you two later, I'm sure," Vaughn said before shifting and taking to the sky once more.

He wasn't sure how long he flew before he saw the loch. It was so still, it looked like glass. A mountain stood on one side, a thick forest on two others. The last was undulating fields. It was simply too beautiful to pass up. Vaughn landed and took in the area. The sound of dragons nearby made him sigh in contentment. He waded into the water and swam around the large loch first as a dragon and then as a human.

When he finally came onto shore, he lay naked near the forest beneath the bright sun. He laced his hands behind his head and closed his eyes as he enjoyed the silence. There were no planes, no cars, no trains, no horns, no people talking on their mobiles. No hum of electricity ran through the wires strung around the world. The wonderful, blessed peace lulled Vaughn.

How would he ever return to Earth after this paradise? It wasn't only because the dragons were here—although that played a big role. It was because he could live as himself—a dragon. He wouldn't have to pretend or hide who he was. He wouldn't have to worry about humans learning that he had magic, or only flying at night during a storm because the mortals might see.

Then there was Eurwen.

Vaughn opened his eyes as he thought of her. He wasn't sure what to make of her. She had haunted his thoughts and dreams for centuries. He had searched Earth for her again and again, and he would've kept searching. Because he knew he had to find her. Somehow.

Some way.

He spotted a dragon flying by itself. At first, he couldn't see its color because the sun cast a shadow. He slowly sat up, staring in awe at the metallic peach scales and gold wings. He caught sight of two gold horns curling outward and straight up from atop its head. The long, peach tail had a gold tip. It was Eurwen. He was sure of it.

Vaughn didn't know when he had gotten to his feet. He was about to shift and fly with her, but something stopped him. He knew the minute she spotted him. His heart thumped, wondering if she would come to him. One way or another, they needed to talk. If she wouldn't come to him, then he would go after her.

He took a step, ready to shift, when he saw her turn slightly and head in his direction. He couldn't look away from her. He'd never seen a more beautiful dragon. Then again, Eurwen and Brandr weren't just any offspring. They were descended from Fae royalty and a Dragon King, who was the epitome of nobility. How could Eurwen be anything *but* exquisitely regal and utterly unique?

She landed gracefully, her pearly gaze on him. She tucked her wings against her body before shifting to her human form. He fought the urge to cross the distance separating them and haul her against him for a kiss.

"You're naked," she said.

He blinked, the words not registering for a moment. Then he looked down and realized that he was, indeed, still without clothes. "I seem to recall a time when you couldna get them off me fast enough."

"You remember?"

Vaughn wasn't sure what surprised him more. The fact that she actually thought he could forget her? Or the uncertainty in her voice. "Aye, lass. I've never forgotten you. I looked for you every day."

"Why?"

"Why?" he took a step toward her. "Have you no idea?"

"Maybe I need to hear it."

He looked from her golden blond hair to her silver eyes. "You felt what passed between us that night. I know you did."

"So?" she asked, lifting her chin in defiance.

"Why did you no' come to me? Why did you stay away?"

Her eyes skidded away for a heartbeat. "I belong here."

"You could've told me."

"We were to have no interaction with the Kings."

That made Vaughn frown. "Who told you that?"

"It was something Brandr and I agreed upon," she answered.

"Was that before or after you met me?"

She swallowed. "Before we ventured to your realm."

"To spy upon Con and the rest of the Kings? Rhi? Why would you do that?"

"You wouldn't understand."

He shook his head. "Hard to answer that since you never gave anyone a chance. You and your brother assumed you knew best. Two incredibly powerful beings may have created you, but we have all been alive much, much longer than you and your brother. You're infants compared to us."

"Do you think I wanted to like you?" she shouted, finally losing her cool.

Vaughn looked at the ground and sighed. He lifted his gaze and said, "I know the woman I spent that night with changed my entire life. She has never left my mind, no' for a single day. That woman controls my dreams. I would've given my life for her. That woman had courage and spirit and would've made her own decisions."

Of all the ways he'd thought this encounter might go, it hadn't been like this. He turned and walked toward the forest.

"Where are you going?" she called.

He halted. Without looking over his shoulder, he asked, "Why should I stay? You didna even speak to me when I first arrived. I thought we'd shared something amazing and profound. I guess I was wrong."

Vaughn waited for her to speak. When she didn't, he continued into the woods. He was hurt and angry, and he wasn't sure if it was at Eurwen or himself. How had he not known that Eurwen was a dragon that long-ago night? She must have used some sort of magic. Worse, he'd just told her of his feelings, and she said nothing. All these centuries he'd spent pining after a woman he believed was his mate, only to discover that she wanted nothing to do with him.

Zora suddenly lost its luster. Vaughn needed to go somewhere and lick his wounds. He didn't want to run into Varek, Jeyra, Con, or Rhi. He could find his way back to where they'd come through the doorway, but he wasn't sure where it was exactly. Which meant, he had to wait for Rhi or Eurwen to tell him.

Perhaps it would be better if he spent some time alone. As he meandered through the forest, he realized that for the first time in a very, very long time, he was utterly alone. At Dreagan, he had a manor full of Kings and mates. Vaughn had his own room, but he could still hear others in the house.

Even when he had to travel for his duties as solicitor for Dreagan, mortals were always around. It made him claustrophobic at times. Zora reminded him of a time long forgotten, a period when his only duties had been those of his clan. A time before the humans' arrival.

He sat beneath an oak and leaned his back against it, the bark scratching his bare skin. As much as he felt at home in this realm, like the Teal had said, this wasn't his world. The Dragon Kings might be welcome for a visit, but he was sure they wouldn't be allowed to stay. Not that he blamed Eurwen or Brandr. They ruled this realm. Vaughn wouldn't have accepted anyone else coming to Earth, trying to remove him as King of Teals.

And there was no way the Dragon Kings could live on Zora and *not* rule. It's what they had been born to do.

CHAPTER SIX

Eurwen wasn't sure what had just happened with Vaughn. She had taken to the sky to try and clear her head after her conversation with her parents. Then, she'd seen Vaughn. It had been impossible for her to put off talking to him even a moment longer. She couldn't remember a time when she had been so nervous and edgy.

Finding him naked had shifted her emotions to something more…wanton. After the dream she'd woken to that morning, she needed release.

And she needed it with Vaughn.

Unfortunately, everything had gone wrong the minute she opened her mouth to talk. No matter what she said, it'd come out nearly the opposite of what she *wanted* to say.

Eurwen thought about following him, but she was too upset. First, her talk with Con and Rhi had gone sideways, and then the same had happened with Vaughn. She was no longer sure of herself or her thoughts.

With one last look at where Vaughn had disappeared into the forest, Eurwen turned and jumped into the air as she shifted. She started toward her cottage at Cairnkeep, then realized she didn't want to be alone. She needed to talk, and only one individual would truly understand what she was going through—Brandr.

She changed directions to look for her brother. The problem was, he hadn't wanted any Dragon Kings here. Especially their father. All Brandr would do was tell her, "*I told you so*," and that wasn't what Eurwen needed, either. She started to turn around to fly back to her home when she spotted Brandr with the generals. Curious, she continued toward them to discern what her brother was up to.

By the time she reached the group, the four dragon generals were gone. Brandr stood in human form with his arms crossed over his chest, his long, black hair pulled back in a queue, his black eyes watching her.

"I'm surprised to see you," he said when she landed. "I thought you'd be cozied up to Con and Rhi."

She ignored his smirk as she shifted to her human form and flicked her long hair over her shoulder.

His eyes narrowed, the movement identical to their father's. "You'd better no' be here to try and convince me to talk to them."

"I'm not. They're having a look around." Eurwen wasn't sure why she didn't tell her brother the rest of it. Maybe because she wasn't in the mood for his smugness. She needed someone to lean on, and he was all she'd ever had.

Erith had been amazing and did her best while raising them, but the goddess had her hands full with leading the

Reapers. While Eurwen got along with the other dragons, it wasn't easy being friends with those you ruled. She was never sure if they were friendly because they genuinely liked her or simply because of who she was.

"Sis?" Brandr asked with a frown as he dropped his arms and walked to her. He studied her face as he put a hand on her arm. "What is it?"

Eurwen shrugged in an attempt to brush off his question, but the concern in his eyes caused the dam to burst and the tears to fall.

He pulled her against him and held her as she cried. "Did they hurt you? What did Con say? I know he must have said something to make you cry. Or was it Rhi? Bloody hell. I knew they should no' have come. I'll force them out right now."

"No. No," Eurwen said as she lifted her head from his shoulder and sniffed. "That isn't it. I mean, we did have words, but they didn't hurt me."

Brandr gently wiped the tears from her cheek. "Then who did? Tell me so I can kick their arse."

"I could do it myself, thank you very much," she said with a smile.

His lips softened into a grin as he gripped her shoulders and stared into her eyes. "I know you can. That doesna mean I can no' get my own hits in."

"I have to tell you something."

He grew serious as he nodded. His arms dropped to his sides. "The cliff?"

"Yes."

They flew together to a cliff near Cairnkeep. It was the

spot where they had landed the first time they came to Zora and shifted. It was the spot they used to settle arguments, plan, and talk about anything important.

Eurwen landed and shifted before lowering herself to the ground. Her legs dangled over the side as she gazed out at the vast mountains where the varied greens of the trees and grass met the vibrant blue of the sky. Even after all her years on Zora, it still managed to take her breath away.

Brandr settled beside her. "You're leaving."

"What?" she asked in shock as her head jerked to him. "No."

Relief swept over his face as his shoulders sagged. "Thank the stars."

"You thought I was leaving?"

"You brought our parents here, then came to me crying."

She pressed her lips together and glanced at the mountain range. "I am upset about my conversation with them, but I'm disappointed in myself. I thought I was past the anger that ruled me for so long."

"You mean *my* anger."

She cut him a dark look. "It was both of ours." Eurwen sighed. "What I need to tell you doesn't involve our parents."

"Just say it. Whatever it is, it'll be all right," he said, squeezing her hand briefly to show his support.

Eurwen lowered her gaze to the ground. "Do you remember when we first began visiting Earth?"

"Aye," he said with a wry twist of his lips.

Her gaze lifted to his face. "Then we started going alone."

A small frown furrowed his brow. "Aye."

"We had rules."

"We did."

"I broke one."

Brandr stared at her in silence for a full minute. "What happened?"

"I was in Norway."

"Ah. Your fascination with the Vikings."

It was her turn to flatten her lips. "With how they treated their women. How they allowed them to fight alongside the men. Another culture also did that."

"The Celts."

There was no heat in Brandr's words, but Eurwen wasn't fooled. It was something else he got from their father. "I watched two warring Celt clans fight one day. It was brutal and vicious. A woman led one, the clan I had been studying for some time. They won, and without any interference from me. That night, they celebrated."

Brandr shrugged. "And?"

"Someone new arrived. Someone who wasn't part of the clan."

"You wouldna be telling me this if it was just a human you took to your bed. Which means, it was a King."

Eurwen drew in a deep breath and then released it. "The minute I saw him across the fire, I was drawn to him. Like invisible strings connected us, and some unknown force was pulling us together. I couldn't have turned away had I tried. But…I didn't want to go. That night was…everything. I knew that he would realize who I was or start asking questions I couldn't answer once the morning came. So, I left. Not a day goes by that I don't think about him. Fight the urge to go to Dreagan and find him."

"Why did you no' tell me this before?"

"We promised each other that we'd never be around the Kings."

Brandr swallowed and looked out over the view. "Yes, well, that was a one-time thing."

Astonishment jolted through Eurwen as she looked in disbelief at her brother. "Did you not hear what I said?"

"I heard that you've no' gone to him." Brandr glanced at her. "That's all I need to know."

"No."

He swiveled his head to her, his brows drawn together. "What?"

"I said, no."

"To what, exactly?"

She got to her feet. "I told you that story to lead into another, but you've made your stance perfectly clear."

"We doona need the Kings. We never have. We never will," he stated calmly.

Which only enraged her more. Eurwen fisted her hands as she glared at her twin. "We don't need them, but that doesn't mean they can't be in our lives."

"That's exactly what it means." Brandr slowly got to his feet and dusted off his hands before facing her. "Plenty of dragons would do anything to be your mate. Pick one."

She couldn't believe what she was hearing. "What the bloody hell are you on about? You know we can't just *pick* a mate. That isn't how it works."

"This is our realm. The Kings had their chance on theirs, and they buggered it all. I'm no' stepping aside for them to come and take over. Ruin what we've done. Perhaps you need to think about whose side you're on."

"I'm on *my* side," she retorted.

His nostrils flared, a sign that he was fighting his anger. "Are you telling me that Dragon King is your mate?"

"I don't know what he is. What I want is your support, no matter what happens."

"I love you, Eurwen. We've been through a lot together, but you know my stance. If your mate is a King, then you willna be ruling Zora any longer."

Her eyes widened in incredulity. "You can't be serious."

"I willna give them a foothold here. And if you're mated to one, that's exactly what will happen. If that means I banish you, then so be it."

"You forget we rule together. You can't banish me anymore than I can banish you."

"Figure out what is more important." A muscle ticked in his jaw before he walked away.

"Why is everyone walking away from me today?" she asked herself.

Eurwen faced the view and took a deep breath, but that didn't alleviate her emotions that had been in upheaval since the start of the day. It felt as if everything were falling apart when she had believed this first step in a new direction was what she was meant to do. How could she have been so wrong?

It wouldn't have mattered if she and her parents had shared an amazing conversation and bonded because nothing would change Brandr's mind. He'd laid it out for her. She could choose Zora and him, or she could have their parents and Earth.

And possibly Vaughn.

Very few times in her life had she not known what to do. Where she felt as if she were adrift in a sea of uncertainty and doubt. But today, she was drowning in that ocean with no way out.

Zora was her home. She hadn't had a conventional birth or upbringing. Nothing about her and Brandr had been normal. She wasn't sure of anything anymore, and she was beginning to wonder if she had ever known anything.

She did know one thing. And that was how Vaughn made her feel. But could she decide about the rest of her life based on one night that'd happened lifetimes ago? She didn't know Vaughn, and he didn't know her. They had physical chemistry, but that didn't equal compatibility. Maybe she was overthinking things. Perhaps she thought there was something between her and Vaughn that really wasn't.

There was only one way to know for sure.

CHAPTER SEVEN

"Want to talk about it?"

Vaughn blinked and looked at Varek, who stood beside him. "What? No."

Varek raised a brow. "I'm no' sure keeping whatever is wrong to yourself is a good idea."

As if on cue, Rhi and Con came out of the shadows, heading toward the fire. Vaughn was thankful because the last thing he wanted to do right now was talk about Eurwen. Especially when he wasn't sure what to think.

He'd spent most of the day wandering the forest, and the other half flying around Zora. He'd seen many dragons, but he hadn't approached them, and they hadn't come near him. He also hadn't seen Eurwen again. It had been nearing dusk when Varek used the mental link and told him where he and Jeyra were living.

Vaughn sat back while Varek introduced Jeyra to Con and Rhi. Though the two wore smiles, they didn't come as easily as usual. Something had happened with Eurwen. Or had Brandr been involved? Vaughn felt for his friends. He knew the couple had endured a great deal since learning about their twins and seeing how their children hadn't wanted to see them. There had been such hope in Con's and Rhi's eyes this morning. That was gone. Replaced by pain and distress.

"Shite," Varek said as he looked between Vaughn, Rhi, and Con. "What happened to you three today?"

Rhi accepted a mug of wine from Jeyra. "Let's just say that it's going to take longer than I realized before we can have a cordial discussion with Eurwen."

"Did you get to meet Brandr?" Jeyra asked.

Con shook his head as he accepted his wine. "Apparently, our son doesna want any Dragon Kings here."

Varek and Jeyra exchanged a look before Varek said, "He wasna too pleased with my being here, but he didna tell me to leave."

"I think that was before Eurwen created the doorway," Vaughn said.

Rhi swallowed the wine and nodded. "Precisely."

"Does that mean we have to leave?" Jeyra asked Varek.

Con sat on one of the six cut tree stumps around the fire. "None of us wants a war, and I think that's exactly what Brandr expects. If we're asked to leave, then we'll go. Peacefully."

Vaughn turned his wine mug in his hand. "I agree. For the moment, we're allowed to stay. Let's learn what we can in case we're no' allowed to return."

"That bloody well can no' happen," Varek stated. "The other Kings need to experience this."

Rhi put her hand on Con's shoulder as she stood beside him. "You have to understand where Brandr and Eurwen are coming from. This is their home. They rule this place."

"And they're worried we're coming to take it," Vaughn said.

Jeyra snorted as she grabbed the wine jug and refilled her mug. "That's what I'd think if I were them."

"That's no' what we're doing. Is it?" Varek asked with a frown.

Con turned his head and kissed Rhi's hand, looking up at her before saying. "No. That isna what we're about. Eurwen was right this morning. We had our chance, and I bungled it."

"That isna only on you, Con. We all did," Vaughn said.

Con's black gaze met his over the dancing fire. "The responsibility lies with me. I ordered—"

"That's bollocks," Vaughn interrupted. "You lead us. We follow your orders, but you know as well as we do that if we hadna believed in you and agreed with you, we would have made our thoughts known."

Varek said, "Hear, hear."

"Besides," Jeyra added. "The past is the past. Nothing can change it."

Rhi leaned down to kiss Con's forehead before sitting beside him on a stump. "I agree. Unfortunately, it's the past that has turned our children against us."

"How long are you staying?" Vaughn asked.

Con shrugged as he stared into the fire. "Until we're told to leave."

"What about you?" Varek asked Vaughn.

Vaughn blew out a breath. "I'm no' sure."

"I thought you found what you were looking for," Rhi said.

When Vaughn looked up, both Con and Rhi were staring at him, knowing looks in their eyes. "I might've been wrong."

"This might be your only chance. Be sure before you do anything hasty," Con advised.

Varek leaned forward to rest his forearms on his knees. "I feel like I've missed something."

"You have," Jeyra said with a teasing laugh.

Con caught Jeyra's gaze. "I admit, I wasna sure what to think of a woman who went out of her way to have a Dragon King captured on Earth and brought here. Now that I see you and Varek together, I understand. Whatever might have driven you before, you did it so the two of you could be together."

Jeyra smiled as she looked at Varek. "That's right. Otherwise, we never would've met, and I wouldn't know what it means to love a Dragon King."

"I think it's time we hear your story," Rhi said to Jeyra.

Con nodded. "Absolutely."

"Over dinner. With more wine," Varek added with a wink.

Vaughn watched the two couples with a smile. The Dragon Kings might live like billionaires because they were thanks to Dreagan Industries, but they didn't need such luxury. Varek and Jeyra lived in nothing more than an elaborate tent, much like the Bédouins used. And they were happy.

Their meal of venison might have been prepared with magic, but sitting around the fire out in the open was something that each of them not only enjoyed but craved. Vaughn missed the simple life.

When each of them had their plates and were eating, Varek

began his story about waking up chained and being carried into a cell.

"When I was alone, I tried to use my magic, but I couldna," he explained.

Jeyra shrugged. "I thought it was because of the manacles I put on him. Supposedly, they stop anyone with magic from using their abilities."

"It took some convincing, but I got her to trust me," Varek said with a smile directed at his mate.

Jeyra leaned forward and kissed him before looking at the rest of them. "Things just weren't adding up. I knew he wasn't the dragon who killed my family, but I wanted justice. I needed it. Unfortunately, in my search for it, I uncovered things that I wasn't meant to find."

"Like?" Rhi pressed.

"The man who raised me said that we created the barrier that kept the dragons out. Yet, when I asked when that'd happened and who had done it—since none of us have magic—he couldn't answer."

Varek nodded. "Then she was told I wouldna be executed as she had thought. They wanted to use me. Planned to marry me off so they could get more land."

"You must be joking," Con said in disbelief. "They actually believed that would get more land?"

Varek snorted. "Just like with Earth, the humans will do anything for more land."

"The thing is, they don't need it," Jeyra told them. "There's plenty. As long as the rich stop hoarding it."

Vaughn could only shake his head.

"Eventually, Jeyra and I came up with a plan for my

escape. It was tricky, and we nearly didna make it. The only reason we did was thanks to one of the councilwomen. It wasna until we exited the gates of the city that I heard the screams."

Vaughn watched as Varek closed his eyes, as if the mere memory had brought him pain. "What screams?" he pressed.

"Dragons." Varek opened his eyes and looked between Vaughn and Con. "There were dragons in the city, and they were being tortured."

Con jumped to his feet, fury emanating from him. "Still?"

"We released them," Jeyra told him.

"With Erith's and Cael's help," Varek added.

Rhi reached up and tugged on Con's hand to get him to sit back down. Then Rhi said, "It seems Erith leaves out quite a lot about what she does for dragons."

"I told her to let you know everything," Varek said.

Con rolled his eyes. "This is Erith we're talking about."

"Get back to the dragons," Vaughn said.

Varek issued a single nod. "Right. As we were setting up a plan to rescue them, Jeyra's people started chasing both Jeyra and I. We crossed onto dragon land, and I thought they might want to help me free the dragons."

"They didn't?" Rhi asked with a concerned frown.

Jeyra shook her head sadly. "It was left up to Varek, Erith, Cael, and me."

"The three of them got into the city. I couldna use my magic within its borders, but Erith—as a goddess—and Cael —as a god—had no problems."

Jeyra set her mug on the ground. "Turned out it was the lead councilman was torturing the dragons and using their magic so no one could use magic within the city. The dragon that killed my family had escaped somehow. That's when I learned that my family had been hunting and capturing dragons. That's why it'd killed my family and not me. I was raised to fear and hate dragons and any being with magic. But...when I saw the state of the red and pink dragons—"

"Pink?" Vaughn and Con said in unison.

Varek's smile was wide. "Aye. They're no' extinct like we thought. We rescued one."

"Just one?" Con asked. "Are there more?"

Varek's smile lost some of its luster. "I've no' seen more. I hoped to, or at least to learn *how* there was another Pink."

"That's amazing news," Vaughn said.

Varek made a face. "It was. Is. I'll admit that. But knowing what had been done to those dragons for decades left a sour taste in my mouth. I doona want to think about how many dragons the humans have killed."

"What about the head councilman?" Rhi asked, fire in her eyes.

Jeyra grinned. "You don't need to worry about him. Erith killed him."

"While Jeyra rescued the Pink," Varek said.

"I knew I liked you," Rhi told Jeyra.

"Erith and Cael teleported the dragons here because they were weak," Varek continued. "That's when I met Brandr. He wasna exactly welcoming, but he didna force me to leave. He thanked us for rescuing the dragons."

Con scratched his eyebrow. "What of your people, Jeyra? How did they come to be here?"

"That's something I was hoping one of you could help

decipher," she answered.

Varek exchanged a look with Jeyra. "Every human here was brought as an infant. No one knows who brings them or why."

"Did you ask Erith?" Rhi questioned.

Jeyra nodded. "We did. She didn't have an answer."

"How is the population?" Con asked.

Varek linked his hand with Jeyra's. "No one can bear children here. We know that isna affecting the dragons. It could be because of the barrier the twins erected to keep the humans on their land, or it could have something to do with how and why they're brought here."

Con was silent for several moments. Then he said, "I know you wanted some time alone, but I'd like for you to return to Earth. Varek, let Sophie check Jeyra out to see if something in her blood can explain what's going on."

"I get to see Dreagan?" Jeyra asked happily.

Vaughn laughed. "You'll be inundated with the other mates wanting to talk to you."

"Oh. I'm not really great with other women," Jeyra said with a frown.

Rhi laughed and shook her head. "Everyone there is wonderful. It might be overwhelming at first, but you'll soon learn that each of them has a special gift. There are other warriors, too, like you, so you needn't worry about that."

"Looks like we're headed to Earth," Varek said to Jeyra.

She glowed with happiness as she leaned forward to kiss him again. "I told you. Anywhere you are is home. I don't care where we are."

Vaughn felt more than ever that he was missing the other

half of himself. The part he believed he'd found with Eurwen. He looked at the empty seat on the other side of him and wished that she was there.

He thought about their earlier conversation as the others talked. Maybe he'd been too hard on Eurwen. After all, she was taking a big chance allowing a doorway to connect Zora and Earth. Of course, she would be guarded. Of course, she would be defensive.

She might have opinions about his past, but she hadn't been there. It wasn't right that she judged something she hadn't been involved in. But had he not done the same to her? Had he not judged her and lashed out, simply because he hadn't liked what she'd said?

Vaughn set aside his uneaten plate and now-empty mug and tried to slip away unseen. He got two steps before he heard someone behind him. He turned and found Con.

"You going to her?" he asked.

Vaughn nodded. "Is that a problem?"

"She's in a difficult position."

"I realize that. It's one of the reasons I'd like to talk to her again."

Con crossed his arms over his chest. "I can no' say I particularly like knowing what transpired between you and my daughter, but I only learned of her existence a few months ago. I have no right to get in your business."

"She is your daughter, no matter the circumstances. But I need to know if she's my mate, or if I'm hanging onto one night that happened eons ago for no reason."

Con smiled and placed a hand on his shoulder. "Good luck. I can no' imagine a better King for her."

CHAPTER EIGHT

Everything was wrong.

Everything had gone wrong.

Eurwen paced her cottage, resentment and hurt mixing into a potent, intoxicating fusion. The conversations with her parents, Brandr, and Vaughn kept running through her head on a loop until they blended.

She paused and put her hands to her head. "Stop," she demanded.

Everything cleared away but Vaughn.

She dropped her arms to her sides and swallowed past the lump of emotion in her throat. How had everything gone to shite so spectacularly today? Every conversation she had seemed to be on a collision course with a wrecking ball—even Brandr, who she had needed to lean on, to have his support. Eurwen had never been in this position. Her twin had always been there to listen and talk to her.

He'd never given her an ultimatum before.

But she realized that what she felt had nothing to do with her brother or her parents. Or Vaughn. This was about *her*. She loved Zora, deeply. But for a long time, she had felt as if something were missing in her life. Could Vaughn be the answer? Or was she so caught up in the fantasy and memory of their shared night that she couldn't see past it to the actual answers?

There was only one way to find out.

Eurwen stalked to the door and yanked it open—only to find Vaughn standing there.

Her heart leapt into her throat. "What are you doing here?"

"Coming to see you," he answered in his deep, velvet timbre. He quirked a thick brow. "Where are you going?"

"To find you."

She couldn't look away from his gaze. Her skin tingled all over as her blood ran fast and hot through her veins. The memory of the dream made her sex throb with need.

"I doona like the way we left things," he said.

Eurwen nodded in agreement. "I didn't either."

When his gaze lowered to her mouth, she found it impossible to breathe. She fought not to throw herself at him and kiss him.

"Lass, you've got to stop that," he said in a strained voice.

A slow smile curved her lips. Eurwen didn't pretend to misunderstand what he was talking about. "Oh?"

"We'll get to the loving. But first, I'd like to talk."

She let her gaze slowly run down his hard body from his broad shoulders in his form-fitting shirt to his trim hips and long legs encased in denim. He was unimaginably gorgeous in human form. But in dragon form, he was magnificent.

"Eurwen."

Her stomach fluttered at the raw longing in his voice. She briefly closed her eyes and pulled herself together. If he wanted to wait, then she would wait. It might be the most painful thing she'd ever done, but she would do it.

"As you wish," she replied as she met his gaze again. "Please. Come in."

She turned to walk away and let him close the door. She didn't get two strides before he spun her and clasped her against him. His blue eyes flared with desire so deep, so palpable, that she forgot to breathe. Then she felt his arousal pressed against her stomach, thick and hard.

"In case you doona think I want you," he said in a low, husky voice.

Her fingers gripped his upper arms tightly. Eurwen was overwhelmed by a myriad of emotions she couldn't even begin to name. But the one thing she did know was that having Vaughn near, letting him hold her, was something she hadn't even realized she needed.

"What?" he pressed as he searched her face.

Eurwen swallowed, trying to put what she was feeling into words. "I–I didn't fathom how the sound of your voice would…" She shook her head, unable to find the word.

"Would what, lass?" he pressed, his voice gentle and soft as if he knew how difficult this was for her.

"That it would ease something inside me I hadn't even known was there."

"I know the feeling." He wrapped his arms around her again, bringing her closer.

Eurwen closed her eyes as they held each other. She rested

her cheek on his shoulder and accepted the embrace. Nothing about it was sexual. It went much deeper than that. And it was profound.

This wasn't her first hug. She'd had many over her lifetime from her brother and even Erith, but this felt entirely different. This wasn't brotherly or motherly. This was…stronger, richer. *Deeper*. It was the same connection she'd felt the first time she'd seen Vaughn across the fire in the Celtic village. A familiarity she couldn't explain. An ease that didn't make sense.

A closeness she innately knew—and sought.

"I've missed you," she whispered.

His hold tightened. "And I've missed you."

Minutes passed as they simply stood there, holding each other. Finally, Eurwen leaned back to look at him. "You want answers."

"There are a few I hope you can give me. But more than anything, I just want to talk. I want to know you—as well as I know your body," he said with a sexy smile.

She quirked a brow at him. "Now look who's teasing."

His expression grew serious. "I searched the world over for you. I never stopped looking because I knew you were out there somewhere, waiting for me to find you."

"You should be angry about what I did."

He blew out a breath and stepped back, his hands moving down her arms to take hers. "A part of me is, but I also know that people usually have a reason for the things they do."

"That reason could've been to hurt you."

Vaughn shook his head, a lock of light brown hair falling onto his forehead. "If you had wanted to wound me, there were many ways you could've done it by sticking around and playing with my heart."

"I'm not so sure I could be as polite as you if the situations were reversed."

"I've had centuries to learn patience. Though, I'll admit, it's still one of my shortcomings."

Eurwen couldn't help but smile. She led him to the sofa with one hand and pulled him down beside her. "Would you like anything?"

"You," he replied. "But I'll wait."

He was entirely too charming. Then again, she knew that. "I have a confession. I've returned to Earth a few times since our night."

"I assumed you had."

"I watched you handle a couple of legal matters for Dreagan. You're a force. With one word, you can make your opponents lose their cool in the most embarrassing ways. It's mesmerizing to watch. You're charming but savage at the same time."

He glanced down at their still-interlocked hands. "I wish you would've approached me."

"I couldn't. I wasn't supposed to the first time, but I was unable to resist you. I saw you walk into the village and couldn't take my eyes off you. I knew who you were, and I couldn't believe you were there."

One side of his lips lifted in a grin. "Like it was Fate?"

"Exactly."

"Because it was."

She tucked her legs against her as she turned to face him.

"I wanted to approach you the other times I visited, too. You have no idea how much."

"What stopped you?"

"A pact Brandr and I made. After we came to Zora, we spent decades sorting things out with the dragons. We barely got that under control before the humans began arriving."

Vaughn's brows snapped together. "No' bairns?"

Eurwen paused, searching her mind. "There were a handful of adults, both men and women, and each of them had infants."

"Curious," he murmured. "Go on."

She licked her lips. "We knew what had occurred on Earth with the mortals. Erith told us everything."

"A second-hand account, I might add."

"True. But she was on your side. She has a deep love for dragons, and especially my parents."

Vaughn blew out a breath. "Then you know how she saved Rhi?"

"I do. The point was, Brandr and I refused to make the same mistakes that happened in your realm. We approached the humans only once and told them about the planet. Said that it was ours. We asked them to leave, but they didn't have any idea how they had even gotten here. Brandr actually took them to another realm, but the next day, they were back. We tried that thrice more with the same outcome."

"That tidbit is interesting," Vaughn said.

"We had no choice but to leave them here. Still, we put up the barrier and warned them to stay inside it. We clearly marked it for them so they knew where it was. We also gave them a good-sized area so they didn't feel constricted and want to go through the barrier. About six months later, two more infants arrived, seemingly out of nowhere."

Vaughn's frown was deep. "You've never seen anyone?"

"Never."

"Is it on your side of the barrier?"

She shook her head. "Both Brandr and I have tried to see who it is, but we've never been able to. There's no rhyme or reason for when the bairns arrive, or even how many. Somehow, the mortals always know."

"Jeyra said they have people checking certain places several times a day, just in case. I doona think they're warned. I think they've learned that it happens and to be prepared."

Eurwen shrugged. "Makes sense."

"Knowing what happened with us and the mortals colored your view of them."

"Are you really telling me that if you had it to do all over again, you wouldn't do things differently?"

He twisted his lips. "Maybe. It's easy to say that now, but it wasna so black and white when we were going through all of it. But that story is for another time. You were telling yours."

"It wasn't just my brother and me who were wary of the humans. The dragons were, as well. They all knew the stories of why their ancestors had come to this realm. Their hatred runs deep."

"How do they feel about Jeyra being here?"

Eurwen had hoped he wouldn't ask that question. "Let's just say it's a good thing she's with a Dragon King."

"I thought you might say something like that. The other Kings on Earth need to know this."

"I understand why the rest of you need to come here and see the dragons firsthand, but I hope you also appreciate how things have changed for the dragons since leaving your realm."

He nodded slowly and gave her a reassuring smile. "I'll make sure of it. Con needs to know this, too."

"I intended to tell him, but things didn't go as planned."

"Things rarely ever do."

She chuckled. "That's very true."

"So, the dragons were no' happy with the mortals being here."

"That's another reason we put up the barrier. Brandr and I ordered the dragons never to cross it. A few disobeyed and wreaked havoc on the humans. We disciplined them, of course. It wasn't easy, but Brandr and I made things work. There were no excuses, no leniencies for either the humans or the dragons. Finally, eventually, things calmed down. Everyone stayed on their side of the barrier."

Vaughn smiled, his eyes crinkling in the corners. "Impressive."

"Not that impressive since you now know about the recent dragon rescue from the human city."

He wrinkled his nose and half-heartedly shrugged. "It was resolved. When did you start visiting Earth?"

"Before the humans came. Brandr and I wanted to see our parents and your world for ourselves. We never stayed longer than a few hours."

"Did you see Dreagan?"

"From a distance," she said with a nod. "The magic there is so strong."

Pride shone in his Persian blue eyes. "That's why we chose it as the Dragon Kings' home."

"The pact I had with my brother was that we would never speak to any of the Kings."

"Ever?" Vaughn asked in surprise.

She smiled sadly. "Ever."

"No' even your father?"

Eurwen shook her head. "After a while, we began splitting up so one of us was always here with the dragons. Neither of us asked the other what they did while on Earth. I think we both assumed that we did the same things as we had done together."

"Except, you didna."

"No." She swallowed and glanced away. "I've never kept a secret from my brother. Until my time with you."

Surprise flashed in Vaughn's eyes. "You didna tell him?"

"Not until today."

"I gather he didna take it well?"

"Not in the least." She didn't want to talk about Brandr and his thoughts right now. "I never intended to meet you. Or any of the Kings. I followed Rhi around a few times in recent years, watching her shop and get her nails done. But you...that night..." She shrugged. "I couldn't have walked away had I wanted to."

Vaughn linked his fingers with hers. "And in the morning?"

"I woke in your arms. I didn't want to leave, but I knew if I didn't, you'd wake and start asking me questions."

"Like how I didna know you were part dragon?"

She winced, scrunching her face. She got up to walk off

some of the energy building inside her. She paced, glancing at him to see his expression. "That was my doing. When I knew I couldn't walk away from you, I used magic to shield myself from you."

"So I wouldna clearly recall your face, the color of your hair, or what kind of magic you had?"

Hearing it made it sound awful, but at the time, it had been the easiest choice. "If you had known who I was, *what* I was, you would've bombarded me with questions and tried to force me to Dreagan. Or, worse, called Con to the village."

"We know firsthand how strong a mix of dragon and Fae blood can be. You and Brandr are no' the first."

"You're speaking of Melisse. The first Dragon Queen."

"Is that no' what you are?"

Eurwen laughed and shook her head. "I wouldn't claim that role. Nor would Brandr claim to be a Dragon King."

"You both can shift. You lead the dragons. I'd say you fit those roles exactly."

"I've not really thought about it. We did what we were called to do."

Vaughn got to his feet to step in front of her. "Like it or no', you're descended from royalty. I would call you a Dragon Queen."

Could she? Why hadn't she ever thought of herself as a Dragon Queen. Like Vaughn said, she could shift. Only Kings could do that. "I don't have a clan. Not like you or my father."

"You have all the clans."

She smiled. "Yet, there's only one Dragon King I want."

He didn't utter a word as she walked to him and placed her hands on his chest. She looked up into his eyes to see them smoldering with need. Her lips parted as her heart skipped a beat.

"We're no' done talking," he murmured before pulling her against him, his mouth descending upon hers.

His lips ravaged hers with a kiss that could've set the entire realm on fire. Her arms wound around his neck, and his hands gripped her ass and pressed her to him so he could grind his cock against her.

Nothing had ever felt so good.

Nothing had ever felt so *right*.

And she knew that everything was about to change.

CHAPTER NINE

DRAGON
KINGS

This was so much better than the dream. Vaughn feared he would never let Eurwen out of his sight again. She was his mate. He just wasn't sure if she was aware of that or not.

Her lips were pliable, her skin smooth. Her body soft. Desire pulsed within him, demanding release, commanding the pleasure he knew awaited them both.

He groaned when her fingers slid into his hair, her nails gently scraping his scalp. The taste of her was heady, her harsh breaths making his blood run hotter than before. With a thought, he removed their clothes so they were skin to skin.

Eurwen tore her mouth from his and stared up at him, her pulse rapid in her throat. "You have no idea how much I want this."

"Oh, I verra much do," he said as he kissed her once more.

She turned him and began backing him from one room to another. When he felt the soft give of a mattress behind him, he lifted her off her feet, turned around, and set a knee on the bed as he lowered her, catching himself with a hand. He broke the kiss long enough to rise on both hands and look down at her.

Golden hair spread around her like a crown. Silver eyes ringed with pewter gazed up at him with the same yearning he felt. She was the most beautiful thing he had ever seen. To finally have her in his arms once again, to know her name, only made the connection he felt for her grow firmer. Purer.

"You're exquisite."

She reached up and touched his face as she smiled softly. "No more talking," she said and pulled him down for another kiss.

He moved his hand between their bodies and cupped her breast to gently massage it. His finger brushed over a turgid nipple, causing her to gasp. He thumbed the peak until she ground against him.

Then she flipped him onto his back and straddled him. He raked his gaze over her pale, unblemished skin. Her shoulders were slim, but the muscles in her arms, abdomen, and legs were defined. Her breasts were full, just barely overflowing his palm. Her dusky nipples were hard and waiting for his tongue.

He set his hands on the swell of her hips before caressing up to the indent of her waist and continuing to cup both breasts. Eurwen's eyes closed, and her head dropped back, her hair brushing his legs as he began teasing both nipples. He lifted his hips so his cock rubbed against her sex.

She suddenly leaned forward, their eyes meeting as she braced her hands on his chest. She leaned down and softly brushed her lips over his before crawling backward. The moment she reached for his arousal, Vaughn grabbed her and pulled her back up.

"You did that to me this morning in the dream. I need to be inside you," he said.

She gaped at him. "The dreams are real, then?"

He frowned. "What?"

"This morning. I had you in my hand and mouth."

"Shite," he murmured. "How?"

"I was going to ask you that."

He shook his head. "I doona want to think about that now. I'd rather be inside you."

"I agree," she replied with a seductive smile.

When she rolled onto her back and lay there waiting for him, Vaughn could only look on in amazement. He wasn't sure why such a stunning being wanted him, but he wouldn't question it. No, he planned to grab her with both hands and be grateful.

He rolled toward her but settled between her legs.

"I thought we decided that…"

Her words trailed off when his tongue swirled over her clit. Vaughn inwardly smiled at how he was able to silence her. He lavished undivided attention on her, making sure she was inundated with so much pleasure she couldn't form a coherent thought. By the soft cries falling from her lips, he was doing just that.

It was too much.

It wasn't enough.

Vaughn kept her seesawing between sensations with every lick and lave of his tongue. She both reached for the climax and pushed it away because she knew the longer she held off, the greater it would be.

The joke was on her, however, because she had no control over her body when it came to Vaughn. He was the master of pleasuring her, and she happily granted him that. She'd had lovers before, but none had touched her—*knew* her—like Vaughn.

Her thoughts vanished as the pleasure intensified. Desire swirled low in her belly, growing tighter and tighter. Just as she felt herself about to reach that final hurdle, Vaughn changed the speed of his tongue.

It was maddening.

It was amazing.

She didn't know how he could touch her so expertly. It was like he knew exactly where to give her the most pleasure and what she desired.

Her hands fisted the covers as he drew her closer and closer again. Closer than before. She held her breath, wanting to tell him to wait yet beg him to continue. No sound passed her lips as he continued his teasing.

Right up until the climax claimed her.

Vaughn held Eurwen's hips still as her back arched off the bed and she cried out. He continued swirling his tongue over her until she lay limp. His cock jumped eagerly as he rose on his hands and knees.

She looked up at him with half-lidded eyes and reached for him. Vaughn guided himself to her entrance and pushed inside her. She gasped in pleasure as her body stretched to accommodate him. He slowly filled her, pausing when he was fully seated. Their gazes met. He wanted to tell her how much she meant to him, but something held him back.

Her hands flattened on his chest as her eyes lowered to his dragon tattoo. Her fingers lightly ran from one shoulder to the other, following the curve of the dragon as it lay curving from collarbone to collarbone with the tail laying over his left shoulder. Her gaze lifted to his then, and he saw the stark, blatant desire.

He began moving his hips. The friction of their bodies soon had their skin slick with sweat. She wrapped her legs around his waist and began meeting his thrusts. It didn't matter how many times he'd made love to her in his dreams, it couldn't beat the real thing. His hunger, his need was so great that he soon found the climax upon him. He shouted and buried himself deep within her as his seed filled her body.

For several minutes, they didn't move. Vaughn looked down at her to find her smiling at him. He grinned. Life would be so good now that he'd found his mate.

"We're going to be doing this a lot," she said breathlessly.

He chuckled as he pulled out of her and plopped onto his back. "We certainly are."

Vaughn began reaching for her to pull her against him when she turned the other way to move a pillow. That's when he saw her tattoo. The dragon ran gracefully, seductively down Eurwen's spine as if winding around it. It was in the same special red and black ink that made up the Kings' tats.

"This is stunning," he said and ran his hand down it.

Eurwen glanced at him over her shoulder and smiled. "I like how it feels when you touch it."

"I know exactly what you mean," he said with a smile.

She turned to him and rested against his chest, her long eyelashes brushing his skin as he stared at the ceiling. There was so much he wanted to say but he wasn't sure how to even begin. Their first words hadn't been good ones, and he didn't want that to happen again. At least, not so soon. He wasn't averse to arguing. That was a natural part of any relationship. But a lot was going on outside of just him and Eurwen.

Suddenly, she sat up, her eyes wide. "I told Con and Rhi they could come here anytime. What if they walk in on us?"

"They willna," Vaughn assured her before glancing down at her glorious breasts.

Her silver eyes narrowed on him as she frowned. "How can you be so sure?"

"Because Con knows I'm here."

"He knows?" she squeaked.

Vaughn wasn't sure if she was outraged, embarrassed, or both. Regardless, he'd obviously said the wrong thing. "I had to convince Con to allow me to come with them on this first trip. Every King wanted to come."

"Did you know it was me before you stepped through the doorway?"

"Nay, lass. I'd hoped, but I wasna sure."

She sighed. "My parents know…everything?"

"They doona keep secrets from each other. I'm sure Rhi knows by now, as well. I left them with Varek and Jeyra. Con knows you and I had words earlier. I told him I wanted another chance to talk with you. They willna be disturbing us tonight."

Eurwen visibly relaxed. "That's good. I guess."

"You doona like them knowing?"

"I'm not used to others knowing my business."

Vaughn put one arm behind his head and touched Eurwen with his other. He couldn't stand not touching her. "What about your brother?"

Her gaze slid away, and she fell silent for a moment. Then she curled up next to him once again, resting her cheek on his chest. He wrapped his arm around her and simply held her. Vaughn, like most of the Dragon Kings, had been so wrapped up in his problems on Earth with the mortals, Fae, and Others that he hadn't stopped to consider Eurwen and Brandr and what they might have endured. None of them had.

Vaughn was ashamed to say that he'd believed their problems on Earth were much larger than anyone else's. That was not only shortsighted but also wrong. She had told him a little, but he suspected she had only glossed over the facts instead of delving into them. Not that he blamed her. It had been Eurwen and her brother against everyone. He'd most likely have acted the same in her position.

Eurwen sighed, her cool breath brushing against his skin. "There was a time I could've told you exactly what he was thinking. It hasn't been that way for some time."

"You're both a mix of two verra powerful people. I imagine you have magic from both the dragons and the Fae. Since you were able to gain control of the dragons, you two can obviously speak to them."

She nodded her head and absently traced figure eights over his chest and stomach with her finger. "The mental link. Yes, we're able to do that. You saw me shift from dragon to human."

"And Brandr? Can he?"

"Oh, yes."

Vaughn kissed her head softly. "Can either of you do Fae magic, other than creating doorways?"

"Like teleporting? Yes. Only short distances."

"Bloody hell," he murmured with a grin. "Sounds like you got the best of both." When she was silent, he said, "Siblings are difficult. Sometimes, you're close. Sometimes, you are no'."

"I've watched enough families to know that. But twins are different," she explained. "There's a connection that other siblings don't have and never will."

That's when it hit Vaughn. "You miss that connection."

"No. Maybe. I don't know. He doesn't understand why I wanted our parents here."

"He's no' ready."

She shifted her head to meet his gaze. "I fear he never will be."

"Will that create a problem?"

"It already has."

Vaughn rolled onto his elbow to look down at her. "How so?"

She looked away and shook her head.

A yawning pit formed in Vaughn's stomach as he realized that she was talking about telling Brandr about her night with him. "What did your brother say, exactly?"

"It doesn't matter," Eurwen said as she sat up and hugged her knees to her chest.

Vaughn wasn't going to accept such an answer when he knew something was going on. He sat up beside her. "It does matter. You're hurt."

"We have something beautiful and special here." She turned her head and met his gaze. "Something I know the Dragon Kings want."

"Wish to experience," he corrected. "This is your world. We're no' coming to take it."

She raised a blond brow, her expression disbelieving. "Really? Do you want to leave?"

He hesitated.

Her lips flattened as she faced forward. "Exactly. Varek asked to stay. Any King who comes will ask the same thing."

"We're no' challenging you or Brandr."

"Who says we won't challenge any of you?" she asked in a dry tone.

Vaughn blinked, taking in her words. He wasn't sure what to think…or do. Finding her was supposed to be the difficult part. He was coming to realize that he'd been dead wrong.

"We don't have any idea if the magic on this realm is the same as yours. When Erith created—"

"What?" Vaughn asked in shock, his head swinging to her.

Eurwen wrinkled her nose as she glanced his way. "I forgot you weren't there when I told Con and Rhi. Erith created this realm to give the dragons a place to go."

"Shite," he murmured, surprise and amazement running through him.

"Erith tried to mimic Earth for the dragons, but there are

differences. They're subtle. You'd probably miss them if you weren't looking."

Vaughn ran a hand down his face. "We know verra little of the magic of our realm, other than it's powerful. We know from our battle with the Others that magic can be drained from a planet, but I have no idea where it comes from. There is magic here. I feel it."

"It's Erith's," Eurwen explained. "It's why the clans don't have Kings."

He looked at her, waiting until her silver eyes met his before he asked, "And you're worried that might change if the Kings are here?"

"It's possible. I don't want any Teals challenging you for the right to be Dragon King."

"We were never meant to be Kings this long. We were only meant to stay in power until someone stronger came and the magic chose them."

Eurwen shrugged. "I don't want to challenge you, my father, or anyone else."

Ah. So that was her real fear.

For both her and Brandr.

Vaughn put his hand over hers. "The best way to ensure that doesna happen is if we can all sit down and talk. Including your brother."

"That's never going to happen."

CHAPTER TEN

There was so much going on inside Rhi that she wasn't sure which way was up. At least, she had Con by her side. The thought of going through any of this alone made her nauseous. She would've done it, because when you had to do something, you had to do it. But that didn't mean she would've liked it.

"What?" Con asked when his black eyes swung to her.

She smiled and walked to him, wrapping her arms around him. "I love you."

"I love you," he said before giving her a soft kiss. "Now, what's wrong?"

She couldn't hold back her laugh. "You know me so well."

"Stop stalling and spit it out," he said with a wink.

"I have a bad feeling."

His brows drew together. "What do you mean?"

"Our children, the dragons, the humans, this realm, the babies appearing... Take your pick, my love, but something isn't right."

Con blew out a breath and ran his hands up and down her upper arms. "You're so used to having something or someone to fight that you doona know what it is to have peace. Besides, if something were going on, Varek would've known by now."

"Need I remind you that he spent most of his time on this realm in a prison? Without magic," she stated.

Con paused and issued a nod. "Fair point. But after—"

"It's only been a few days. What do you think Varek could've seen? Not much. Also, he's otherwise occupied with his new mate. Case in point, where are they now?"

"Is it too much to ask for things to go right?" Con asked.

Rhi gazed up at him, understanding his worry and dismay. "I want things to be simple and easy, but that isn't our world. It never will be because of the power and magic the Dragon Kings have."

"You are no' the only one feeling as if something is off," he admitted.

She flattened her lips and gave him a pointed look. "You were just going to keep that to yourself?"

"I was expecting things that wouldna be there. Force of habit kind of thing."

"What are you always telling me?"

"To trust your instincts."

"Exactly. What were you doing?" she pushed, forcing him to admit the truth.

His nostrils flared as he glanced away in irritation. "I get your point."

"Say it."

His black eyes looked into hers. "I was ignoring my gut."

"And we can't do that."

"Nay, love, we can no'," he said with a grin. "Now, tell me what you've seen."

She looked around the grove, the trees circling them, and the mountains beyond. "The absence of our son raises a huge concern. If Eurwen opened the door against his wishes—"

"You're worried there will be repercussions," Con finished.

Rhi nodded. "To start, yes. Eurwen wouldn't have opened the doorway unless she wanted to, but her attitude today tells me that she's unsure if she made the right decision. We need to tread carefully. After all, this is their realm."

"I'm acutely aware of that. Dragons have been circling us all day, but none have approached. The few I've tried to converse with willna engage. Vaughn had a brief conversation with some Teals, and it wasna friendly."

Rhi took Con's hand and led him to the fire as they sat on the cut stumps facing each other. "This realm may look similar to ours, but it isn't the same."

"The magic isna, either. It isna even close. It feels more like..." He paused as if searching for the right word.

"Erith?" Rhi offered. "She *did* create it."

Con nodded. "Exactly. That's why none of the dragons have challenged our children. Why there are no' any Kings or Queens."

"Will that change with our arrival? Has it changed with Varek being here? Was there a bigger reason for our children not wanting us here, other than their anger at something neither of us had control over?"

Shock fell over Con's face. "Bloody hell. Do you think?"

"I'm not ruling anything out. I understand that the twins

are upset that we weren't in their lives, but why take it out on us? Neither of us knew of their existence until recently."

"Why no' be angry at Erith for putting all of us in this situation?" Con asked.

Rhi shook her head as she glanced at the fire. "I don't want to ask that. But, yes. Everything looks perfect and beautiful, but you and I know from experience that things rarely are as they seem."

"Surely, Eurwen would've told us."

"What if she doesn't know? What if neither of our children knows?"

Con released her hand and quickly stood as he paced. Rhi watched the unease and suspicion begin filling her mate. It was rare for Con to let any kind of emotion show if anyone but she was around, but he didn't seem to care right now.

"I might be reaching," she said with a shrug. "Maybe you're right. Maybe I am seeing things that aren't there."

He shook his head and halted in looking at her. "My thoughts didna go down that road, but that isna to say you're wrong. I've been troubled since Jeyra and Varek told us about the infants. There doesna seem to be a rhyme or reason for their arrival, nor why some live a regular life span of a mortal, and others, like Jeyra, live several hundred years."

"We need to get Jeyra to Dreagan so Sophie can look her over. Maybe do some bloodwork. I don't sense any magic within her, but that doesn't mean it's not there."

"I doona sense magic, either, but it could be a new kind that dragons can no' detect."

Rhi saw his brow furrow deeper. "There's something else."

"All these millennia, none of the Kings has been able to have children."

"We did," Rhi said with a smile.

He didn't return it. "Would you have carried our children to term?"

"Yes."

"You can no' know that for certain, love."

Rhi hated that she was getting defensive. "I'm not the first Fae to get pregnant with a Dragon King's bairn. Need I remind you of Melisse."

"Between her and now, there have been none. Yes, Eurwen and Brandr are alive. Who is to say that if we had all made different decisions back then that you wouldna have lost the bairns?"

"Or had them," she interjected.

A muscle ticked in Con's jaw. "Back on Earth, Claire and V are going insane every day waiting to see what will happen with the babe she carries."

An idea suddenly struck Rhi. "Bring Claire here."

"What?" Con asked, visibly taken aback.

"The dragons here have no problem having children."

"Claire isna a dragon. And the dragons didna have problems on Earth, either."

Rhi shot him a dark look. "I know Claire isn't a dragon, but she's carrying the child of one. Add in the fact that Usaeil used magic to ensure that Claire would get pregnant, and I think she should come here. She's overdue anyway."

"Why here?" Con pressed.

"Because there might be something on our realm that

prevents humans from having a child with a dragon," Rhi said, just shy of shouting.

Con searched her face for several minutes before his face paled. "Shite."

"There was always a fifty-fifty chance the bairn wouldn't survive," Rhi continued. "Claire is human, and I'm not sure what going through a Fae doorway will do to her or the babe. Everything might go as planned on Earth, allowing their child to survive."

"Or it might be stillborn like all the others," Con replied.

Rhi shrugged. "I say we leave it to V and Claire to make the decision."

"That's bringing another King and his mate to Zora. If you think things are precarious now, I can no' imagine they'll get better."

"We'll send Varek and Jeyra to Dreagan like we spoke about. Claire and V will come in their place."

Con walked to her and pulled her into his arms. "We'll tell Eurwen in the morn. Hopefully, she'll agree."

"Or we could go now."

"That might no' be a good idea."

She leaned back to look up at him. "This doesn't have anything to do with Vaughn leaving and how neither he nor Eurwen could take their eyes off each other, does it?"

"Nothing gets past you," Con said with a grin.

Rhi playfully punched him in the arm. "You know I hate being left out of things."

"Love, I was going to tell you everything."

"Next month?" she asked with a roll of her eyes as she tried to turn away.

Con chuckled and dragged her back to him. "Come here," he said in a husky voice before his mouth descended on hers.

Rhi was powerless to resist him. She wrapped her arms around him and sank into the kiss. "I'll never get tired of your kisses," she said when it ended.

"You better no'," he said as he rubbed his nose against hers.

She smiled, her heart filled with so much joy. "I know this day didn't turn out like either of us wanted, but we got to see one of our children. We're in their realm, getting a glimpse of how they live. It's enough. For now."

"You're a special woman, my love."

"I know," she teased. The smile dropped as she looked into Con's eyes. "We're going to need to take it slow with the twins. And by slow, I mean at their pace. It goes against everything I want to do, but I think it's the only way."

Con pulled her against him and held her tightly. "I agree. We hoped for the best, but we didna get the worst. It was somewhere in between. I think we could call that a win."

"Yes, we can," she said, blinking back tears. Then it became too much, and she couldn't stop her shoulders from shaking as she bawled.

Con kissed the top of her head. "It'll be fine, love. I promise."

"I never got to hold them. Feed them," Rhi said through her sobs. "I never got to see their first steps or hear their first words. We missed everything."

"But they're alive. You're alive," Con said. "I'd much rather have all of you."

She buried her face in his shirt and sniffed. He was right,

as usual. Erith could've let the twins die that day. Instead, she'd saved the bairns as well as Rhi. Still, Rhi couldn't simply ignore all the things she wished she would've gotten to experience as a mother.

"Who's to say we can no' have more children?" Con whispered in her ear.

Rhi slowly lifted her head. "What?"

A slow smile pulled at Con's lips. "I want to experience all those things as a father, too."

"I–I don't know why I didn't consider that before."

He tucked a long, black strand of hair behind her ear. "We both deserve to know what it is to be parents."

"What if—?"

He placed a hand over her mouth to silence her. "There are always things to consider. I'm no' saying we should start now. I'm telling you that I'm open to whatever you want."

"It's hard to answer that because I have what I've always wanted—you."

"You never lost me. I know it seemed that way, but I was always yours."

Rhi wiped at the tear streaks on her face. "We both made so many mistakes."

"The past is the past. It doesna do either of us any good to keep looking back. You forgave me."

"And you forgave me."

"Hopefully, our children will forgive us eventually, as well. Until then, we'll keep showing them that we willna give up."

Rhi smiled and leaned forward to kiss him. "How long do you think we'll be allowed to stay here?"

"No' long."

She saw his gaze lift to the skies. "Dragons?"

"Golds."

"Do you want to fly with them?"

"With every fiber of my being."

She stepped out of his arms. "Then go."

"They willna speak to me," he said with a sad smile. "Flying with them is out of the question. It's enough that I'm allowed to see them."

Rhi moved to stand beside him, their arms locked as she looked up and searched the dark sky for the dragons. They must have been high up because she couldn't see them. "There's another issue we need to address."

"The Silvers in Dreagan," Con said as if reading her mind. He glanced down at her and winked. "They belong here with the others. I'm going to broach the topic with Eurwen in the morning. Once I have her approval, I'll go to Ulrik."

"Surely, Ulrik will say yes."

Con shrugged. "What if no other Kings are allowed through the doorway? What if none get to see the dragons? The Silvers are our link to the past. Ulrik might have a hard time letting go."

"Whether we get to return to Zora or not, releasing the Silvers will be difficult. It's the right thing, though. Dreagan was meant to be a place of happiness and hope, not a prison. For anyone."

CHAPTER ELEVEN

Waking up next to Vaughn was amazing. Eurwen didn't want to open her eyes. She loved how he had held her all night. Whether she was on his chest, he was curled around her, or she him, they had never stopped touching each other.

When she finally lifted her lids, it was to see Vaughn awake and grinning at her. "What?" she asked.

"You have the cutest little snore."

She gaped and covered her mouth with her hand. "I do not."

He nodded, his smile growing. "You do. It's adorable."

"How long have you been awake?"

"All night. I didna want you to leave again."

She frowned. "I wouldn't."

"I wasna going to chance it." He leaned forward and placed his lips on hers for a lingering kiss. "Besides, I got to listen to the dragons all night. It was…"

He trailed off as if saying the words were too much. She shot him a smile. "I can't even imagine."

"I hope you never have to find out." He blew out a breath. "I suppose we must rise."

She stopped him from getting out of bed. "Can't we just stay here all day?"

"I'd like nothing better, but I have a feeling we're going to get some guests soon."

Her parents! Eurwen couldn't believe she had forgotten about them. "Right."

"Doona frown," Vaughn told her. "We have plenty of time to spend together."

She watched him rise from the bed and begin dressing. Eurwen wanted to spend time with Vaughn. Brandr was the problem.

"You're frowning."

Her gaze jerked to Vaughn's face. "What?"

"You're frowning. Whatever you're thinking of isna good."

She shrugged and sat up before slowly swinging her legs over the side of the bed and getting to her feet.

"I know Con and Rhi want to talk to you some more, and you should talk with them," Vaughn said. "But, afterward, I'd like to see you again. I think we should do more talking."

Eurwen nodded since she didn't know what else to do. They'd had all night to talk, but he had wanted to hold her. And she'd been fine with that. She was a little wary that he might ask to stay on Zora. That simply couldn't happen. Ever. Just as Varek couldn't remain.

But there was also a chance that Vaughn would ask her to

go back to Earth with him. She liked being with him, but she wouldn't give up her home for…

Say it.

She couldn't even think the word. Vaughn was special. He'd captured her attention that long-ago night and had held it for untold years. That didn't mean they were destined for each other. It didn't mean anything.

Or did it?

Eurwen needed some time to think. Unfortunately, she wasn't going to get it. She walked into the bathroom and, with a thought, cleaned her body and hair. She chose a blush skirt that hung loosely and just grazed the floor. The matching top draped off one shoulder and hugged her waist. Eurwen finished the outfit with a pair of gold sandals. She walked back to Vaughn to find him staring at her, longing radiating from him.

"Bloody hell, lass. That material is see-through," he said in a low voice, rough with desire.

She walked up to him and rose on her tiptoes to kiss him. "Is it?"

"You know it is," he said with a grin as his arms went around her.

Just as their lips were about to meet, they heard voices approaching. Eurwen wasn't ready for their interlude to end, but neither of them had a choice.

"It's going to be fine," Vaughn assured her.

She gazed into his Persian blue eyes. "I wish I could be as optimistic."

A knock sounded on the door. Eurwen stepped out of

Vaughn's arms, but before she could turn away, he stopped her and kissed her once more.

"Trust me," he pleaded.

That was the thing. Eurwen didn't think she could. Instead of answering him, she walked to the door and opened it to see her parents. The two larger-than-life individuals held hands. Rhi wore a smile while Con bowed his head to her in greeting.

"I hope it isna too early," Con said.

Behind her, Vaughn replied, "It is."

Eurwen didn't look at him. She moved to the side and said, "Please, come in."

Rhi entered, followed by Con. Eurwen then looked at Vaughn. He started toward the door when Con said his name.

"Before you go, there's something I'd like both you and Eurwen to know," Con said.

Eurwen's heart thumped in her chest. She prayed this wasn't anything about Vaughn spending the night with her. She could barely think about it herself. The last thing she wanted was to discuss it with the two people in front of her. Or Vaughn.

Instead, Con's black eyes slid to Eurwen. "Your mother and I have a request."

"What is that?" she asked.

"We're asking for an exchange of sorts."

Eurwen immediately became wary. "Explain."

Rhi put her hand on Con's arm and then said to Eurwen, "I'm sure you know of V and his mate, Claire."

"The pregnant one," Eurwen said with a nod.

"Her babe is due, and we're concerned."

Eurwen looked between her parents. "You want to bring Claire here? Why?"

"We want to give Claire and V every opportunity to have their bairn born alive," Con said. "It may no' mean much to you, but since you and your brother are the last dragons—"

"Half," Eurwen corrected him.

"—born, there is call for concern."

Vaughn said, "None of us have had children since the dragons left our realm."

It was on the tip of Eurwen's tongue to say that was their fault, but she managed to keep the comment to herself. "The exchange would be what, exactly?"

"I'd like Varek to take Jeyra to Dreagan and get her looked over by one of the mates who is a human doctor. Test her blood and the like to see if we can determine why she ages differently than the others on this realm," Con explained.

Rhi shrugged. "And maybe try to decipher where and why the babies are brought to Zora."

It seemed like a fair trade, though Eurwen wasn't sure Brandr would agree. But he wasn't here. She was. Yet, if she continued in that vein, it was a slippery slope. If the situation were reversed and Brandr made a decision she disagreed with, she wouldn't just sit back and accept it. They had always ruled Zora together. Why did it feel like that was about to change?

"Eurwen?" Vaughn pressed.

She looked his way, all the while trying to decide if she would let Brandr know what was going on or not. Eurwen knew Brandr would refuse more Kings coming to Zora for any reason. And while she understood his side of things, she also empathized with Claire and V.

"All right," she finally agreed.

Con smiled. "Thank you. The final decision rests with Claire and V."

"As it should. Are you returning to Earth to tell them?"

"We were hoping to stay and speak with you," Rhi said.

Con glanced at his mate. "Varek can tell them."

"Unless you'd like to go," Vaughn said.

Eurwen's head snapped to him. "What?"

"You've never been to Dreagan. This could be your chance to see that side of things. I could accompany you."

The thought of getting to walk on Dreagan land, to feel the magic beneath her feet, was entirely too tempting. The indecision must have shown on her face because Vaughn gave her a soft smile.

"I'll let you talk to Rhi and Con first. Then you can make your decision," Vaughn said before walking out and closing the door behind him.

Eurwen stared at it, not at all sure what to think of someone coming into her life and making decisions for her. Vaughn wasn't actually making the big decisions, though. He was only maneuvering her in a way that she could reach conclusions.

Brandr would no doubt call Vaughn manipulative.

Was it? Or was she looking for something that wasn't there? She didn't like how out of balance she felt. Everything was tilting one way and then the next. She didn't feel as if she had any say in any of it. Which was ridiculous because she was the one who had begun it all by opening the doorway.

Eurwen finally remembered that she wasn't alone. She turned to her parents to find them watching her. In an attempt to stop any questions, she smoothed her brow and motioned to the same seats they had taken the day before.

"I want to apologize for yesterday," she began.

Con shook his head as he sat beside Rhi. "You spoke your mind, as you should."

"It wasn't how I wanted our first conversation to go."

Rhi grinned and put a hand on Con's leg. "I think all of us felt that way. We wanted you to know that we understand your and Brandr's concerns."

"We only ask that you give Rhi and I a chance to get to know both of you," Con added.

Eurwen crossed one leg over the other. "I can't promise anything for Brandr. If I didn't want to know the two of you, I wouldn't have created the doorway."

"But?" Rhi pressed.

Eurwen shrugged and folded her hands in her lap. "It has created a rift between my twin and me."

"Siblings fight," Con said.

Rhi nodded. "All of them."

"This is different," Eurwen told them. "I can't pinpoint exactly what it is, but I feel it. Brandr and I have argued before. It isn't harsh words we've exchanged. Instead, it feels as if he's…" She paused, trying to find the right word. "Cold. Indifferent, almost."

Con's gaze was intense as he leveled it on her. "Is this about us being here? Or is it about Vaughn?"

Eurwen lowered her gaze to her lap. So much for her not wanting to talk about Vaughn. She took a deep breath and raised her eyes to her parents. "I didn't tell Brandr about my encounter with Vaughn until yesterday."

"He must be hurt," Rhi said.

"Maybe." Eurwen shrugged. "I can't tell if it's because you two are here or if it's Vaughn."

Con scratched his forehead. "Or a combination."

"Is that why you're hesitant to go with Vaughn to Dreagan?" Rhi asked.

Eurwen didn't like being put on the spot, but maybe it was better if she answered. "I've seen Dreagan from afar. I would like to walk it."

"But?" Con asked, a blond brow quirked.

"I don't know."

Rhi caught Con's gaze and jerked her chin to the door. After a moment of frowning, his brow smoothed, and he got to his feet. "Excuse me for a moment."

Eurwen watched him leave before her eyes swung to Rhi.

"I thought we could have a moment alone together," her mother said.

"About?"

"Vaughn."

Eurwen felt her anxiety rising. "I don't have anything to say."

"You've not asked for my advice, and my mum always told me never to give it unless someone asked, but I'm going to make an exception." Rhi leaned forward in her seat and smiled. "The wonderful thing about you and Brandr is that you weren't raised with the Fae or Dragon Kings. You don't have any of our issues or preconceived notions. While you are a part of both worlds, that may make some things difficult for you."

Eurwen found herself wanting to know what Rhi was talking about. "Like?"

"You know from being around dragons that they mate for life. They know, here," she said and pointed to her heart, "when they've found their chosen. I'm not a dragon, and Fae don't mate for life, but I felt it. I knew the instant I saw Con the first time that he was going to change my life."

"He nearly broke you."

"And I nearly destroyed him. Everyone has a path they must travel. Sometimes, two people walk together for a time and have to take different roads to become the people they were meant to be so they can return to each other."

Eurwen gaped at her mother. "You truly believe that?"

"I wouldn't be with Con, otherwise. I can look back and see how much I've changed since that horrible day that I not only lost him but also you and your brother. The difference was, I didn't know about my children. Although, perhaps subconsciously, I did. I mourned deeply for Con, our love, and the future I thought I had planned out. I also believe that I mourned you and your brother."

Eurwen lifted a shoulder in a half-hearted shrug. "Vaughn and I have had two nights. That's it."

"He's searched for you. He never stopped looking."

"You believe he thinks I'm his mate."

Rhi laughed and sat back against the cushions. "It's obvious. Don't you think?"

"If I thought he was my mate, wouldn't I have returned to him many years ago?"

The smile faded from her mother's face. "As someone who fought against what I knew in my heart on many occasions,

I'll say that sometimes we only see the things we want to see. You have many responsibilities here. Aside from that, you kept a big secret from Brandr, and I suspect that has weighed heavily upon you all this time. Just those two things alone could be enough to keep someone here instead of going after what they really want."

Eurwen couldn't argue her mother's words.

"What would it hurt to go with Vaughn, Varek, and Jeyra to see Dreagan?" Rhi asked. "You could meet other Dragon Kings and their mates. I know they will have a lot of questions for you. Whether you answer them or not is another matter entirely."

The more Eurwen thought about it, the more she wanted to go. "You're right. Nothing's stopping me from going."

CHAPTER TWELVE

There was a dozen different reasons Vaughn thought that
Eurwen should come with him to Dreagan.

And a dozen why she wouldn't.

He wanted to pace, fly, roar, do *something*. Instead, he
stood calmly in the same spot she had been in when he, Rhi,
and Con had emerged from the doorway the day before.

"You doona fool me," Con said as he walked up
beside him.

Vaughn looked at him and grinned. "Oh?"

"The stiller you are, the more torn-up you are inside."

"When did you learn my secret?" Vaughn asked with a
frown.

Con laughed and clasped his hands behind his back.
"Long, long ago, brother. It's what makes you so formidable
as a lawyer."

"What are you doing out here?"

"Rhi wanted to talk to Eurwen."

Vaughn wrinkled his nose. "Is that good?"

"I can never guess these things. Rhi saw something, and she obviously believed it would be better if she were alone with Eurwen. Did last night go well?"

"I thought so. Now, I'm wondering if I was wrong."

Con's gaze locked on a trio of Violets flying in the distance and followed them. "There are many explanations for why Eurwen would refuse to go to Dreagan. The main one, I suspect, is Brandr."

"Varek speaks highly of him."

"I'd like to meet my son, but I'm no' sure that will happen this trip."

Vaughn turned his head to Con and waited until the King of Kings met his gaze. "Will you force it?"

"It would be beneficial to everyone if I didna. It'll crush Rhi, but getting to spend even a little time with Eurwen will make up for it somewhat."

"Maybe you and Rhi should take Eurwen to Dreagan," Vaughn offered.

Con shook his head. "We're going to remain in Zora. I want Brandr and the dragons to know that we're no' coming to take control."

"I doona feel good about leaving you without backup," Vaughn said as he faced Con.

"You think my son might challenge me?"

Vaughn's brows rose. "He could."

"If he does, he does."

"You want to subject Rhi to witnessing a fight between her son and husband? Knowing that one will lose? What if it's you? Then she dies. And if you kill Brandr? What would that do to your relationship?"

Con's eyes lowered to the ground as he stayed silent for a time. "I know my words make it sound as if I've no' considered any of this. I have. Rhi and I have spoken of it several times."

"Speaking of it and being here are two different things."

Finally, Con looked at him. "I'm no' sure it's sunk in with Rhi yet. But I became acutely aware of things when the Golds wouldna answer me."

"You could've made them."

Con smiled sadly. "Could I have? I'm no' so sure. We may be Dragon Kings on Earth, but what are we on other realms? What are we here?"

"We're Dragon Kings."

He shook his head. "We're dragons who can shift. Nothing more. Nothing less."

"You and I both know that we Kings could take back control of the clans if we wanted."

"Is that what you want?"

Vaughn hesitated, unsure of his answer.

"Exactly," Con replied. "We want to return to normal, but after seeing the dragons, it's hard to think of forcing them into a life they no longer know. The world we knew and loved, the one we fought for, is gone. The dragons we knew and loved, those we sent away to save them, are gone. They have a beautiful, protected place here. I willna take it from them. Nor will I allow anyone else to take it from them."

Vaughn nodded in agreement. "What reason do we have to stay on Earth?"

"It's our home. No being has more magic than us there. We're the realm's protectors. Perhaps that was what we were destined for all along."

"Some Kings will want to live here."

Con's lips flattened. "My children willna accept that. The dragons willna accept that. Something has to be set up so the Kings and their mates can come for short periods of time, never interfering with how Eurwen and Brandr reign here."

"Seems logical and fair. I hope the twins feel the same."

"They willna," Con said softly.

Vaughn saw movement out of the corner of his eye. When he turned his head, he spotted Eurwen's pink skirt blowing in the breeze. Across the distance, their gazes met. His heart began pounding when she started toward him.

Please, he inwardly begged.

He didn't know why it was so important that he show her Dreagan, but it was. She had been to Earth many times, but this would be different—if she decided to go. Vaughn knew she was troubled over Brandr's reaction to her being with a Dragon King. Personally, he thought Brandr could shove it.

Vaughn managed to remain where he was until Eurwen reached him. She briefly looked at Con before her gaze returned to Vaughn. The sunlight on her hair made it look like spun gold. Her beauty was stunning, and her smile made him tongue-tied.

"Hi," he said.

She grinned, causing his heart to jump in his chest. "I'd like to accept your offer to go to Dreagan."

Vaughn couldn't remember the last time he had been so happy. "When do you want to leave?"

Eurwen glanced to the side, reminding him that Con and Rhi were there. Though he couldn't remember when Rhi had walked up.

"We plan to stay," Con told Eurwen. "If that willna cause any problems."

She shook her head. "Use my cottage. Brandr knows both of you are here. Hopefully, he'll come to see you." A frown furrowed her brow as she slid her gaze back to Vaughn. "How long will we be gone?"

"As long or short as you want," he answered.

Con grinned. "I just told Varek. He and Jeyra will be along shortly."

Eurwen licked her lips as she hesitated, looking between Con and Rhi. "Please, don't do anything while I'm gone."

"I'll make sure he doesn't," Rhi said as she wrapped her arm around Con.

When Vaughn looked up, he spotted Varek, his lichen scales flashing in the sun, Jeyra upon his back. After Varek landed and shifted, he and Jeyra walked to them.

Eurwen bowed her head to both. "I'm Eurwen."

"I was hoping I'd get to meet you," Jeyra said.

Varek grinned at his mate before turning to Eurwen. "I've heard a lot about you. Are you coming?"

Eurwen met Vaughn's gaze. "I am."

Varek's smile widened. "That's good to hear."

"Ready?" Vaughn asked everyone.

Jeyra looked pale and a bit green. "I'm nervous."

Varek laughed. "You captured a Dragon King, prepared to fight me to the death, and you're nervous about going to another realm?"

"Yes."

"You'll be fine," Eurwen said with a wink. "Promise."

Jeyra visibly swallowed and linked her hand with Varek's.

"Follow us," Eurwen told them as she started down the hill.

Vaughn stayed by her side. He wanted to grab her hand, but he held back. Then, suddenly, she took his and met his gaze as they passed through the doorway. In the blink of an eye, Vaughn found himself back in the Dragonwood on Dreagan.

He couldn't say why, but it seemed vitally important that Eurwen be here with him. He pulled her closer and lowered his gaze to her lips. She had no idea how tempting she was. He wanted to kiss her right then, to remove her clothes and make love to her in the woods.

"No," she said with a grin.

He blinked. "What?"

"Your feelings are in your eyes," she whispered.

That made him smile. "Really?"

"Yes. Stop grinning."

"I'm not sure it's my feelings in my eyes. I think you're feeling the same things I am."

She glanced at Varek and Jeyra, who were off to the side, talking. "Maybe. Can we come back here? Alone? At night?"

"Absolutely," he said, right before he lowered his head and pressed his lips to hers.

For just a moment, she sank against him. Then she pulled back.

"You have to know how I feel about you," he said.

She shook her head. "I don't want to talk about that now."

Vaughn was disappointed, but he didn't press. Not now. Later, he would have the conversation. But she was right. They weren't alone. Now wasn't the time to talk about his feelings or the fact that he knew she was his mate. As part dragon, he assumed that she felt the same thing. Given the way she kissed and made love to him, she felt *something*.

Varek and Jeyra were laughing when they started toward the manor. Vaughn let the couple get ahead of them before he asked Eurwen, "Ready?"

"Yes," she said breathlessly.

They meandered through the forest. He heard Jeyra gasp when they emerged from the trees. Vaughn hid his smile when Eurwen's steps quickened. Her gaze searched, her head tilted to the side as she tried to catch a glimpse of whatever was outside the wood. Then, finally, they cleared it.

Vaughn paused, watching Eurwen as her eyes moved over the mountains in the distance to the rolling hills dotted with sheep and cattle. He knew the moment her gaze landed on the manor because her lips parted in surprise.

"I've seen it in pictures," she said. "But this is different."

He squeezed her hand. "Wait until you see the inside."

"The magic here is…"

He chuckled. "I know. It can be a bit overwhelming."

"I've felt it every time I came to this realm, but here, on Dreagan, it's like I'm standing in the middle of it," she said as she looked at him.

"Because you are."

"How do you leave?" she asked in wonder.

He shrugged. "It isna easy. I think it's knowing that we can return that allows us the ability to leave."

"This is where you came after you sent the dragons away?"

He pointed to the mountains surrounding them. "Dreagan is sixty thousand acres. Most of it is comprised of mountains. Each of the Kings has their own mountain, a place we go to be alone. For many of us, we slept away centuries. Only two Kings never slept."

"Which ones?"

"Ulrik. And your father."

Her lips twisted. "Somehow, I knew Con would be one of them."

"He takes his duties as King of Kings seriously. He's always protected us, Dreagan, and the world."

"Including the humans, even though it meant sending the dragons away."

Vaughn sighed as he nodded slowly and looked to his mountain. "That's right."

"You were right, you know."

He jerked his head to her. "About what?"

"Telling me that just because I heard the story didn't mean I knew what happened. Or how it made any of you feel."

"I'm sure Erith did her best while sharing the story."

"I'd like to hear it from you. If you want to tell me."

He flashed her a smile. "I doona like to talk about it. None of us do. But you have a right to know. All the dragons have a right to know everything."

"I agree."

"There is something I'd like from you, though."

Her lips curved. "What would that be?"

"For you to explain why you and your brother hate us so much."

"I think you deserve to know. Brandr might not agree with me, but he hasn't agreed with me in some time."

Vaughn turned her toward him. "You're twins, siblings. For the longest time, it was only the two of you. Whatever created the rift surely can be mended."

"I'll make sure of it," she said with a nod.

Vaughn glanced to Varek and Jeyra, who were almost to the manor. "Are you ready? There will be a lot of people. We could bypass them, and you could teleport us to my room."

She laughed, her face lighting up. "I want to do this properly."

"Then proper it is," he said as they faced the manor and began walking.

CHAPTER THIRTEEN

Zora

Brandr placed a knee on the ground as he looked around, his eyes searching the area. For what, he didn't know. It was just a feeling that had been growing inside him for days now. A gnawing uncertainty that wouldn't let him rest.

He'd sent his dragon generals to look for anything out of the ordinary, hoping, praying that whatever he felt had nothing to do with his sister opening a doorway to Earth for their parents. And any other Dragon King who wanted to venture to Zora.

Brandr didn't like keeping secrets from Eurwen. At one time, they had known everything about the other. As time passed, they each began their lives while ruling the dragons together. It had worked. He hadn't known every detail of her life, but she hadn't known his, either. It was better that way. At least, he had thought that. Now, he wasn't so sure. Especially after he'd learned of her night with Vaughn. He didn't want to think what might happen if they were mates. All he could do was pray that Vaughn was purely an infatuation for his sister.

He trusted Eurwen with his life. Partly because they were twins and connected on a deeper level than other siblings. But it also had to do with the fact of how they had grown up, found Zora, and got the dragon world ordered again. They'd only ever had each other. Erith had been there, but merely as a peripheral figure.

Brandr blew out a weary breath. Zora was supposed to be free of the troubles that had—and always would—plague Earth. Yet he couldn't push aside the suspicion that whatever had disrupted the peace was somehow connected to Earth and the Dragon Kings.

He knew how important it was to Eurwen that she have a relationship with their parents. The last thing he wanted was to tell her that he'd been right all along, and that their parents and anyone else from Earth could never return. Because he feared if he told Eurwen that, she would leave Zora.

Or worse—he'd have to banish her because of Vaughn.

Brandr had hated the Dragon King immediately. He knew the basics of all the Kings, and he'd never felt one way or another about Vaughn. Until now. What had the bastard said to Eurwen to make her keep a secret from him for so long?

"Enough," Brandr said to himself as he shook his head to dislodge his thoughts.

He spread his fingers and placed his right palm on the earth as he closed his eyes. He wasn't sure what he searched for. He only knew that he would find it in the ground—or the absence of something. Brandr had started near his and

Eurwen's cottages at Cairnkeep and then expanded out in a
circle. The farther from the center he moved, the more
troubled he became. All he could do was hope that whatever
this was, it hadn't gotten a foothold on Zora and could be
eradicated quickly.

When he found nothing, Brandr rose and continued
walking. He was getting closer to the border with the humans.
He had no interest in being around any of them. It was one of
the reasons he had stopped visiting Earth. In his opinion, they
were mortal enemies of all dragons. If he came across one, he
wouldn't hesitate to take action—in any way that was needed.

As he reached the stream at the edge of their domain, he
knelt and put his hand upon the earth. That's when he felt it,
the coldness that hadn't been there before. Brandr walked
along the edge of the water, stopping every fifty meters and
testing the ground, his concern growing. But he found no more
answers.

He backtracked and went the other way. To his shock, the
ground grew colder and colder the closer he got to the spot
where the crone had managed to pull Varek from his realm to
theirs.

Brandr straightened and dusted off his hands. "It's time I
find this crone."

The instant he learned of her existence from Jeyra, Brandr
had been curious about her. Unfortunately, Jeyra couldn't give
him any answers. Brandr hadn't been able to do a proper
search for the crone, but perhaps it was time he focused on
locating her. She might very well be the cause of everything.

Whatever—or *who*ever—had disrupted the balance on
Zora would be dealt with. Swiftly and severely.

He turned and was about to shift when his enhanced
hearing picked up the sound of someone approaching from the
woods across the stream. Brandr ducked behind a tree and
waited. He swallowed his disappointment when it turned out
to be a couple of human teenagers wanting to get a look at the
border. Brandr shook his head because adolescents were all
the same, no matter what species. They always got into
trouble, pushed boundaries, and went places they had no
business going.

Brandr thought about scaring them. If they wanted to see a
dragon, he'd show them one. Maybe then they wouldn't get
near the border again. Before he could carry out his plan, he
heard more footsteps coming up behind the lads. Was it more
of their friends? Given how the two laughed and talked, they
had no idea that anyone approached.

A deep, gruff voice called out to them, causing both boys
to jerk in surprise and spin around awkwardly. The two lads
were visibly shaken. Whoever the man was, the boys were
terrified of him. Several seconds passed before the man
emerged from the forest.

He was tall and barrel-chested. His long, red beard hung
nearly to his chest. He dressed in the style of the other
humans, though the material of his outfit was of good quality
that consisted of a dark brown sleeveless tunic paired with a
lighter shade of trousers stuffed into tall boots. Two thick gold
armbands were clearly visible. Brandr saw a design on them
he couldn't quite make out.

"Get home," the man ordered the teenagers.

They were in such a hurry to get away, they slipped on the
damp ground.

"And don't come back!" he shouted after them.

Then he looked across the stream. Brandr committed the man's image to memory. From his red hair and beard to his brown eyes and voice.

The man stood still as stone for a full minute, moving nothing but his eyes. Finally, he let out a whistle, mimicking a bird. Three men came out of the woods to join him. Each of them as menacing as their leader. Brandr frowned because he hadn't picked up that there were four of them. They didn't have magic, which meant they had used another kind of skill to hide how many they were.

"You sure about this, Yannick," the big blond on the man's right asked.

The leader cut him a dark look. "It's the only way, Tuft."

"Sateen ordered none of us to cross the border," the black-haired one stated.

Yannick's lips flattened at the mention of the council leader's name. "What she doesn't know won't hurt her."

"He's right," said the auburn-haired man next to Yannick. "We have to find the crone. If she can capture a Dragon King, she can get what we need."

Brandr's heart clutched in his chest. What would the humans want with the crone? Another Dragon King? Surely, not. Capturing Varek had done nothing for them. In fact, they had lost a lot by taking him prisoner.

The humans might want to leave Zora. If that were the case, Brandr would help them. But he had a suspicion that things wouldn't be quite so simple. Most likely, they were after a way to strike at him, Eurwen, and the dragons.

Had he not felt something was amiss, he wouldn't have

ventured to the border and discovered all of this. As much as
he wished this was the cause of his unease, he knew it wasn't.
Whatever he searched for was aiding in disrupting everyone
on the realm.

The four wordlessly headed away from him. They stuck
near the stream but didn't cross it. He wanted to follow them,
but he would eventually run out of cover. He called for one of
his generals through the mental link, ordering the dragon to
follow the group and see how far they went, and to make sure
they didn't cross the barrier.

Brandr waited until the men were out of sight before he
retraced his steps. He loved flying, and there were times he
made use of his ability to teleport, but sometimes he liked
walking, too. It gave him time to think and be alone. The
dragons rarely bothered him when he was on a stroll. It was as
if they knew he didn't wish to be disturbed.

Sometime later, he reached Cairnkeep and his cottage. He
paused before entering and looked in the direction of Eurwen's
home. He knew Con, Rhi, and Vaughn had arrived, though
Brandr had made sure to stay out of their way. Were things
going as well as Eurwen had wanted? He was still angry at her
about Vaughn. Enough to keep him away from her cottage and
stop him from communicating with her.

Maybe after their parents departed, he would talk to her.
He couldn't remember the last time he had been so furious
with her—or hurt.

If she stays.

He hated the voice in his head. He didn't need to be
reminded that Eurwen might well have found her match with
Vaughn. Then again, if he were her mate, she wouldn't have

stayed away from him for so long. That made Brandr smile.
Vaughn was just a dalliance for his sister. He wasn't happy
about it, but at least she wasn't falling in love with Vaughn.
Brandr wouldn't forgive that. Not after everything they had
dealt with when they'd found the dragons.

Brandr was just entering his cottage when he heard
laughter. He looked into the sky and saw a woman with black
hair atop a gold dragon, gliding through the air. His parents.
They hadn't tried to approach him. That should make him
happy. It was what he wanted.

Wasn't it?

Without another look at them, he walked inside his home
and shut the door.

CHAPTER FOURTEEN

Dreagan

Eurwen was finally on Dreagan. She could hardly believe it.
The pictures she'd seen of the distillery were nothing
compared to the unbelievable beauty of the land. And the
magic. She was almost dizzy with the force of it.

The need to explore the mountains was overwhelming. She
wanted to see each one, to know which King had which
mountain. Especially Vaughn's. But that would come later.
She was about to meet everyone now. She was tense and
anxious, all to encounter the Kings she had watched for untold
centuries. Then there were the mates.

"We doona have to do this now," Vaughn said.

Eurwen smiled at him. "I'll be fine."

"That doesna mean we have to do this now."

"Jeyra and I will be sharing the spotlight, which will make
things easier for both of us."

Vaughn's lips curved into a sexy grin. "That it will. Just say the word if we need to leave."

She nodded and focused her attention on the four-story gray stone manor. There were windows everywhere. So many. Large, small, and every size in between. She loved that it had been built into Dreagan Mountain.

"The manor is set apart from the distillery by two overlapping hedgerows," Vaughn told her. "There's a hidden entrance that only those from Dreagan are aware of. A designated path so we can navigate it and reach Dreagan."

She was impressed. "No mortals have ever gotten near the manor?"

"No' unless they were invited. Which, of course, is rare."

Eurwen saw Jeyra and Varek enter the manor through a side door. Vaughn slowed his steps to give them more time. "Which floor is your bedroom on?"

"Top right." He pointed to a group of windows. "Those right there."

"Will I get to see it?"

Vaughn's blue eyes met hers. "I hope so."

Eurwen looked at the imposing structure of Dreagan Mountain that towered over the manor. "Why build the manor into the mountain?"

"There is a hidden entrance from the house to the mountain with tunnels and caverns we use. The largest one is for the mating ceremonies."

Eurwen didn't look his way when he mentioned that. She didn't want to give him any ideas.

"There's also a large portion at the back of the mountain that's wide enough for us to fly into."

Her head jerked to him. "Really?"

"Aye. I'll show you all of it."

She could hardly wait. By the time they reached the manor, Eurwen was ready to go inside. Vaughn opened the door and stepped aside for her to enter first. He didn't release her hand, which she was thankful for.

A small group of people surrounded Jeyra and Varek. No one had seemed to notice them yet. Eurwen wasn't sure if they were being polite, or if they genuinely weren't aware of her arrival. It didn't matter, though, because it gave her time to look around. Colorful rugs covered the dark wood floors. Some of the walls were paneled in the same dark wood, while others were painted lighter colors and had dark molding.

Everywhere she looked, she saw dragons. Some were obvious, like the paintings or the banister, but others were less so. The manor was massive and, at times, opulent. But at the heart of it was a home. Now that she was inside, Eurwen couldn't ignore the relaxed, comfortable atmosphere. It was due in part to the occupants, but it really came down to the Kings since they had built and adorned the manor themselves.

That's when it hit her. The house was an homage to the way of life they had lost. A blow of melancholy struck her suddenly. Vaughn was right. She had no right being angry over something she knew very little about. She hadn't lived it. She didn't know anything.

But it was all right here. Every drop of pain, tears, blood, and anger for the loss of the dragons—for the loss of their home.

She turned to Vaughn.

Before she could say anything, he smiled sadly and nodded. "You feel it, do you no'? I can see it in your eyes."

"Why didn't you warn me?"

"I wanted to see if it would affect you."

She deserved that after everything she had said to him and her parents. "If I hadn't, would you have thought less of me?"

He shook his head. "Never. It speaks to how prominent your dragon is that you feel it."

A man with long, black hair and gold eyes came into view, diverting Eurwen's attention. She hadn't expected to meet Ulrik so soon. The King of Silvers had traveled down a bumpy road for a long time, but he was now back in the fold with the other Kings.

"What an honor," Ulrik said. "You look so much like Rhi. Only with Con's hair. I'm—"

"Ulrik," she said before he could.

The King of Silver's gold eyes widened slightly. "Of course, you know who we are. It's a shame we're just learning of you and your brother. Is he here?"

"Just Eurwen," Vaughn said.

Ulrik's gaze dropped to their joined hands. Eurwen had forgotten that she still held onto Vaughn. She loosened her fingers, but he held her tighter as if to say that they had already been seen, so what was the point?

Ulrik bowed his head. "Perhaps we'll get to meet your brother soon. For now, my mate is ready to tackle me to get to you."

"Stop it," a woman with an American accent mixed with Irish playfully chastised Ulrik. She came up beside him and held out her hand. "I'm Eilish."

Eurwen had seen the dark-haired beauty before, though she knew very little about her. They clasped hands. "I'm Eurwen."

"A beautiful name."

Eurwen stared into Eilish's green-gold eyes and smiled, liking her immediately. "So is yours."

"We're delighted you're here. Since there are so many of us, we didn't want to overwhelm you or Jeyra, so we're approaching in shifts." Eilish flipped back her long locks.

Ulrik chuckled. "Trust me, you want us in turns. Otherwise, you might disappear with Vaughn, and we wouldna get to know you."

"How long are you staying?" Eilish asked.

Eurwen shrugged. "I'm not sure."

"Maybe we'll have some time for us girls to get together," Eilish offered.

"That sounds nice." Eurwen had never had friends. Not like this. She was close to some dragons, but that was different. She suddenly realized that she didn't just want friends, she needed them.

Vaughn caught Ulrik's gaze. "We're here for Eurwen, but we also need to speak to V and Claire."

Ulrik's smile vanished. "I hope you have a solution. Claire isna doing well."

Eurwen looked between the two. "What's wrong?"

"She's uncomfortable, for one," Eilish explained. "But with every day that passes, and she doesn't go into labor, she grows more frightened."

"How's V?" Vaughn asked, concern tingeing his voice.

Ulrik lifted a shoulder as he shook his head. "He's holding

it together for Claire, but he's hanging on by a thread. They both keep saying they're aware that the bairn could be stillborn, but it's eating them up."

"We brought something we hope will help," Eurwen told them. "But there's no guarantee."

Ulrik blew out a breath. "At this point, they'll take any help they can get."

"Perhaps we should speak to them now," Vaughn said.

Ulrik and Eilish turned as she and Vaughn fell into step behind them. Eurwen glanced at the crowd with Jeyra and Varek and smiled at anyone who looked her way. She took in as much of the manor as she could on her way up the stairs to the third floor to V and Claire's room.

After a knock, V opened the door. Eurwen stared into ice blue eyes filled with concern that he was desperately trying to hide. V's dark brown hair hung around his shoulders. The instant he laid eyes on her, hope filled his face.

"Can we speak with you and Claire?" Vaughn asked.

V quickly moved out of the way. Upon entering the room, Eurwen spotted a pretty woman with long, blond hair and kind brown eyes sitting on the edge of a chair rubbing her extended stomach. She had dark circles under her eyes from stress and worry.

"V, Claire," Vaughn said. "This is Con and Rhi's daughter, Eurwen."

Eurwen smiled at the couple. "It's nice to meet you both. My parents, along with Vaughn, have told me so much about you."

"Please tell us you have a way for us to have our child," V pleaded.

Claire clicked her tongue as she frowned at her mate. "Vlad. Don't put that kind of pressure on anyone. Please."

Eurwen watched as the King of Coppers moved to his mate and knelt beside her. "I'll do whatever it takes for you and our bairn."

Vaughn cleared his throat. "What we bring you isna a guarantee."

"Then why have you come?" V snapped.

Eurwen understood his distress. He felt helpless, desperate. The woman he loved had Fae magic used on her to ensure that she would become pregnant without her knowledge. Eurwen had seen many dragon births on Zora. Since she didn't spend any time with the humans in her realm, she didn't know what it was like for them not to bear children.

Most likely, it was worse for the Kings and their mates because the mates could become pregnant, giving everyone hope that a child could be born—though no human-dragon hybrid had ever lived.

"To give all three of you a fighting chance," Eurwen said. "One we know you won't have here."

Claire looked at her with determination. "Usaeil's magic created this child. It was that same magic that allowed me to remain pregnant. Maybe the same power will let this child be born alive."

"Fae magic or no', Claire, no human-dragon bairns have ever been born alive," Ulrik said.

V sighed loudly before looking between Vaughn and Eurwen. "What is your suggestion?"

"Come to Zora," Eurwen said. "I don't know what walking

through the doorway to another realm will do to Claire or the babe, though."

V frowned. "Then why go?"

"We know what will happen here," Vaughn said.

Claire asked, "And the humans on Zora? How are they?"

Eurwen had hoped they wouldn't ask about that, but the couple needed to know everything. "They're unable to have children at all. We don't know why. You would remain in our domain. Rhi and Con, as well as Vaughn and I, think you might have a chance in my realm."

Claire turned her head to V. "What do you think?"

"I'll do anything, go anywhere to keep you and our child safe and alive," V told her.

"And if I want to go to Zora?"

V smiled at her. "I'll be right beside you."

A tear fell from Claire's eye onto her cheek. "Let's go."

"The sooner, the better, I think," Ulrik said.

Vaughn nodded as V stood.

Eurwen walked to Claire and held her other hand as she got to her feet. "Steady, now."

"I've got her," V said as he carefully lifted her into his arms.

Eurwen watched them. "I'll teleport us to the doorway. Once you walk through, Con and Rhi will be nearby. If you don't see them, call for them."

Claire laid her head on V's shoulder. "I'm ready."

Vaughn touched her shoulder as Eurwen reached for V. In a blink, they were at the doorway. V didn't linger. With a quick farewell, he walked through and out of sight.

V held his breath as he passed through to the new realm. When Claire didn't cry out in pain or wince, he breathed easier. But his worry didn't lessen.

"It's going to be all right, beautiful," he told her.

She touched her hand to his face. "It will be because you're beside me. No matter what happens. We have each other."

"Never forget that," he said as he kissed her temple.

V looked up the mountain and saw Rhi standing there. The sound of dragons all around should have been enough reason for him to rejoice, but all V could think about was his mate, his love. Before he could shift to fly them to the top, Rhi was beside him.

"I'm so glad you're both here," she said with a smile.

V didn't look away from Claire's face. "She needs to lie down."

Rhi touched him. In a blink, they stood inside a cottage. V strode to the bed and gently set Claire down. She rolled away from him onto her side and cradled a pillow against her before closing her eyes. V smoothed her hair away from her face. He hadn't seen Claire this at ease in weeks.

"Let her sleep," Rhi said and tugged his arm.

V begrudgingly left his mate, but he wouldn't be far.

CHAPTER FIFTEEN

Vaughn turned away from the doorway, emotions churning inside him. The distress and apprehension that surrounded both Claire and V were unmistakable.

"What?" Eurwen asked.

"I wouldna want to be in V's shoes."

Eurwen cocked her head to the side. "With every pregnancy in every being, there is always a chance the child won't make it—or the mother."

"I'm aware of that."

"This is about the Kings being unable to have children with mortals."

Vaughn met her gaze. He could tell her, but it would be better to show her. "Come with me."

Their return to the manor was silent. He took her around to the back of the mountain so she could see the entrance they used in their true forms. Once inside, he studied her, waiting until she noticed the carvings. The minute she did, her gaze drank in all of the dragons that had been drawn, carved, and etched into the stone.

"There are thousands of these throughout the tunnels," Vaughn told her.

Eurwen walked to one of the carvings and touched the stone. "Just like the dragons within the manor, these are a tribute."

"To what we once had. To what we lost. Aye."

Her silver eyes met his. "What does this have to do with children?"

"This realm was never perfect, but it was damn close before the humans arrived. They were frightened, starving, and in need of protection. Especially because they didna have magic. The Kings gathered to approach them, but because they couldna understand us, the magic shifted us to their form. It was the first time any of us had that ability."

Eurwen nodded. "Erith explained that to me."

"Did she tell you how painful it was for us? Did she tell you we were suddenly thrust into a new role that we all desperately tried to figure out? Bodies we didna understand how to work properly?"

Eurwen glanced at the ground. "She didn't."

"The shift happened without warning," Vaughn explained. "The pain was excruciating, but thankfully didna last long. Our magic allowed us to understand any language, so we had no trouble talking to the mortals. But learning to move our new bodies? Well, that was something else entirely. No' only did we each have a sword, but we also had tattoos. Were the markings always there, and we just never saw them beneath our scales? That isna something anyone can answer."

She watched him, listening intently.

Vaughn took her hand and led her through the tunnels. "We're protectors. It's something innate in every King. We didna see the humans as a threat. We saw them as those needing defending. So, we helped them. We gave them land, helped them build structures to keep them sheltered from the elements, and showed them what could and couldna be eaten. We believed we were doing the right thing."

"How could you open your home to them? There were no mortals on your world before."

He quirked a brow at her. "I could say the same for you and Zora. The humans didna arrive until after you did, yet you and Brandr didna destroy them."

"We thought about it."

"We're no' killers," Vaughn told her. "We made a vow, and we stuck to it. Even when the humans began to multiply at an alarming rate and spread. Even when they hunted the smaller dragons. We believed we could keep them in check."

Eurwen glanced at him. "You weren't harsh enough with their punishment."

"And when a dragon ate a human or two? What were we supposed to do?"

She twisted her lips.

"We tried to be fair with everyone involved. It worked on occasion, and other times it didna. During all of this, many of us Kings grew closer to groups of mortals on our land. Many took human females as lovers."

A muscle ticked near Eurwen's lips. "Did you?"

"I had several."

"At once?" Eurwen asked in surprise.

Vaughn grinned, wondering if that was jealousy he heard in her voice. "No. Over a five-hundred-year span, three mortals became pregnant by me. Two miscarried almost immediately."

"The third?" Eurwen asked as she halted and faced him.

The soft glow of the magical lights on the tunnel walls cast half her face in shadow. "She carried the child to term. None of the Kings used magic to prevent the pregnancies, at least no' at first. So, the thought of having a child was exciting. She was one of the first to carry a half-dragon bairn to term. The instant she went into labor, I was by her side."

Vaughn's memories took him back to that day immediately. He could hear his lover's painful screams, feel her hand squeezing his as she pushed during a contraction. More than that, he remembered the hope that had filled the room. Until...

He closed his eyes, trying to halt the memories, but it was too late. Vaughn lifted his lids and looked at Eurwen. "After over twenty-two hours of labor, the bairn made his way into the world. Unfortunately, he was stillborn. His mother swore that she had felt him move inside her. None of us could determine when the lad had passed. My grief was palpable, but hers was gut-wrenching. She never recovered from losing our child. Within a few months, she, herself, was dead."

"I'm so sorry," Eurwen said in a soft whisper.

"After that, I made sure to use magic to ensure that I couldna get anyone with child again. No' only because of what it had done to the mortal, but because of the pain I endured, as well."

Eurwen briefly pressed her lips together. "Then came the war with the humans."

"There was a lot of heartache and anger on both sides. It might have begun with Ulrik's mortal female who betrayed him, but it ended with us. Few Kings didna side with Ulrik and attack the humans. Myself included. Eventually, Con got all of us back on his side, one by one, until Ulrik stood alone."

"And my father banished Ulrik."

Vaughn snorted, shaking his head. "It was much more than that. The two were the closest of friends, brothers for all intents and purposes. Con was King of Dragon Kings, and Ulrik refused to obey, leaving Con no option. No one, especially no' your father, wanted to strip Ulrik of his magic or banish him from Dreagan, but Ulrik wouldna listen to reason."

Vaughn walked to one of the carvings. "Ulrik is responsible for most of these. He did the largest one at the opening. We all wanted to save him, but we couldna. Then he ordered his Silvers to ignore Con. Four of them did. Those are the ones we captured and put into a deep sleep here in the mountain. Humans killed more and more dragons, those trying to protect the mortals from the Silvers. Those dragons didn't defend themselves because we had ordered them to safeguard the humans. Their murders broke us."

Eurwen took his hand in hers and squeezed.

"Everything we did, we did for the humans. The hate and fury that filled us when we saw the slaughtered dragons, when we watched one being hacked by hundreds of mortals as it screamed in pain, was too much. Every King understood in that instant that there couldna be peace. No' now. The humans had a taste for blood, and they wouldna stop. There was nowhere the dragons could go and be safe. There were too many mortals. And we wouldna lose any more."

Her voice broke when she said, "You sent them away."

"It was the single hardest thing any of us has ever done. They didna want to go. We didna want them to go. But in order to regain our world, we had to do something. Our only other choice was to annihilate the humans. We considered it, but as I said before, we're no' murderers."

"You would've been protecting your people."

Vaughn smiled sadly. "And destroying the very thing that made each of us Dragon Kings. Maybe that's what we should've done. The dragons would've remained, and the magic would have chosen others to challenge each of us, defeating us and thus becoming new Kings. But that isna what happened. We sent the dragons away and hid on Dreagan for a handful of millennia, waiting for the time when humans would forget us."

"Without your involvement in keeping them contained, their population exploded," she said.

Vaughn made a sound in the back of his throat and started walking hand-in-hand with her. "The way they fought each other over meaningless, insignificant things…we thought for sure they would eradicate themselves, and we could bring the dragons back. Yet, somehow, the mortals have managed to remain and continue their spread around the globe, happily destroying natural resources and slowly killing the planet. We watched it all from the sidelines and under the radar while mourning the realm we once ruled. But, more importantly, our dragons and the ability to have families."

"Some of the Kings have married humans, be they Druid or not."

"And Fae," he pointed out. "It's only recently that we learned of the first pairing of a Dragon King and a Fae that produced Melisse. The other King of Kings held her prisoner for eons until Con released her. Then we heard about you and your brother. All the time in between, we believed we were the last of our kind. That we would never know what it meant to hold our children in our arms or watch them grow."

She was silent for a moment. "I never thought of it that way."

"Then perhaps you can try to imagine how your parents felt when neither you nor Brandr would see them."

Shame flashed across her face. "It's one of the reasons I created the doorway."

He paused outside of the entrance to the cavern. "You did a good thing."

"I hope so."

"Come," he told her and pulled her after him to where the four Silvers slept.

She gaped and rushed to them, putting her hand on each of them one by one. "They've been here all this time?"

"Aye."

"They should be with the others on Zora."

He nodded. "We agree, but they're Ulrik's clan. He gets the final say. None of us have liked keeping them like this, but having them here has been a balm during the hardest times. But it's time they get to enjoy freedom and carry on with their lives."

"All of you deserve that," she said as she met his gaze over the dragons.

"That willna happen as long as we remain here. And we willna leave. This is our home. The magic that created us thrives here. Our dragons have found a new home, which makes all of us happy, but we're still protectors of this realm and everyone in it."

She walked around the cage to stand beside him. "Do the humans know you waged war against the Dark Fae for them?"

"You know they doona, and they never will. It doesna matter how advanced the mortals get, they can never know of us. If they learn, the majority will want to throw us in cages and dissect us to figure out how we do what we do."

She looked at the Silvers. "So, you hide."

"So, we hide."

CHAPTER SIXTEEN

Eurwen didn't know if it was hearing about what'd happened from Vaughn, being at Dreagan, or a combination of both, but the story impacted her in ways she hadn't been prepared for.

She knew the story. Erith had told her and Brandr multiple times, but the goddess either hadn't known some details or had chosen not to tell them. Whatever the reason, learning the specifics altered Eurwen's perception. She had seen the pain in Vaughn's eyes, heard the distress in his voice.

Felt the bitterness and ire through his grip on her hand.

Walking through Dreagan Mountain and looking at the dragon carvings had been like a punch in the gut. They were so detailed, so beautifully done that even a blind person would've seen the hope and promise in them. All of that, coupled with learning that Vaughn had had a stillborn with a mortal, nearly brought Eurwen to her knees.

The raw emotion as he spoke of that event, even so many millennia ago, choked her.

They stood with the Silvers for a long time, silent and lost in their respective thoughts. Eurwen wanted to take the dragons back with her. However, she wanted all the Kings to come with her to see her world—a place like they had once had. She knew it wasn't possible, but she wished she could make it happen.

Despite everything the Kings had endured, they remained optimistic and sanguine. She wasn't sure she could in the same situation. And if she were to believe Vaughn, that was all because of her father. Constantine, King of Dragon Kings.

"Show me more," she urged Vaughn.

With a smile, he turned and drew her with him as they walked from the cavern back to the tunnel. She glanced down at their joined hands, wondering why it felt so right that they were touching. Without Brandr there to judge her, she accepted not only enjoying Vaughn's touch but also craving it.

He took her through a door out of the mountain that brought them to the conservatory in the manor. Eurwen was amazed at the number of plants in the room. Each was lovingly cared for. She walked through them, unable to contain her smile.

Vaughn grinned at her. "It's one of my favorite places."

"It would be mine, as well. There's something peaceful about being surrounded by plants."

Once they left the conservatory, he took her on a quick tour of the downstairs, showing her the enormous kitchen, the dining room with a table that went on for days, the jaw-dropping library, sitting room, and on and on. Eurwen couldn't wait to explore both the library and the kitchen more. Though, she was curious about the dining room. She'd like to take a closer look at the pictures and pieces of art.

But she forgot all of that as Vaughn led her up the stairs to the fourth floor. There were so many doors.

He pointed to the left. "Ryder's computer room is all the way down there. He's our computer and electronic expert, and his mate, Kinsey, is nearly as good. If you ever need something from him, bring him some jelly donuts, and he'll do anything you ask."

Eurwen laughed, wondering what the computer room looked like. Most likely, it held all the latest and greatest gadgets from the tech world.

"My chambers are this way," Vaughn said as he led her to the right.

Eurwen's blood pumped faster with every step. Finally, he paused midway down the corridor, stopping in front of a room on the left. His Persian blue eyes met hers as he turned the handle and pushed the door open. He swept his hand before her, urging to go first.

Eurwen stepped inside and let her eyes roam over Vaughn's possessions. To her right was a black marble fireplace with a jet-colored decorative mantel. On it was a large picture of a beautiful stag with a dark background. On the left side of the painting were two gold and two silver candlesticks with simple cream candles. On the right side was a single gold candlestick and two silver. The darkness of the frame and the picture sinking into the black fireplace made it almost appear as if the buck were jumping out at them.

Two striking and unique leather chairs with a lived-in and worn look were situated near the hearth. Beneath them lay a simple cream rug that added texture to the wood floors. Her gaze swept along the outside wall, painted an off-white, the windows framing a stunning view of the mountains. A sword hung between the two windows, its blade pointed down, a focal point of the room. The baseboards, crown molding, doors, and window trim were all done in a stunning shade that fell somewhere between black and charcoal gray.

Then she saw the bed. The king-sized frame sat large and impressive against the soft cream color of the walls. Somehow, Eurwen wasn't surprised to find that his bedding was tweed. The texture and colors complemented Vaughn perfectly.

When she was able to tear her gaze away from the bed, she spotted two doors. One was most likely the toilet, and the other his closet. She wondered what kind of clothes he had within. As if reading her mind, he walked to a door and opened it with a smile.

Eurwen happily walked in, then came to a halt as she saw the size of it. His suits were hung perfectly spaced apart and color-coded. His dress shirts, regular shirts, jeans, and jackets...everything was pristine. His sweaters were folded neatly and set on shelves. His ties rolled and settled in a pull-out drawer. But it was his footwear that awed her. One entire wall from floor to ceiling was filled with shoes.

She would've remained, opening other drawers, but he took her hand and led her to the other door. Eurwen's mouth fell open. Just like the bedroom, the bathroom was Vaughn. The floor was white tile. A black clawfoot tub with a white interior rested against a black wall. A black vanity with white double sinks sat below a mirror with a black frame that hung

on a wall with tan houndstooth wallpaper. Black towels hung
on black rods near a shower of black tile with white and tan
accents.

"What do you think?" Vaughn asked.

She turned to him. "It's beautiful. And very you."

"Will you stay with me here tonight?"

"Yes," she replied with a nod.

There was no way she could refuse. She wanted it too
badly.

Vaughn walked closer, his blue eyes catching her gaze.
"We could remain here for the rest of the day."

Eurwen's heart leapt at the idea. She didn't have to worry
about Brandr walking in or what he might say because he
wouldn't know any of it. This trip was a holiday of sorts for
her. She could forget who she was, the responsibilities she
had, and who wanted answers. For now, it was all about what
she wanted.

And that was a glorious thing.

"No one will miss us," Vaughn said in a whisper as his
hands came to rest on her hips, and his head began to lower.

She lifted her face to his, needing his kiss more than she
was willing to admit—even to herself. While she was at
Dreagan, she would let herself feel everything for Vaughn
instead of locking it away. Accepting and acknowledging it
had a profound effect on her.

His lips pressed against hers, firm and insistent. She placed
her hands on his chest and leaned against him as she sank into
the kiss. Desire heated her blood as his arms slowly wound
around her and pulled her tightly against him. His tongue slid

between her lips to duel with hers. She felt his arousal against her stomach, making her sex clench in need.

A knock sounded, interrupting them.

Vaughn groaned as he ended the kiss and pressed his forehead to hers. "This better be life or death."

Eurwen couldn't help but laugh. "It's fine."

"It isn't." He lifted his head, a frown marring his face.

"It is," she assured him.

When he turned to the door, Eurwen realized that she hadn't decided how much time she would spend at Dreagan. However, she didn't expect to spend more than one night. Any longer, and Brandr would likely start a search for her. That meant Eurwen really only had that day and night of freedom.

She winced when she thought of it as freedom. Sharing duties with Brandr on Zora wasn't a punishment. She considered it an honor. But…this pull that Vaughn had on her was impossible to resist, even if it did anger her brother.

Vaughn opened the door. His lips flattened as he stared at whoever stood in the corridor. "We'll be out shortly."

"Right," replied a sultry voice with an American accent. "We both know that's a lie."

Eurwen watched as a beautiful woman with curly, shoulder-length blond hair and hazel eyes pushed past Vaughn. The woman was dressed immaculately in couture, from her Chanel earrings and necklace to her Jimmy Choo shoes.

"Eilish didn't lie. You're stunning," the woman said. "I'm Alexandra, by the way. My friends call me Alex."

Eurwen glanced at Vaughn to see him rolling his eyes. She returned her gaze to Alex. "I'm Eurwen."

"I'm sorry for intruding. I know both of you want some alone-time, but a lot of people are dying to meet you."

Vaughn walked to Eurwen, his lips twisting. "We'd better go down before they come up here."

Alex stopped Eurwen before she could walk out. "I'm not sure how long you're staying, but we do girls' days as often as we can. We'd love for you to join us if you'd like."

"That sounds like fun." And it did. More than Eurwen would have guessed. The invitation thrilled her.

A lot.

It must have shown on her face because as they walked from the room, Vaughn leaned down and said, "Of course, they want to spend time with you."

"I wouldn't know what to do."

He winked at her. "Sure, you would."

They followed Alex down the stairs, where another group waited. Eurwen went through, meeting Dragon Kings and mates. The Kings she knew, and some of the mates she recognized, but it was nice to meet them officially.

Everyone was nice. And she noted many accents— American, British, Scottish, Romanian, and even Greek. Everyone wore smiles. Happiness and love were in abundance at Dreagan. Somehow, she hadn't thought about any of that when she thought of Dreagan. She should have, though.

Just because she carried around so much hate and anger didn't mean others did. Being at Dreagan and meeting everyone had opened her eyes to that and much more. She couldn't wait to tell Brandr. He wouldn't believe her, not until he saw it for himself—if she could ever get him to Dreagan.

Eurwen had no idea how long she talked to the Kings and

mates before Vaughn finally called a halt to it and led her away to the library. He closed the doors behind them and blew out a loud sigh.

"Thank you," she said with a grateful smile.

"I knew you'd be a hit."

His grin made her stomach flutter. "I'm a curiosity."

"Doona sell yourself short."

She sank onto the Chesterfield sofa and dropped her head back. "I'm Con and Rhi's daughter. That's all this is."

"It wouldna matter whose daughter you were. You're one of us." He pushed away from the door and strode to her, a small frown furrowing his brows. "I hope you realize that."

She shrugged. "I don't know anyone here. I barely know you. What little time I've spent on this realm has been to observe mortals. And since I stick with the dragons and my brother on Zora, I don't have anything to compare it to."

"Then learn from those here."

"I'm not going to live here," she said as she lifted her head.

Vaughn shrugged and sank onto the cushion beside her. "I'm no' saying live here, but you could visit. Often."

"Do you remember ruling your clan?"

"Of course," he stated, slightly offended.

She shifted to face him. "Did you like leaving them?"

"You know I didna."

"How about if you did it over and over."

His lips compressed.

"That's how I feel when I venture away from Zora," she told him.

"I see."

She studied him, noting the hard lines of his face. "Do you?"

"Of course."

"I think one of the reasons Brandr and I stayed away from Dreagan all these years is that we realized everyone would want something from us. I'm not talking about Rhi and Con. I mean every King. Every mate."

He tilted his head to the side, confusion filling his eyes. "No one you met today wants anything from you. They only want to get to know you. No' only are you a product of a great love that went through so much, you're also half-dragon, half-Fae."

"I'm not the only one of those."

"Trust me. Everyone wants to learn about Melisse, as well. They're curious and interested. I wouldna call that wanting things that you can no' give."

Eurwen shrugged. "And when I say it's time to return?"

"Everyone will respect that."

"This time. How many more times until someone asks me to make a decision?"

Vaughn's face hardened for the briefest of moments. "You mean, how long until I ask you to choose?"

"I didn't say that."

"We both know that's what you were alluding to."

She licked her lips and tried to shift the conversation. "We're having a bit of fun."

"That's where you're wrong. This means much more to me." Vaughn got to his feet and walked out of the library, leaving her alone.

When the door closed behind him, Eurwen stared at it. "Well. That didn't go well."

How had she expected it to go? She wasn't sure. But she had thought to have a pleasant time with Vaughn, not argue. Though, she *had* suspected that he was more serious about things.

"Suspected?" she asked with a roll of her eyes. "No, I knew."

Yes, she knew he thought that she could be his mate. Did she feel the same? Was it something she wanted?

"I don't know," she whispered.

And that was the rub. She didn't know her feelings about anything. She knew what she should do, what others expected of her, and what the right thing was. But she hadn't thought about what *she* wanted.

CHAPTER SEVENTEEN

"Did she leave?"

Vaughn halted at the sound of Darius's voice. He drew in a breath and got control of his irritation.

Darius came around to his front, his face lined with a deep frown, his long, blond hair pulled back in a queue. "What's going on?"

"Nothing."

"Liar," Darius replied without any heat to his words.

"Eurwen is still here. Or at least she was a moment ago when I left her in the library."

Darius crossed his arms over his chest, his chocolate eyes intense. "I see."

"She's alone. Go talk to her."

"I'd rather you come with us."

"I doona need to be there."

Darius quirked a blond brow. "Had a row, aye?"

Vaughn ran a hand down his face. "I've stood in front of

entire boardrooms of people and never lost my cool. With her, one word sends my anger rising."

"She's your mate."

Vaughn squeezed his eyes closed for a heartbeat. "I've suspected for a long time. I knew it when I saw her on Zora."

"You've met her before?"

Vaughn inwardly winced. "It's no' something I told anyone. Con just learned of it. I didna know who Eurwen was when we shared that night eons ago. I've been searching for her ever since."

"Now, you've found her. She just needs some time to see what you do."

"It isna that simple." Vaughn blew out a breath and leaned against the wall. "Neither her brother nor the dragons want us on Zora. No' even to visit. They fear we'll try to take over or want to live there."

Darius's face grew grave. "What does she want?"

"She's the one who formed the doorway for Con and Rhi, but I think Eurwen has doubts. Our arrival caused some waves throughout the realm. They've gone to great lengths no' to repeat the mistakes we've made here on Earth."

"And are probably making new ones."

"No doubt. I've no' mentioned that to them, and I doubt Con or Rhi have either."

Darius shook his head. "Wise to keep it to yourselves for the time being. So they doona want us there. She's discovering that she's welcome here."

"She made a point of telling me that she willna stay for long. Her place is on Zora."

"If you're no' allowed there, and she doesna want to be here, how are the two of you going to be together?"

Vaughn twisted his lips and shrugged. "Maybe I'm wrong. Maybe she isna my mate. Perhaps I was so caught up in trying to find her after she disappeared that I've spent all this time only thinking she is mine."

Darius dropped his arms to his sides. "The two of you have had verra little time together. Perhaps that is all you need to see the truth—whatever that may be."

"That willna happen on Zora. She was uncomfortable with me there. It could've been because of Rhi and Con or Brandr. Her brother's no' our biggest fan."

"Neither she nor Brandr were raised as a dragon should be. There's much they doona know."

"Ah, but they're no' only dragons. They're half-Fae, as well. Who's to say they'd even recognize a mate."

Darius's brows snapped together. "Bloody hell."

"Precisely," Vaughn said with a nod. "There's a chance she doesna know we're mates. If she's against it, she'll refuse me. I'm no' as strong as Con. I'll no' survive without my mate."

"We're no' there yet."

Vaughn inwardly shook himself. "You're right."

"You and Eurwen need to spend more time together. Even if it is in the company of others. Sophie wants to talk to Eurwen. Why no' join us?"

Vaughn thought about it for a moment, then gave in because he wanted to be with Eurwen. He wanted to spend time with her, listen to her speak, and watch her facial expressions. This might be the only time he got with her. He wouldn't waste it being angry. "All right."

"Good," Darius said with a nod. "I'll get Sophie and meet you there."

Vaughn pivoted and returned to the library. He paused outside the doors, wondering if Eurwen would still be there or not. He steeled himself and opened the door. His eyes immediately went to the sofa, only to find it empty.

Disappointment filled him instantly. It churned violently in his stomach, mixing with sadness and anger at himself for snapping at her. She had been unsure of her role at Dreagan, and because of his worries, he had given her reason to leave when he should've done the opposite.

He sighed as he walked into the library. Vaughn debated whether to try and locate her when movement caught his eye. His gaze jerked to the second floor, where he spotted Eurwen's pink skirt before it disappeared behind a bookshelf. The relief that surged through him was so intense, he became lightheaded.

At the sound of approaching footsteps, he looked over his shoulder and saw Darius and Sophie. He gave them a nod to let them know they could enter. Vaughn then returned his gaze to where he'd last seen Eurwen. He'd wanted to show her Dreagan so she could see what a beautiful place it was. He hadn't thought about sharing her with everyone until it had been too late. One way or another, he would find a way to get some time alone with her before she returned to Zora.

"Eurwen," he called.

She poked her head out from around a bookshelf. "I thought you left."

"You have company," he answered.

She stared at him for a heartbeat before her gaze slid

behind him to where Darius and Sophie had walked into the library. "I'll be right down."

Vaughn didn't take his eyes from her as she made her way to the spiral staircase and descended the steps. She smiled in greeting to the couple she'd met earlier before Sophie had left to continue Jeyra's exam.

"How are you doing?" Darius asked Eurwen. "I hope we've no' overwhelmed you."

She smiled easily and shrugged. "I expected it."

"Expecting it and going through it are two different things," Sophie said in her cultured British accent.

Eurwen nodded. "Too true. How did things go with Jeyra?"

"It'll take a bit before I know specifics."

Darius looked at his mate with pride. "Sophie is great at what she does."

"It helps to have my own clinic," she replied after giving Darius a quick kiss.

Eurwen asked, "Doesn't that hamper things? Eventually, those in the area will realize you don't age."

"We'll face that when the time comes," Sophie said.

Darius glanced at Vaughn before telling Eurwen, "We were hoping you might be able to help us."

"Help with what, exactly?" Eurwen asked.

Sophie clasped her hands in front of her. "You're half-dragon, half-Fae. There's much I could learn from you in hopes of helping any mates who might get with child."

Eurwen's gaze slid to Vaughn. She stared at him for a long minute before returning her attention to Sophie. "What do you want to do?"

"Take some blood, do some x-rays. That sort of thing," Sophie said with a shrug.

Vaughn couldn't shake the feeling that this wouldn't go as well as Sophie hoped.

Eurwen nodded slowly. "Have you done those tests on the Dragon Kings here?"

"Well, no," Sophie replied hesitantly.

"What about with Melisse?"

"I–I've not had the chan—"

"But you felt you could come to me with this?" Eurwen demanded in a soft voice so like Con's.

Vaughn stepped forward to dispel the growing tension. "I believe Sophie was more interested in the fact that you're from another realm."

"My brother and I were conceived here," Eurwen said flatly.

Darius shrugged. "By two powerful figures."

"Are you saying that Sophie isn't powerful?"

Vaughn held up his hand. "No one said that."

Eurwen's silver gaze slid to him. "Actually, that's exactly what Darius said."

"She has a point," Sophie interjected.

Everyone looked at her.

A short laugh escaped Sophie's lips as she eyed Darius. "You're a Dragon King."

"I'm your King," he told her.

She smiled and touched his face gently. "That's true, but I have no magic. I'm not a Druid or Fae. I'm just me."

"You have skills," he insisted. "Look how you can heal."

"With medicine, not magic." She shook her head and

glanced at Eurwen. "Shara is Fae. Rhi isn't only Fae, she's royal. Several mates are Druids or have Druid blood in them somewhere. I have no power. Perhaps that's why we've not been able to get pregnant."

Vaughn was so shocked that his mouth fell open. "You've been trying? Even knowing what could happen?"

Darius nodded without looking at him.

"Why would you do that?" Eurwen demanded. "Sophie, you were tending to Claire. You saw her fear. Her anxiety."

Sophie turned her head to Eurwen. "Because we want a child. I'm fully aware of the risks."

"No," Vaughn said, louder than intended as he slashed his hand through the air. "You say that until you're holding your stillborn bairn in your hands. That kills something inside of you. Something you can never get back."

Sophie lifted her chin. "We're aware of—"

"You're no'!" Vaughn bellowed as he looked between Sophie and Darius. "You can no' possibly fathom the depths to which you'll sink. All of us have watched V and Claire go through this hell Usaeil put them in, none of us able to do anything to help."

"They may yet have a child," Darius stated.

Eurwen softly released a breath. "And they may not. Although, that could be said of any being who gets pregnant. There are numerous accounts of miscarriages and stillborn deaths between dragons and humans. As well as two instances of actual births between dragons and Fae. That isn't enough data to put yourselves through what could be a traumatic event."

"If Claire and V are able to have a child, then we've learned something," Sophie said.

Vaughn's stomach clenched painfully. "What's that?"

"That we need Fae magic to help us conceive."

Vaughn couldn't comprehend what Sophie was suggesting. He lifted his gaze to Darius. "You're in agreement?"

"Our dragons are gone. Forever now. Who knows if we'll get to see them again? I suspect the Silvers will be sent to Zora, which is only right. What else do we have? I found my mate. That was a feat in itself. If that's all we ever get, I'll be satisfied. But there's no harm in trying for a bairn."

Vaughn briefly closed his eyes as he fisted his hands. "You'll wish to take back that last sentence if you lose a child."

"The important word there is *if*," Sophie said.

CHAPTER EIGHTEEN

Zora

Brandr paced his cottage until he could stand it no more. He walked out the door, and even though he told himself not to look toward Eurwen's place, his head turned anyway. There was no movement outside. He didn't know if his parents were there or somewhere else.

He was tempted to find Varek. He hadn't wanted to like the Dragon King, but the simple fact was that he did. It helped that Varek had freed the dragons from imprisonment.

Brandr opened his mental link and reached out to his generals to see if they had learned anything.

"The four humans I'm following have remained on their side of the river. They've no' found the crone as of yet."

"Thanks," Brandr said.

Nundro, another of his generals said, *"More and more*

dragons are growing uneasy. Tempers are flaring. I've broken up two fights already."

"*Fights are no' uncommon,*" Brandr reminded him.

Nundro snorted. "*These are no' common skirmishes.*"

"*I see.*"

And Brandr did see. Whatever he'd felt was causing more and more disruption on his realm. The answer seemed simple enough: Get the Dragon Kings off Zora immediately. That should right things instantly. He'd known that Eurwen had been wrong to create the doorway. If she really wanted to meet their parents, she could've done it on Earth. No one needed to come here.

He didn't care about the Kings' wishes to see the dragons. In his mind, they'd lost that right when they sent their clans away without finding them a proper home. He didn't care that they'd never left their realm. To blindly open a dragon bridge to some unknown place was tantamount to murder in his mind.

Brandr stilled when he heard a woman cry out in pain. He frowned, wondering if it was Jeyra. He didn't know much about the mortal, other than that she was Varek's mate. She appeared quite capable, however. In fact, she would've been someone Brandr would have considered entertaining as a lover. But he didn't tread on other's territory.

The woman shouted again. This time, he was certain it came from Eurwen's cottage. Instantly, he reached out to her via their mental link. No matter how many times he said her name, Eurwen didn't respond.

"I'll kill each and every one of them if they harm her," he vowed as he strode angrily across the expanse to his sister's home.

Brandr threw open the door to find Con, Rhi, V, and a pregnant female. The woman was propped up on Eurwen's bed, her long, blond hair stuck to her face from sweat. Her lips were pulled tight in pain as she gripped V's hand as if her life depended on it.

The King of Copper's face was set in determined lines as he softly urged the woman on. But Brandr saw V's fear.

Rhi sat on the bed near the woman's feet. She had her hand on the mortal's protruding stomach. "Breathe, Claire. That's it. Just breathe."

In an instant, Brandr realized what was happening.

Con suddenly stepped into his line of sight. "I hoped to meet you, son. These are no' the conditions I expected to see you under, however."

"Where's Eurwen?"

Brandr saw the briefest of frowns on his father's face. "She didna tell you?"

"Would I be asking if she had?" he snapped.

Rhi suddenly said in a clear, authoritative voice, "Enough, you two. Outside. Now."

Con walked past him without hesitation. Brandr hesitated a heartbeat before turning on his heel and following his father outside. Brandr closed the door and realized that Con had strode farther away from the cottage.

Growing more irritated by the second, Brandr lengthened his strides to catch up with him. When he did, Brandr glared at him. "Where is my sister?"

"She went with Vaughn, Jeyra, and Varek to Dreagan."

"She wouldna."

Con stoically stared at him. "She did."

Brandr didn't want to believe it, but Eurwen would never go without answering his call no matter how angry she was with him. The fact that she hadn't answered earlier confirmed what Con had said.

"I didna know she left without telling you," his father said.

First the doorway, then Vaughn. And now, this. Brandr felt as if he were losing his sister. He wasn't sure how or why it was happening. They'd always had each other's backs, but she was doing things completely out of character lately. And he wasn't sure what to do.

"She's merely getting a tour of Dreagan," Con told him. "Something you're welcome to do anytime."

Brandr shook his head. "Nothing on your realm interests me."

"As I told Eurwen, we're no' here to try to take over or invade your realm. Rhi and I are here to see the two of you."

"You've seen. Now, leave."

A muscle ticked in Con's jaw, the only thing that let Brandr know he was irked. Con's face remained impassive. "Leaving at the moment is impossible."

"Because of the pregnant woman?"

"That is V's mate," Con said, his voice dipping lower. "Claire is here in hopes the bairn can be born alive."

Brandr crossed his arms over his chest, his fury building with every second. "This is why I didna want the doorway built. You all think you can just come and go as you please."

"Contrary to what you might believe, we asked for Eurwen's permission."

And the hits just kept coming.

Con blew out a breath. "You know about us. You know

that only three bairns have been born alive. Melisse, you, and your sister. All three of you are half-Fae. Claire isna Fae. She isna a Druid. But a Fae ensured she conceived. Usaeil wanted to hurt us. Most unions between dragons and humans end in a miscarriage fairly soon. It's uncommon for a mortal to carry a bairn to term. Claire and V have the right to see their child born alive."

"All of that is your problem. Things from your realm. What gives you the right to bring any of it here?"

"You want to keep our realms separate, but that isna possible. You're my son. The dragons you rule are here because of me. Our two realms are tied together, whether you want to believe it or no'."

Brandr snorted as he dropped his arms to his sides. "You talk so nobly, but when it came right down to it, you didna try very hard to get here to know your children, did you?"

Fury filled Con as he narrowed his black eyes. "You know nothing of what you speak."

"Oh, I speak the truth. Something you're unable to do."

Con's nostrils flared. "Your mother and I knew nothing of you and your sister. Erith took you from Rhi to save the three of you, but when it came time to return you to Rhi's womb, you two would have none of it. At least, that's what Erith told us. She took you from us. We never knew the joy of your birth, never got to name you, watch you crawl. We missed it all. Yet, you and Eurwen knew of us the entire time. You came to Earth. You watched us. You're the ones who made it clear you wanted nothing to do with us. Could we have stormed Zora? Could I have made you talk to me? You're bloody right I could have!"

Brandr saw for the first time why the magic had chosen Con as King of Kings. He was formidable, clever, and astute. His calm demeanor belied the fierce dragon he was.

"Rhi and I respected your wishes," Con continued. "Even though it tore us both apart. Your utter disregard for our feelings and the lack of control we had in any of this is appalling and inexcusable. You're better than that." Con walked past Brandr back to the cottage.

Brandr swallowed, pretty sure his father had just firmly put him in his place. He hadn't liked what Con had said, but he couldn't deny the truth of it.

"By the way, we're no' leaving until Claire has the bairn," Con threw over his shoulder.

Brandr turned, but Con had already continued walking. He stared at his father's retreating back, unsure of what to do. He didn't want any Kings on Zora, but they were already here. Brandr couldn't, in good conscience, send Claire away now that her labor had begun. He thought it was foolish for them to think that having the child on Zora would make a difference in whether it lived or not.

Claire cried out, the sound filled with agony. Brandr recalled V's face and the panic there. A King and his mate were attempting to bring a life into the world. Whatever anger Brandr felt toward the Kings didn't apply to an innocent child.

He returned to his home, but he could still hear Claire's screams, even across the distance. The hours progressed, with day fading to night, but Claire's cries only grew louder and longer. She was in tremendous anguish. Finally, he'd had enough and teleported from his place to Eurwen's. He wasn't sure why.

Brandr quietly opened the door and stepped inside. V sat behind Claire, supporting her as she reclined against him. Rhi was between Claire's spread legs, guiding her and telling her when to push. Con stood off to the side, watching it all with a worried expression. Something in his father's face made Brandr realize how important this birth was. He'd been too wrapped up in his anger to comprehend that until now.

"Come on, baby," V urged Claire. "You can do this."

Tears fell down her cheeks. "I'm tired. So tired."

"I've got you," V said and kissed her temple. "I'll always have you. No matter what happens."

Claire's face scrunched up as she bore down, her teeth bared as she strained. Brandr wasn't sure he should be here, but he couldn't make himself leave. No one had noticed him yet. It felt as if he were intruding.

Another twenty minutes passed as he watched Claire pushing without any movement from the baby. Suddenly, Brandr felt the urge to go to her. He fought it, not understanding. Until he could no longer ignore the feeling within him.

He started forward. Out of the corner of his eye, he saw Con's head jerk to him. As he neared Rhi, she looked up in surprise. Brandr looked at V, then Claire. The human mate met his gaze. He paused, waiting for her approval. He had no idea why, but it was important. Then, she nodded once.

A cry tore from her as a contraction hit. He could see her stomach moving from the cramp. Brandr lifted his left arm. He watched it as if from outside his body as he rested his hand upon her belly. The moment his palm made contact, he felt the Fae magic.

He jerked back in shock.

"Whatever you did, do it again!" V shouted.

Brandr looked at the Dragon King. Claire screamed as if in more pain than before. Brandr returned his hand to her belly, and she quieted. He felt the contraction moving through her body, but more importantly, he discovered why the bairn had yet to be born.

He swallowed and looked at the couple once more. "Usaeil's magic caused you to conceive. That magic guaranteed the babe would live to term. But it's also her magic that's causing the bairn to remain in your womb."

"If she wasna already dead, I'd kill her again," Con said from behind him.

Rhi caught Brandr's gaze. "Can you help?"

"Do you feel the Fae magic?" he asked.

Rhi shook her head. "Usaeil must have made sure none of us could."

"I have no' felt it," V said. "And I've tried."

Brandr shrugged as he looked at Claire and then V. "I've never done this. I'm no' even sure I can."

"Please," Claire begged as her face scrunched in pain with another contraction.

Brandr drew in a deep breath and closed his eyes as he focused on the Fae magic. He called it to him. It clung to the infant in Claire's womb, refusing to let go. Brandr felt it draining the life from the bairn.

He deepened his focus and demanded that the magic listen to him. The first time it brushed against him, he nearly gagged. It was Dark Fae magic. The evil was sickening, and the more it obeyed him, the more he felt as if he were suffocating. But he didn't stop. He had to get all of it or the baby would die.

Little by little, he gathered the magic until he had all of it. When he lifted his hand from Claire's stomach, the magic covered his arm like a black mist. He tried to look at Claire, but his eyes were fuzzy, and his knees started to buckle.

"I've got you," Con said as he supported him.

Brandr suddenly found himself in a chair, dimly aware of the shrill cry of a bairn.

"You did good, son."

He wanted to tell Con to shove it, but oddly, the words affected him. Brandr didn't have the energy to think about that now. He concentrated on the magic that crept up his arm. He wanted it gone. His attempts to shake it off were in vain. Then he felt himself falling, sleep pulling him under.

CHAPTER NINETEEN

Dreagan

Eurwen couldn't stop thinking about when Vaughn had told her the story of his stillborn child. His pain had been there for all to see. He no longer hid it. Unfortunately, Darius and Sophie either chose to ignore that or didn't recognize it for what it was.

"Are you the only two attempting to have a child?" Eurwen asked the couple.

Sophie looked at Darius and smiled. "We've not spoken to anyone else about this."

"At least you spared V and Claire that," Vaughn said.

Darius's gaze cut to Vaughn. "Would you really have all of us live forever without children?"

"I would spare you the agony of losing another one," Vaughn snapped. He sighed, visibly distressed. "I would expect you, of anyone, to understand what it means to lose a child."

Darius's nostrils flared in anger. "I'll never forget that pain. Ever."

"Then why?" Vaughn demanded in exasperation. "Why would you put yourself and Sophie in such a position?"

Eurwen looked between the two, suddenly realizing what Vaughn was saying. Darius had also lost a child. Now she understood why Vaughn was so distraught about Darius's and Sophie's seemingly flippant decision.

Darius drew in a deep breath and turned his head to Sophie. His lips softened as he gazed into her eyes, his love evident. "I can't change the past. Nor do I wish to. The love I share with Sophie is more than I ever thought I would have. She's helped to heal the broken pieces of my heart. I didn't spare any details of what I went through. We've had numerous discussions about the odds and what could happen. It isn't an easy decision. But it's something we both want."

Sophie smiled, her eyes glittering with unshed tears. Eurwen's heart was torn. She saw the affection between Darius and Sophie and why they wished to attempt to have a child. Eurwen's gaze slid back to Vaughn, and her heart broke all over again for the pain reflected in his eyes. This kind of decision was one that would have to be made by each couple once they knew the facts of both sides.

Eurwen realized this conversation wasn't going anywhere. It was time she stopped it. She caught Sophie's attention. "You think I'm different because I was born on Death's realm and have lived for some time on Zora, right?"

"I do," Sophie said as she turned her attention to Eurwen. "I gather you don't?"

Eurwen shook her head. "You know my parents."

"And that in itself is something to consider," Darius said.

Vaughn pinched the bridge of his nose between his thumb and forefinger. "Darius, you're my brother. We've stood together for countless millennia. Sophie, I hold you in high regard for your ability as a doctor. You've done great work. I understand why you want to study Eurwen, but as she told you, she's no different than Melisse."

"I'd like the opportunity to find out," Sophie stated.

Eurwen shook her head. "No."

"What are you hiding?" Darius asked.

Eurwen raised her brows, surprised at the vehemence in his words. "Nothing."

"Then it won't hurt for me to examine you. Take some x-rays as well as blood," Sophie said.

Vaughn moved closer to Eurwen. "She's given her answer. Perhaps you should start gathering data from Melisse or us first."

Darius said nothing as he took Sophie's hand, and the couple exited the library.

Once they were gone, Eurwen turned to Vaughn. "Are you all right?"

"It's like they couldna hear me."

"It isn't that they couldn't. It's that they didn't want to."

Vaughn shook his head as his Persian blue eyes met hers. "If you had been here for the last nine months of Claire's pregnancy, you would understand how shocked I am."

"I might not have been here, but I heard your and my

parents' words about the couple. I also saw V and Claire for myself. Why do you think I agreed to let Claire go to Zora? If there's a chance the child could be born alive, I want them to have it. It's the least they deserve after what Usaeil did to them."

Vaughn walked to the sofa and sank onto the edge of a cushion as he rested his forearms on his knees. "Please doona think I doona want my brethren to have children."

"I don't think that," she told him. "I know why you hold that opinion."

He turned his head to her. "If Claire and V's bairn is born alive, more Kings and their mates will start trying for their own."

"Maybe that's what is supposed to happen."

"Eurwen, I lost a child with a woman who wasna my mate and it nearly broke me. Magnify that a hundred times, and that might come close to what it would feel like between a King and his mate."

She sat beside him, wanting to comfort him in any way she could. "They will lean on each other."

"Some will. Some willna. That kind of loss can destroy once-strong bonds."

Now it made sense to her. "Dragons mate for life, but humans and Fae don't."

Vaughn slowly nodded his head. "Con has long feared how mortals might respond mentally to being immortal. It isna in their DNA to live that long. Though that wasna his only concern. At one point, he actively tried to dissuade the Kings from taking mortals as mates."

"How did that turn out?"

"As you'd expect. Once a dragon finds his mate, there is no one else for him. Con knew that. He understood it. But he looked to the future, as he always does."

Eurwen scooted to the cushions on the sofa to support her back. "There is no divorce for dragon mates."

"Dragons know this. Con tried to explain it to the mates, but all of them swore their love for their King. I believed them. We all did. Even Con."

"But that doesn't stop him from worrying that something might eventually tear one or more couples apart," she guessed.

Vaughn slowly sat back as he sighed. "When I first became King of Teals, I remember looking at Con and thinking it couldna be that difficult to be King of Kings. I've learned from watching him over the eons that I had no idea what I was thinking. Con shoulders a great responsibility. He's put his happiness to the side for ours, time and again. He's always thinking about our continued survival and how we can find fulfillment and love while remaining hidden from the humans."

"If any of the mates leave their King, it would mean death for both of them. A dragon can't survive without its mate."

"And the mates are tied to the King through the ceremony." Vaughn's lips twisted. "Every King here would like to have a child. But at what cost?"

"That's what irritates you with Darius and Sophie, isn't it?"

He nodded. "We all resigned ourselves to never having children. We expected to live out eternity alone. Then the unexpected happened, and some of us began finding mates."

"Perhaps more change is coming. Brandr and I were born. Granted, not of a human but rather a Fae."

Vaughn's gaze was focused on a spot before him, though he absently nodded.

Eurwen knew he was most likely entering a dark place with memories of his lost child. She put her hand atop his to get his attention. "Take me to your mountain."

"What?" he asked as he turned to look at her.

"Your mountain. Take me to it."

His face softened. "All right."

She got to her feet and pulled him up by a hand. "Let's go."

"Now?"

"Why not?" she asked.

He smiled and linked his fingers with hers. "Why no', indeed."

When Vaughn turned her toward the door, she tugged on his arm to stop him. Then she shook her head. "I've another way."

In the next breath, she teleported them to the back of Dreagan Mountain.

"It's still too light for us to fly," he told her. "We'll have to walk."

"Which direction?"

Vaughn pointed to the west.

Eurwen focused on one of the mountaintops as far as she knew she could teleport and jumped them there. One mountain at a time, she teleported with Vaughn directing her until they finally reached his. She watched as the tension from the manor fell away from him. He took her hand and led her down one side of the rockface until they reached a boulder that hid an entrance to the mountain.

"I never wanted to be caught and no' be able to get into my mountain," Vaughn explained. "There's an entrance at the base, one I use in my true form, and this one."

Eurwen had always wanted to go into one of the mountains on Dreagan. Neither she nor Brandr had ever used one for themselves, but other dragons on Zora did. She often wondered if her Fae blood made it so she didn't yearn for a mountain.

The instant she entered Vaughn's mountain behind him, something moved through her. The sensation was one of comfort and solace. The deeper she went into the tunnel, the darker it became. Her dragon sight took over, allowing her to see easily.

Her hand was still linked with Vaughn's. He led her through the tunnel that wound slightly downward. She spotted a couple of forks in the passageway but decided to ask about those later. Just as in Dreagan Mountain, carvings of dragons were prevalent all through the tunnel.

"Did you do these?" she asked.

Vaughn glanced at her over his shoulder. "I did."

They were impressive. Some were lone dragons. Others clustered together. Some stood while more were in flight. Some were done as closeups, and still more were carved as if seen from a great distance. But they were all Teals.

The tunnel widened, emptying into a cavern. Eurwen paused to take it all in when Vaughn released her hand and walked ahead of her. A moment later, a ball of light emerged from his hand. It began rising into the air, growing larger and brighter until it touched the ceiling above.

Eurwen looked from one end of the cavern to the other. The floor was smooth and bare except for the occasional boulder. It almost looked as if someone had rolled them out of the middle. The arched ceiling that came to a point was high enough that a dragon could stand without hitting its head. The curved walls were absent of dragon carvings, but what stood out were the scorch marks made from dragon fire. And the scratches from Vaughn's claws.

"This is where I slept away many centuries," Vaughn said.

She made her way to one of the scorch marks and lightly ran her fingers over the burnt rock. "You did more than sleep."

"I had to release my anger somehow. Allowing it to fester would've only made things worse."

Eurwen turned her head to him. "And you couldn't take it out on those you felt responsible."

"Humans." He shot her a lopsided grin. "That I couldna."

"Why did you choose this mountain?"

He seemed to think about that for a moment and then shrugged. "I can no' answer that. After the dragons were gone, Con brought us here. He urged us to find a mountain and sleep. I remember flying this way, but I doona have any memories of choosing a particular mountain. I was weary and outraged. I knew I had to sleep. I think I took the first mountain I came across."

Eurwen watched how he gently touched the rock as he walked. She didn't believe anything had been done carelessly. He might not have chosen this mountain, but it had chosen him.

"Con came to us every ten years and updated us on things as we slept," Vaughn continued. "Then, one day, I woke. I wasna yet ready to leave the mountain, but I was done sleeping. I walked every inch of this place. When I couldna go farther, I made tunnels. It wasna long after that I started the art. I had no concept of time. I didna leave, didna even look outside. I would get restless and sleep, only to wake sometime later and begin the process all over again."

Eurwen studied Vaughn, the way he smiled when he talked about the mountain, how he stroked the rock. "Do you return here?"

"Aye." He met her gaze and smiled. "We each have chambers at the manor, and they're somewhat private. However, it's hard to get real privacy in such a place with so many people. When I need to center myself, I come here. I can block out the world and feel the magic."

"Sounds perfect."

"Do you have such a place?"

She glanced around the cavern. "Nothing like this. When Brandr and I first arrived on Zora, we were intent on calming the dragons. It wasn't long after that we created Cairnkeep. While it might not be as grand as Dreagan, it's our home."

His brows shot up in his forehead. "That place is spectacular. The views alone are sublime. You sit atop a mountain. I would say it is grand."

"We don't have a manor."

He gave her a dry look. "We both know if that's what you wanted, you would have it. Dreagan and Cairnkeep might be different, but each is beautiful in its own right."

His words warmed her heart. "I like it here. There's something very calming about your mountain."

"I always thought so. I feel it each time I come here."

"I felt it," she told him in amazement.

His lips turned up in a smile. "Somehow, that doesna surprise."

"It does me. I've never been drawn to mountains. Not like you and the other Kings."

Vaughn shrugged nonchalantly. "That doesna make you any less of a dragon. It only means you need something different."

"Why did I feel something when I walked in here?"

"I wish I knew."

"Does every King feel something when they enter their mountains?" she asked.

Vaughn's smile widened. "I've never asked any of the others."

"Really? I would've thought you would."

"We might be as close as brothers, but we must have our privacy. You know that. Otherwise, you and Brandr would share a house."

Eurwen nodded in agreement. She walked to the middle of the cavern and spun with her arms outstretched. She lifted her head and saw the scorch marks above her. Halting, she stared at them, trying to imagine the pain Vaughn suffered.

"Trying times," he said from behind her.

She whirled around and met his gaze. "You had a realm all to yourself. Then you welcomed new beings that changed everything."

"We expected them to treat us with the same respect we did them."

"Instead, you lost everything. Locked on a magical land but unwilling to take back your world. You remained here, furious and hurting, with no way to do anything about it."

His shoulders dropped. "I can forget what the humans have done. It's just a wee moment. Then I remember everything once more. We're living in Hell. One we created, but Hell nonetheless."

Eurwen placed her hand on his cheek. "How do you survive?"

"I searched for you."

Her heart skipped a beat at his words.

Then he yanked her against him, his mouth ravaging hers.

CHAPTER TWENTY

The instant his lips touched hers, Vaughn burned to be inside Eurwen.

The heated kiss grew feverish, frenzied. Their hands clawed at each other, trying to get to bare skin. Then, finally, the clothes were gone. His next breath locked in his lungs when she reached between them and wrapped her fingers around his cock.

Vaughn groaned at the sensation of her hand moving up and down his length. He was powerless to move when she ended the kiss and dropped to her knees in front of him. He couldn't take his eyes from her. His lungs locked as she leaned forward and wrapped her lips around his arousal. Pleasure surged through his body as she used her hands and mouth on him.

When he could take no more of the exquisite bliss, he grabbed her by the shoulders and pulled her to her feet: He kissed her, backing her against the nearest boulder. Then, it was his turn.

He kissed down her jaw to the base of her throat. Her pulse jumped, and he flicked his tongue over it. Then he slowly kissed his way to her breast. He licked around her nipple before taking it into his mouth and suckling the nub. Her nails dug into his back as her hips rocked against him. Vaughn moved to her other breast and teased that nipple. Only then did he kiss down her stomach to her navel.

Her breath hitched when he knelt before her and lifted one leg over his shoulder. He glanced up at her to find her hooded eyes watching him closely. Vaughn smiled before his tongue swirled around her clit. A soft cry fell from her lips. He continued his assault by pushing a finger inside her, moving it in time with his tongue.

"Please," she begged. "I want you inside me."

He ignored her, doubling his efforts. Her cries grew louder. The leg holding her began shaking, and still, Vaughn continued.

She stiffened and let out a shout as she peaked. The sound was music to his ears. They'd come together only in his dreams for so long. She had been like smoke, hard to hold. Now, he got to feel her, see her, taste her. And he couldn't get enough.

Vaughn rose, grabbing her by the hips and lifting her. Their gazes met, locked as he slowly entered her. Her lips parted on a sigh. Her arms wrapped around him as he pushed in deeper. He began pumping his hips. Their breaths mingled as their damp bodies rubbed against each other. She leaned forward and kissed him.

He held her beautiful body against him as he thrust faster, deeper, seeking the pleasure he knew awaited them both. Her nails lightly scraped his scalp as her tongue brushed against his. With every movement, it confirmed that she was his mate.

His lids lifted as he ended the kiss. He looked deep into her silver eyes. Something passed between them. Something deep and intense. It went through him like lightning, sinking into every fiber of his being and pushing him to orgasm. He gripped her hips and plunged deep, spilling his seed within her.

For long minutes they stayed locked together. Eurwen smoothed the hair from his face. He lifted his head and looked at her to find her smiling. He then pulled out of her and set her on her feet. Instead of walking away, she took his hand and sat down. Before her bottom touched the floor of the cavern, a thick fur blanket appeared. He let her pull him down beside her. Then, he lay back and tugged her onto his chest.

"I've spent a lot of time in this mountain," he told her. "I never thought I'd be here with you."

"Do you regret showing me?"

"No' at all. What I was trying to say—badly, apparently— is that I'm verra happy."

She smiled as she lifted her head to kiss him. "So am I. I didn't know what to expect coming to Dreagan. With you."

"I'm glad you came."

"I am, as well. I hope that I can talk Brandr into coming, eventually."

Vaughn held her tighter against him. "I'd rather talk about you."

She laughed softly. "Oh? What about?"

"How I feel about you."

The instant the words were out of his mouth, the atmosphere changed. The easygoing attitude Eurwen had disappeared, replaced by tension. But Vaughn wouldn't be denied. He had to tell her.

"I've tried to tell you before, but you wouldna hear me. I have to say this."

She shook her head, her eyelashes brushing against his chest. "Please, don't."

"Why?"

"Why must you? Why can't things stay like this?"

Vaughn tried not to take her words wrong, but it was hard not to. "Because I've searched for you for ages. Now that I finally found you, I need you to know."

"Vaughn, please. Don't."

"You're my mate, Eurwen."

She sat up, keeping her head turned away from him. Her long, blond hair tumbled around her shoulders and hung down her back to brush her hips. Vaughn reached up and touched his finger to the silky strands.

"Eurwen," he called.

She released a long breath. "I begged you not to say anything."

"Why?" he pressed. "I know you feel something for me. It was there the first night we met. It's been there the entire time I searched for you. It's there now. Why is it so hard to admit that?"

She rose to her feet, clothing herself as she did. Then, she faced him. "I've known where you were. Always. Don't you think if I had believed you were my mate, I would've come to you?"

Vaughn should've known that she would strike ruthlessly. He sat up, bracing himself with his hand. Hurt bloomed like a blackness inside him, growing larger with every word she spoke.

"You should've left things as they were. We could've had a nice time. Why couldn't you leave it?" she cried, her face scrunching with sadness.

"Because I know what I feel."

She shook her head. "I'm sorry."

Vaughn watched her walk away. He didn't call out to her, didn't beg her to stop. She had said her piece, just as he had. He wasn't sure how he could've gotten it so wrong. She wanted to be with him. He wasn't mistaken about that.

Or maybe he was.

He lay back and laced his fingers behind his head. This cavern had seen his rages, his pain, his suffering and misery. It had never before seen his pleasure. But even that was now gone before it had even taken shape.

Of all the things Vaughn had experienced throughout his long life, he'd never known heartbreak like this. His mate, the one meant for him, had refused him. It was a death sentence for a dragon. Death would be easier than living without her.

Now he understood how Con had felt not that long ago before he and Rhi reconciled. The emptiness was a yawning void. All these years, he'd never given up on his search for Eurwen. When he found her, he'd thought all his dreams would come true. Instead, they had been dashed carelessly upon the stones of Fate.

He went back through his conversations with Eurwen. She had told him time and again that her place was on Zora—and his wasn't. He'd heard her, but he hadn't actually listened. Not that it would've mattered. Whether he told her about his feelings or not, he'd known the truth. It didn't seem right that he'd finally found his mate, only to be unable to have her.

Vaughn wondered if it would've been better to keep it to himself. At least then he could've had time with Eurwen. As soon as that thought went through his mind, he knew it would've actually made things worse. The more time he spent with her, the deeper his love went.

"It's too late, anyway. I was lost the first night we met," he said to himself.

The only reason he had survived this long was because he had known all he had to do was find her. Now that he had, nothing would ever be the same.

Vaughn rose and found his clothes. He put them on instead of using magic. When he walked out of his mountain, he saw that night had fallen. He hadn't realized he'd been inside for so long. Patrols flew Dreagan's perimeter. It wasn't his night, but the thought of going back to the manor and running into Eurwen didn't sound appealing.

Or worse, learning that she had returned to Zora.

No, it was better if he remained away from the manor. Minutes ticked by, but Vaughn didn't shift. Instead, he sat on the slope of his mountain and listened to the sounds of the dragons flying. He missed the roars from Zora. On Earth, they couldn't roar unless there was a storm to blanket their sound. He missed a lot about Zora. But more than anything, he craved to have Eurwen back at his side.

Vaughn remained seated there throughout the long hours of night. Kings called for him via their mental link, but he didn't answer. He wanted to be alone with his grief and misery.

He rubbed the area over his heart, wondering how something could hurt so bad. He was sinking into a despair so deep, he knew he'd never be able to pull himself out of it—and he didn't want to.

Dragons weren't meant to be alone. It was why they had mates. Why the magic allowed them to find their perfect partner. When the dragons were sent away, the Kings had feared they would be alone forever. Miraculously, many found their mates among the humans and Fae. Suddenly, the Kings had hope again.

Hope could allow someone to continue on long after others would've stopped looking and trying.

But hope could also kill with the dullest of blades.

CHAPTER TWENTY-ONE

Ulrik stood in the Dragonwood with his arms crossed and his feet braced wide. Some might consider it a battle stance.

He would agree.

"This isn't a good idea," Eilish said from beside him. "No one interfered with us. We shouldn't be interfering in someone's life."

He cut his eyes to her. "Every one of them meddled in our relationship. Even before it was one."

"This just feels wrong, babe," she said with a shake of her head.

"I might have been away from Dreagan for too many millennia to count, but some things doona change. Vaughn was always one of the steady ones. He was never quick to anger or to choose a side. He weighs everything carefully. It's what makes him such a good attorney."

Eilish clicked her finger rings together, something she did

when she had a lot on her mind. "This isn't about some legal matter. This is about his heart."

"Which is worse," Ulrik stated.

His mate blew out a breath. "I'm not trying to make light of the situation. I'm merely pointing out that you wouldn't want anyone intruding in our relationship."

He turned his gaze to her, meeting her green-gold eyes. "You've always been wise beyond your years. I value your opinion more than anyone else's, but you doona realize what's coming."

"Con survived those years without Rhi."

"Because that was Con. He did it because he felt he had no choice, that he had to lead the Kings."

Eilish shrugged. "Vaughn is invaluable. Can't we make him think the same?"

Ulrik dropped his arms and faced her. "Sweetheart, it isna that easy. Con survived without Rhi because he's stubborn and shoved all his emotions away. He was a shell of a man. The simple truth is that a dragon can no' survive without its mate."

"What if Vaughn got it wrong?"

"You saw them together. What do you think?"

Eilish started to speak, then changed her mind. She blew out a breath. "I've never seen Vaughn look at anyone the way he does her."

"See?"

"Yet I rarely see any Kings with just any woman. Usually, if they bring someone to Dreagan, it's because there is already something between them that ends up being love."

Ulrik frowned, confused. "Exactly."

"You're missing the point, babe. I'm saying that I don't

see Kings just dating. I don't know how they interact with someone who isn't a mate."

"Oh." She had a point.

Eilish touched his arm, her hand lingering on him. "Maybe Vaughn wants this so badly that he doesn't realize the love isn't there."

"He's looked for her for so long."

"Precisely my point. He's been so intent on finding out who she is, that his emotions have gotten all tangled."

Ulrik slowly released a breath. "I know what you're saying, and anything is possible. But I doona believe that is what's going on with him."

"What's your plan, then? Do you really think you can stop Eurwen from leaving Dreagan? You do realize she can make another doorway and leave anytime she wants."

"I was hoping to talk to her."

Eilish wrinkled her nose. "I'm not sure that's a good idea."

"Then you talk to her."

"What?" she asked in shock.

Ulrik grinned, the idea suddenly clear in his mind. "Aye. You talk to her. Female to female."

"I don't know her."

"Neither do I."

Eilish gave him a flat look. "You're a Dragon King. You have more in common with her than I do."

"She's held a grudge against us for quite some time. Who do you think she'd readily listen to? Me, who she doesna trust nor care for? Or you, a female who came to Dreagan just as she has?"

Eilish rolled her eyes. "I hate when you're right."

Ulrik smiled and reached for her, pulling her against him so he could give her a quick kiss. "You love me."

"I do. Don't let it go to your head," she teased.

"Too late."

She cupped his face and gave him a lingering kiss. "All right. If this is going to work, you need to leave."

"If she comes here."

"She will," Eilish stated.

Ulrik squeezed her hand before walking away. There was much he wanted to say to Eurwen but now wasn't the time. Ulrik had faith that Eilish would be able to connect with Eurwen, even if it were only to keep her at Dreagan for a little longer. He didn't want to think about what would happen if she left.

Vaughn had been chasing a ghost for many lifetimes. He'd finally found Eurwen, confirming what he'd believed all along. The minute Ulrik had seen the couple together, he'd known that Vaughn had found his mate. It was also obvious that Eurwen wasn't aware of that yet. It made sense that Vaughn would tell her while they were at Dreagan.

When Ulrik had seen Vaughn sitting forlornly on his mountain, he'd recognized that his friend had bared his soul — and not gotten the response he'd hoped for. Ulrik had then left his position on patrol to seek out Eurwen. When he hadn't found her, he'd decided to wait in the Dragonwood. Now, all he could do was hope that things worked out for Vaughn. Ulrik couldn't remember the last time a King had died from not having his mate. They'd come close to losing Con. Too close.

Ulrik wouldn't lose Vaughn.

Eilish looked around, feeling uneasy. She didn't want to be
here. She didn't think talking to Eurwen would do any good,
but she would do it for Ulrik. It was evident by her mate's
attitude and words that this was important to him.

She also wanted Vaughn to be happy, but she didn't know
how she could change things for him and Eurwen. Especially
when Eurwen seemed intent on refusing him. At least, that's
what they thought. No one had actually spoken to either of
them. Vaughn because he refused to talk to anyone, and
Eurwen because no one could find her.

Eilish wasn't even sure this was where the Fae doorway
was. She was sure it was in the area, but she hated not being
able to see it.

She'd debated asking another of the women at Dreagan to
come and help her. Too much rested on her shoulders when it
came to keeping Eurwen on Earth. She had no idea what to
say, and if she said something wrong, she could ruin
everything. How could she face the Kings if Vaughn died
because of her?

Eilish turned around to pace and drew up short at the sight
of Eurwen. She stood as still as stone between two trees, her
blush-colored clothes almost glowing. There was no moon that
night, but it was as if a light shone directly upon Eurwen
anyway.

"Hi," Eilish said.

"You think to stop me?"

Eilish inwardly winced. "We both know that while I'm a

powerful Druid, I don't stand a chance against your dragon and Fae magic. I came to talk. Nothing more."

"I don't have anything to say."

"Maybe listen, then?" Eilish offered.

Eurwen's silver eyes regarded her silently for almost a full minute before she relented. "Fine. Talk."

Yeah, this is going great, Eilish thought to herself. "I remember the first time I came to Dreagan. I was overwhelmed by everything and everyone. They meant well, but they had no idea how disconcerting it was. Unfortunately, I was just like them for your arrival. We've been waiting a long time to meet you and Brandr. We might have ganged up on you."

"It wasn't too bad."

Eilish saw Eurwen relax a little and gave herself a small pat on the back. It was a tiny victory. "The mates hoped we'd get some shopping, eating, chatting, and all of that in. It might seem so mundane, but—"

"I'd like that. I really would," Eurwen replied over her.

Eilish blinked in astonishment. "Really?"

"I don't get to do any of that on Zora."

"But you've come to Earth. Surely, you've done it while here."

Eurwen shrugged and glanced away. "It isn't nearly as fun by myself."

"No, that it isn't." Eilish looked at Eurwen with new eyes. Here was a powerful being who ruled the dragons on another realm, but she didn't have any female companionship. "We could go now. Just you and me."

"Now?"

Eilish shrugged, smiling. "Why not? I can take us anywhere," she said and wiggled her fingers with the finger rings that allowed her to teleport. "Your choice."

"I wouldn't know what to choose."

"Oh, I have so much to show you," Eilish said with a grin. "The one thing a girl needs is friends. All of us here lean on each other a great deal. There have been times I wouldn't have gotten through a day without the other mates. I'm not saying we always get along. Quite a few of us have different personalities, but we're a family. We always have each other's backs."

Eurwen's lips softened in a sad smile. "That sounds amazing."

"You're part of that family, as well. You and Brandr."

"My brother would never come here."

"Things change. Give it time."

Eurwen looked at the sky. "I can see the Kings on patrol. It's heartbreaking that they have to remain quiet."

"They've gotten used to it."

"The longer I'm here, and the more I learn, the more I realize why they so desperately want to visit Zora."

Eilish nodded. "To see the dragons."

"How do they do it?"

Eilish thought about Ulrik. "Some days are easier than others. Some are very difficult for them. Dreagan allows them the space they need when it gets to be too much. They can go to their mountains and take to the skies at night. During a storm, they're all up there," she said with a smile, thinking about it. "It's a beautiful sight to see them together. They don't hold back their roars then. Con ensured a safe place for the

Kings. No matter what you think of your father, know that he always had the dragons' survival at the forefront of his mind."

"I've learned much about the Dragon Kings as well as my parents over the last few days. I thought I knew everything. I'm ashamed to even admit that because no being can ever know everything. We're all meant to grow and continue to learn. But Brandr and I judged Con and the Kings harshly."

"And Rhi?"

Eurwen walked closer to Eilish. "Her, as well. How ridiculous is that? Neither of my parents had anything to do with what happened to us."

"Children often blame their parents for things. I did. When I learned who my true father was, I couldn't have been more shocked. Then I learned the truth about my mother and what her family had done to her. I looked for someone to blame. My parents seemed an easy target. They were responsible for me, after all. Then we learn they are much more than our parents. They are people who live and love and make mistakes like everyone else."

"I'm coming to see that."

Eilish wrinkled her nose briefly. "Your parents are amazing people."

"Everyone keeps telling me that."

"Because we want you to know that, without them, most of us would be dead. Rhi risked her life time and again for the Kings and mates. She nearly died in a couple of instances. Even as she battled personal issues, she was always there for us. Do you know she healed the Fae Realm? It's habitable again. A small portion of it, but it's growing each day."

Eurwen's face went slack. "She did?"

"She has the power to destroy worlds as well as heal them. In her darkest days, she could've destroyed all of this in a blink. But she was strong enough not to."

Eurwen sighed softly. "Everything I thought or believed has been turned on its ear."

"Sometimes, that's the best way to find a new path."

Eurwen was silent for a long moment. "Take me somewhere we won't be disturbed. Somewhere we can talk."

"I know the perfect place," Eilish said as she held out her hand.

CHAPTER TWENTY-TWO

The instant Eurwen took the Druid's hand, she teleported them to a tropical beach. The sun beat down from a cloudless sky, sparkling off the vibrant green water that lapped lazily at the white sand beach as mountains rose from the sea, leaving only a narrow space for boats to enter the cove. She turned and looked behind her to the dense jungle beyond.

"I love this place," Eilish said.

Eurwen blinked against the harsh sunlight. "Where are we?"

"Thailand. I can't get enough of these islands. Each one is more spectacular than the next. And the water?" Eilish smiled contentedly. "Ulrik and I get away and come here as often as we can. It's a place we aren't disturbed."

Eurwen lifted her skirts and walked to the water, taking her shoes off along the way. The cool waves rolled over her feet and up to her knees as she waded deeper. Listening to the waves had a calming effect on her.

"Thank you," she said over her shoulder to Eilish.

The Druid came up beside her, now wearing an olive green bikini. "My pleasure."

"Most of my life, I only had Brandr to talk to. We're close —or we used to be. We've drifted apart recently."

"I never had any siblings. I wish I'd had someone to turn to."

"But you had friends." Eurwen turned her head to look at her.

Eilish nodded. "I did. Do you?"

"Not really. There are dragons I would call friends, but their lives are much different than a human's."

"And you're a part of both worlds."

"Not fully in either one," Eurwen admitted aloud for the first time.

Eilish frowned, her green-gold eyes filled with concern. "It's easy for someone to put labels on us. I think we should get to decide who and what we are. If you want to be a dragon, then you're a dragon. If you want to be Fae, then you're a Fae. It doesn't matter who your parents are or what anyone expects of you."

"That's the rub," Eurwen said. "I don't know what I want."

"I think you do."

Eurwen blew out a breath and looked out at the stunning water. "I want to belong to something. I don't know why I'm saying that when I do. I belong to Zora and the dragons."

"Do you really? Or did you and Brandr answer a call the universe sent out? Did both of you take on the responsibility without considering what you wanted?"

Shock went through Eurwen. She slowly looked at Eilish. "I–I've never thought of it that way."

"Perhaps you once belonged to Zora. But maybe now you're seeking something else. We all grow. Sometimes, we outgrow what we've been doing."

"Where does that leave me, then? I've always ruled alongside Brandr."

"But is it what you *want* to do?" Eilish shrugged. "I think you need to step back and consider that."

Eurwen shook her head. "I've never asked myself that."

"Let's start small. What do you want to do right now?"

Eurwen smiled, a laugh bubbling within her. "Swim."

"Then we swim!" Eilish shouted as she ran into the water.

Eurwen snapped her fingers, her clothes gone, replaced by a turquoise bathing suit. She dove into the water and swam beneath it. Spectacularly colored fish darted here and there. She spotted an octopus before it ducked between some coral.

When she finally broke the surface to drag in air, Eurwen looked around for Eilish. She found the Druid lazily swimming back to shore. Eurwen wasn't nearly finished yet. She dove back under to explore more of the wonderful world beneath the waves. She lost count of the number of different fish she saw. Her excitement grew when she spotted some rays and even a couple of smaller sharks.

The final time she broke the surface, she found Eilish reclining in a hammock, strung between two trees. Eurwen swam to shore and walked from the water.

"Now that's a smile," Eilish said when she saw her.

Eurwen chuckled. "I feel great."

"You're so much like your parents, and you don't even

know it. Both of them turn to their duties before seeing to their own happiness. You've done the same."

Eurwen dug her wet toes deeper into the beach, watching the sand cling to her feet and clump. "Yes, I have." She looked at Eilish. "You've not asked the one thing I know you want to ask."

Eilish swung her legs over the side of the hammock and sat up. Then she patted the spot beside her. Eurwen used her magic to return her clothes and dry her hair before lowering herself next to the Druid. They sat in silence for a while, watching the sky grow darker as sunset approached.

Eilish dropped her chin to her chest. "I like you, Eurwen. I'm not saying that just because of who you are. I'd like us to be friends."

"I'd like that, too. I've never had a human friend before."

The Druid turned her head to her and smiled. "We have so much catching up to do to remedy that."

"I'm looking forward to it."

"Me, too," Eilish replied. Then, her smile died. "Your life is your business. I don't want to interfere, but I also want you to know that you can talk to me about anything."

Eurwen drew in a deep breath and released it as she pressed her lips together and looked at the sea. No matter what she had been doing the last couple of hours, she couldn't stop thinking about someone—Vaughn.

"You know about Vaughn, don't you?" she asked Eilish.

There was a small hesitation before Eilish said, "Yes."

"What did you do when Ulrik told you that you were his mate?"

Eilish laughed softly and got a dreamy look on her face.

"We went through quite an ordeal. Neither of us trusted the other, but we couldn't ignore the attraction." She turned her head to Eurwen. "It was always there, at the forefront. At first, I thought it was just lust, but the more time I spent with him, the more I began to care about him. It wasn't long before I depended on him, and then I couldn't remember a time when he *hadn't* been a part of my life. He was there for me at my lowest point. He saved me. He loved me unconditionally. When he told me we were mates, I was overjoyed because I knew I wanted to be with him always."

"And there's the rub. I don't know any of that."

"I'm guessing you didn't know how to respond to Vaughn when he told you?"

Eurwen shook her head. "I could've handled it better. I know that. I didn't want to hurt him. I begged him not to say the words."

"So, you knew?" Eilish asked, shock in her voice.

Eurwen thought about it for a moment and then shrugged. "I knew Vaughn wanted something I couldn't give him."

"I've seen the two of you together. There's no denying the attraction."

"That doesn't mean we're mates."

Eilish nodded in agreement. "What do you think is keeping you apart?"

"We're from two different worlds."

"So were Ulrik and I."

Eurwen rolled her eyes. "You two are from the same planet. That's not true for Vaughn and me."

"But you can overcome that. If you want to."

"Then there's the fact that I have to return to Zora."

Eilish lifted one shoulder in a shrug. "I don't think Vaughn would mind moving."

"We're not allowing any Dragon Kings from Earth to reside there."

"Oh," Eilish said, her eyes rounding. "Really?"

Eurwen nodded. "Brandr would never agree to it. He doesn't even want any more visiting. He also told me that if I choose Vaughn as my mate, he'll banish me."

"Damn. That could be a problem."

"Exactly."

Eilish flattened her lips for a heartbeat. "And you would never want to live here?"

"I have a duty to Zora. Just as Vaughn has responsibilities here."

"It sounds like you've considered things with Vaughn then. You must feel something for him."

Eurwen looked away. "It doesn't matter what I do or don't feel. It can never work."

"If it's meant to be, it'll work. Somehow."

"Spoken like someone who hasn't had to make a choice like mine."

Eilish shrugged, her lips twisting. "Maybe not like yours, no, but every mate has had to make a conscious decision to give up the lives we had—and sometimes even our families— to be with our King."

"You didn't have to give up family immediately, though, did you?"

"Others did. I'm not trying to make light of your situation."

Eurwen dug her toes into the sand. "I realize you're trying

to compare what a mate goes through with what I'm dealing with, but it isn't the same."

"Do you want to be with Vaughn?"

Eurwen hesitated, unsure of how to answer that.

"All right," Eilish said. "Let's try this a different way. Do you like being with him?"

That was easier to answer. "I do."

"That's a step forward. Tiny steps are still steps."

Eurwen smiled at Eilish. Was this what having a friend was like? If so, she had missed out on a lot. The topics she and Eilish discussed now were things Eurwen would never be able to talk about with Brandr because of his hatred for the Kings and everything they represented.

"That smile didn't last long," Eilish pointed out.

Eurwen wrinkled her nose. "Vaughn and I met a very, very long time ago. I knew who he was, but he had no idea of my identity. I made sure of it. We had an incredible night together, and I left while he slept so he wouldn't start asking questions."

"I take it there wasn't much talking that night," Eilish said with a knowing smile.

Eurwen chuckled. "Not a single word. The attraction was too intense."

"So...no talking during cuddling? Surely, the two of you cuddled after."

Eurwen thought back to that night and sighed wistfully. "When we finally grew exhausted, yes, he pulled me into his arms."

"Oh, my God," Eilish exclaimed with wide eyes. "That does sound like an incredible night."

"More than you could possibly know." Just thinking about

it made Eurwen long to return to it. Things had been so simple then. Or perhaps she hadn't realized the complications that she and Vaughn spending time together could cause. Most likely, she was just naïve.

Eilish let out a long whistle. "Sounds like Vaughn made an impact."

"In a manner of speaking."

"How long until you saw him again?"

Eurwen adjusted her hands on the edge of the hammock. "Not until he came to Zora."

"I don't understand," Eilish said, a deep frown creasing her brow.

"Brandr and I made a pact to never interact with the Kings."

Eilish shook her head, her confusion evident. "Any King?"

"Any."

"Ever?"

"Ever," Eurwen confirmed.

Eilish blinked and looked out at the water. "The attraction you spoke of with Vaughn must have been great for you to ignore your pact."

"It was."

"What did your brother say when he found out?"

Eurwen was glad that Eilish wasn't looking at her. "I didn't tell Brandr until Vaughn was in our realm."

Eilish shook her head again as she briefly closed her eyes.

"Exactly," Eurwen said. "If Vaughn is my mate, would I have been able to stay away from him all this time?"

"I wouldn't have been able to stay away from Ulrik," Eilish said as she turned her head to Eurwen.

Eurwen raised her brows, nodding.

"Damn."

The two were silent for a long time. Eurwen kept thinking about Vaughn's face when he left the cavern. The last thing she wanted to do was hurt him, but she should've known it would come to that. She had known he wanted something more. It felt nice to be with him, but by going with him to Dreagan, she had allowed him to think there could be something between them.

"Things change," Eilish said. "You opening the doorway between our worlds and allowing your parents—as well as Vaughn—into Zora might have altered things."

Eurwen looked at Eilish. "I wish it were that simple, but it isn't."

"It all comes down to what you want. Not what your brother wants for you, or even what happens on your world. It's what your heart and soul need. What you can't live without. I think that has already begun to change. You just haven't noticed yet."

"Maybe."

Eilish flashed her a smile. "You *did* come to Dreagan. With Vaughn, I might add."

CHAPTER TWENTY-THREE

"Care if I sit?" Ulrik asked.

Vaughn bit back an angry reply. "I'd rather you didna."

"Too bad."

Vaughn rolled his eyes as Ulrik lowered himself to the ground beside him.

"This isna the Vaughn I know," Ulrik said.

"People change."

"We're no' people."

Vaughn fisted his hands as his irritation spiked. "Dragons change."

"You should be fighting for her."

"If she doesna feel I'm her mate, it's pointless."

"But you think she's yours."

Vaughn turned his head to look into Ulrik's gold eyes. "I know she is."

"Sitting here willna get you your mate. Go after her."

"You make it sound easy."

Ulrik's lips twisted as he issued a half-shrug. "It is."

"She's known who I was from the beginning. She's known where I was the entire time. If she felt I was her mate, she would've returned to me."

"A dragon would've, aye. She's only half-dragon."

Vaughn shot him a flat look. "Do you think I doona know that? I'm all too aware."

"All I'm saying is that she might feel things differently being only half-dragon. Her Fae half may interfere with her discovering her mate. Right? You can no' deny there's a chance."

"There's a chance. But I doona think that's true."

Ulrik frowned. "Why do you say that?"

"They doona want any Kings in Zora. No' to live. No' even to visit."

"But…Con and V are there now. Varek was there. You were there."

"Varek wasna there of his own volition. From what Eurwen told me, Brandr wasna happy she built the doorway to allow Con and Rhi in."

Ulrik's lips flattened as he nodded. "Then you arrived."

"That's when Eurwen told him that the two of us had met long ago."

"I'm guessing he didna take that well."

Vaughn lay back to look up at the sky, linking his hands behind his head. "You could say that. Eurwen willna consider living here. She said her place is on Zora, ruling with her brother."

"And they doona want us there," Ulrik said into the silence. "Shite."

"Precisely," Vaughn replied in a dry tone.

Ulrik released a sigh. "Eurwen might well want you, brother, but she finds herself torn between two places."

"There's no way around that."

"There's always a way."

Vaughn snorted. "Doona throw my words back at me. I said them regarding legal issues."

"You can no' deny it works in this scenario, as well."

"You're trying to give me hope."

"And you're giving up entirely too easily," Ulrik retorted. "The Vaughn I know doesna back down from a fight."

Vaughn rolled his head to look at Ulrik. "This isna a battle, my friend."

"It's a battle of your heart."

"When did you become so romantic?"

Ulrik's gaze drifted away. "There isna a King here who hasna spent lifetimes yearning for his mate. The Fae and even the mortals continually search for the other halves of their souls. We're lucky that we're able to discern it."

"The Fae and humans can—and do—live without their mates, even if they find them. We can no'."

Ulrik's gaze jerked back to him. "You're needed here."

"That isna true, and you know it. Dreagan would continue. The Kings would continue if I died. That is true of any of us. We doona have a purpose anymore. We accepted the mortals here, gave them a home. And then let them dictate how things would be. We allowed them to push us until we had no choice but to send the dragons away."

"That's where you're wrong. We had a choice. We chose to be true to who we are."

"Aye. I've told myself that for a long time. Now, I wonder if I've been telling myself a lie."

Ulrik lay beside him. "You say that because you've been to Zora."

"Eurwen and her brother have the humans contained to a certain place. Dragons doona venture there, and the mortals are no' allowed on the dragons' side."

"Ah, but they do cross."

"No' many," Vaughn argued. "Eurwen and Brandr have given the dragons a place to prosper and grow."

Ulrik drew in a deep breath and slowly released it. "That is working for them now. It willna always. What do you think Brandr and Eurwen will do? What do you think the dragons will do if the humans attack?"

Vaughn's heart clutched in his chest because he didn't want to answer that question.

"They'd stop the humans by any means necessary," Ulrik said for him. "We both know that. Varek told us that Zora is similar to our realm thanks to Erith, but it doesna hold the magic that chooses us as Kings."

"Nay," Vaughn replied softly.

"It's that magic that kept us in line, so to speak. It chose only the bravest and most lethal dragons to lead. But first and foremost, those dragons needed a good heart. There is nothing like that on Zora for the dragons or Eurwen and Brandr."

Vaughn briefly closed his eyes. "The twins are so intent on no' making the same mistakes we did that they willna be able to see that they're making new ones."

"From what you and Varek have said, Zora is beautiful. That will all change the moment Eurwen and Brandr feed their dark side and kill the humans. The Eurwen you know now will be gone."

Vaughn didn't like to even consider that situation.

"Varek likes Brandr, but Brandr willna listen to anything any of us has to say."

"Eurwen might."

Vaughn looked up at the stars above him. "I'm no' so sure."

"We should try."

"There's no reason for either of them to even consider what we're saying because nothing changes on Zora."

It was Ulrik's turn to snort. "Oh? Some person Jeyra called *the crone* managed to pull Varek from our world to theirs. I'd say that's something to think twice about."

"I forgot about that."

"Understandable. You just found the woman you've spent eons combing the Earth for."

Vaughn met Ulrik's gaze. "The crone needs to be found so we can figure out what she did."

"And make sure she can no' do it again. My thoughts exactly."

"I have to return to Zora."

A smile pulled at Ulrik's lips. "That you do. And while you're there, remember why you're so good at being a lawyer. You've got a gift."

"For understanding and using the humans' legal system," Vaughn stated with irritation as he sat up.

Ulrik followed him, shaking his head. "That's only part of it. You have a cool head, Vaughn. You're able to hear what others say. You doona just listen, you *understand*. You're also able to get them to understand you. That isna something to discount. It's time you realized your gifts and used them properly."

Vaughn nodded, a plan beginning to form. "Aye."

"And while you're there, you might also want to spend some time with Eurwen."

"If she'll allow it."

Ulrik grinned as if he were hiding something. "Oh, she will."

Vaughn frowned as he cocked his head to the side. "What's that supposed to mean?"

"You'll see once you're in her realm."

"I'm no' supposed to go back."

Ulrik got to his feet. "Says who? The door isna closed. Besides, Con is still there."

That was a good point. Vaughn stood and faced his friend. "There's still a chance this willna work."

"What would you rather do? Sit here and slowly die? Or go to Zora and fight for your mate and her realm?"

"You know the answer," Vaughn replied tartly.

Ulrik laughed and slapped him on the back. "It's the answer for any King. You just needed to be reminded of that."

"Thank you."

"You would've come to that conclusion alone. I just helped you get there quicker. Shall I bring you to the doorway?"

Vaughn grinned. "Of course."

Ulrik held out his arm with the silver cuff. It had been given to him by a Fae and allowed him to teleport. The instant

Vaughn put his hand on him, Ulrik jumped them to the Dragonwood.

"The doorway is there," Ulrik said, motioning with his hand.

Vaughn knew they were in the right area, but that didn't mean Eurwen had left the doorway open. "Are you sure?"

"Rhi put the two white pebbles on the ground to mark the doorway," Ulrik explained.

"That makes things easier for us." Vaughn took a step, then paused. "There's a chance Eurwen willna be happy to see me."

Ulrik's nose wrinkled as he shrugged. "She feels something for you, brother. The more time you spend together, the more she'll see it. It doesna matter what realm you're on."

Vaughn knew Ulrik was right. It wasn't that he didn't want to chase after Eurwen. He had searched for her all this time. He would continue for as long as he had hope that she cared for him.

Ulrik was right. Eurwen *did* feel something for him. It was there in her kiss, in her touch. Even in the way she smiled at him. Either she didn't know her feelings, or something else was holding her back. It was time he pushed to find the answer —for both of them.

And if she ultimately rejected him and left him without a mate, at least he could look back and know that he had done everything he could.

Vaughn looked over his shoulder at Ulrik. "I doona know when I'll return."

"Con and V will have your back there. We've got you covered here," Ulrik said with a grin.

Vaughn squared his shoulders. It hurt that Eurwen had left to return to her realm, but had he actually expected her to stay after what had transpired between them? He took a deep breath and took two steps. With the third, he was in Zora.

Ulrik released a sigh of relief as Sebastian walked out from behind a group of trees.

"You're playing a dangerous game," Sebastian cautioned.

Ulrik looked into his topaz eyes. "There was no other choice."

"Let's hope Eurwen reacts as we hope."

"And Eilish doesna skin me alive," Ulrik said with a grimace.

Sebastian laughed. "Oh, she will. I just hope I'm there to see it."

CHAPTER TWENTY-FOUR

Zora

Brandr woke with a start. For a second, he couldn't remember why he was in Eurwen's cottage. Then, it all came back to him.

He slowly sat up. Con and Rhi were gone. V was with Claire on the bed, both with their eyes closed. Next to the bed was a bassinet. Brandr stood and walked to it. When he looked inside, he saw the bairn bundled tightly in a blanket. The child looked innocent as it slept peacefully, completely unaware of the turmoil its arrival had instigated.

Brandr couldn't stop looking at the tiny bundle with its wrinkled face. He reached inside and gently brushed the back of one knuckle against the bairn's forehead. Brandr didn't know why he wanted to touch the baby, but once he had, he couldn't pull his hand away. Dragon magic ran through the infant. It wasn't as powerful as V's, but there was no denying that it ran throughout the bairn.

He dropped his arm to his side and looked at Claire and V once more. The look of panic on V's face waiting for his child to be born was something Brandr would never forget. He didn't know why none of them had felt the Fae magic that prevented the baby from being born, but he was glad that he'd been here to help. He didn't want to think about what could've happened had he not.

As a Dragon King's mate, Claire was essentially immortal. The only way she could die was if V died. The way Usaeil's magic had held the bairn would've killed it within Claire's womb. A cesarean would've needed to be performed just to get the babe out. And neither Claire nor V would've ever been the same. Brandr was shocked that his grandmother had been so callous. He had to remind himself that she had been Dark.

It reminded him of the Dark magic. He looked at his arm, but the black, misty smoke that had been there before he fell unconscious was gone. He didn't feel it inside him, but he would be cautious, nonetheless.

Brandr teleported outside to greet the day. The sun was just peaking over the mountain, its first rays lighting the area. He drew in a deep breath, still trying to decipher the confusing emotions swirling within him. Things had been simple once. Easy. Well, as much as they could be in his situation.

As far back as he could remember, he and Eurwen had felt an overwhelming need to get to the dragons. They had been able to talk to each other, but not Erith. The time it took for them to grow and get to the point where they could communicate with the goddess had felt like an eternity. All the

while, both Brandr and his sister had felt the cry of the
dragons within them. It was almost as if they had been born to
find the dragons and restore order once more.

He had accepted that as his life. He thought Eurwen had,
as well. It hurt deeply that she had kept secrets from him
because he knew if she hadn't told him about Vaughn, then
there were other things she hadn't shared.

Obviously, she had sought something more. Why hadn't
she told him? But he knew the answer. Brandr didn't question
her loyalty or intentions when it came to Zora or the dragons.
Or even him. Yet, something was missing from his sister's life.
Something he had missed. And he guessed he hadn't seen it
for some time.

Was it the dynamic between him and Eurwen that'd altered
things on Zora? Was that what he felt now? He wanted to
blame everything on the Dragon Kings, but that was childish.
Varek hadn't asked to come to Zora. He'd had no hand in his
arrival. Frankly, Brandr was impressed at what Varek had been
able to do in the short time he'd been in the realm.

Not to mention that the Dragon King had also found his
mate.

Brandr pushed aside the tightening in his chest each time
he thought about a mate. He knew how dragons discerned
their mates. For many, many years, he'd believed that he
wasn't ready to even consider a mate. Then, as more decades
passed, he started to wonder if he would ever find one. He had
no way of knowing if he would be able to recognize his mate
or not. Had that ability been given to him since he was only
half-dragon?

He hadn't talked to Eurwen about it because she hadn't

mentioned anything about being lonely. Brandr had taken that to mean she was content, and he didn't want her to worry about him being unhappy. Because he wasn't. At least, he wasn't most of the time.

Seeing Claire and V together, though…hell, even his parents, had brought out the staggering loneliness that sometimes overtook him. The yawning, cavernous void of emptiness that loomed ever nearer, trying to swallow him. He hated when it came because it clawed at him, dragging him down into an abyss that threatened to never release him.

Everywhere he looked, beings were paired. None were meant to be alone. And yet, that's exactly what he and his sister had been. Alone. The difference was, Eurwen had found some semblance of pleasure with Vaughn. Brandr couldn't say the same. Instead of facing his feelings and confronting the root cause of his wild emotions, he'd buried all of it and focused on his duties and the dragons.

Try as he might, he couldn't ignore how similarly he had acted to Con. And Brandr wasn't sure how he felt about that. It certainly wasn't something he would discuss with Eurwen or anyone else.

He ran a hand down his face, feeling weary to his very bones. Eurwen was at Dreagan, Dragon Kings were still in Zora, a half-dragon bairn had just been born, and more importantly, something was still off with the realm that he had yet to pinpoint. Not to mention, neither he nor any of his generals had found the crone.

Brandr moved closer to the edge of the cliff and drew in a deep breath in an attempt to release the tension and anxiety building within him. He glanced to the right where Eurwen's doorway was and saw Vaughn emerge. Fury spiked in Brandr with such intensity that he started to shift and charge Vaughn.

Then Rhi was suddenly with Vaughn, enveloping him in an embrace. The sight of his mother stopped Brandr in his tracks. For all the pain she had suffered at the hands of her mate, she had forgiven and moved on. Brandr wasn't sure how anyone could do that. Rhi not only did it with grace that spoke of her noble heritage but also with a smile and a generous heart.

Brandr saw much of Rhi in Eurwen. His sister was more forgiving, more compassionate than he. He would say that Eurwen had gotten the best of both Rhi and Con in many instances, while he had gotten the worst.

"Brandr."

The sound of Con's voice in his head startled him. He thought about ignoring his father's call, but no doubt Constantine was nearby and watching him. *"Aye?"*

"I wanted to see how you were feeling after what you did last night."

Brandr looked away from Vaughn and Rhi and turned to look at Eurwen's cottage. That's when he spotted Con standing outside, watching him. *"I'm doing fine."*

"Thank you for what you did. I know V and Claire also wish to talk to you and thank you."

Brandr shook his head. *"There's no need."*

"There is. And you know it."

"Why is Vaughn here?"

Con raised a brow. *"Ask him."*

Brandr watched his father walk away. He almost called out to Con, demanding that he tell him what he wanted to know. But Brandr knew it wouldn't do any good. Besides, he wouldn't allow Con to know that he was irked about the situation. Not yet, anyway.

He whirled around, intending to tear down the doorway when his gaze landed on Rhi before him. "Did you and Con plan this?"

"No," she said softly. "I've been waiting for you to wake so I could thank you."

Brandr shrugged off her words. "It was nothing."

"That's not true at all, and you know it."

He clenched his teeth. "What do you want me to say?"

She shrugged and smiled. "Nothing. Just listen."

He stared into silver eyes so like Eurwen's that, for a moment, he almost imagined he spoke to his sister and not Rhi.

"Please," she urged, her gaze beseeching him.

Against his better judgement, he gave in.

Rhi's smile was blinding. "Thank you."

"Not here," he said before she continued. "I'd rather go somewhere more…private." He tried not to notice the hurt that flashed in her eyes, but it was too late.

"Wherever you'd like," she said.

"My place."

He turned and started walking, not bothering to wait for her. It was a wanker move, and Eurwen would've called him on it. Brandr slowed his steps until Rhi caught up with him.

Once inside his cottage, she flashed him a smile. "Thank you for this."

He closed the door and leaned against it as he watched her look around his simple home. His cottage was identical in size to his sister's. No one but Eurwen had ever been inside. It was disconcerting to have a visitor looking over his things.

"You like to read," Rhi said as she glanced at him over her shoulder.

He nodded slowly. Two walls of his cottage were covered with bookcases.

Rhi flicked her long, black hair over a shoulder as she faced him. "Have you been to the library at the Light Castle?"

"No."

"I'd love to take you. It's a spectacular place. The library at Dreagan is impressive, as well."

He crossed his arms over his chest, not bothering to answer.

Rhi briefly lowered her gaze to the ground. "I understand." She licked her lips and moved to stand before him. "I know you want us gone. Whatever you may believe, neither Con nor any of the other Kings intend to take over."

"They wouldna be able to."

"Spoken like a King," Rhi said with a grin. Then she twisted her lips. "You might not want to hear it, but Con would've said those exact words."

Brandr didn't want to be reminded, again, that he was like his father.

"We're not bad people," Rhi continued. "We're not perfect. We've made some mistakes." She grimaced. "I've made some doozies, myself. But I hoped you were the type of man who wouldn't judge someone for their past or actions they didn't have any control over. I hoped a child of mine would get to know someone before forming an opinion."

"I'm here, am I no'?"

She scratched her head and swallowed nervously. "The first time I spoke with Eurwen, it didn't go well, but we gave it a second try. I'm asking you to get to know us. Your father and I want nothing more than to learn about the children we didn't even know we had. We've been waiting, not so patiently, for a chance to meet you both."

"I'm no' sure what you want from me. You're here, in our realm, moving about freely."

"I want to know my son."

Brandr dropped his arms and pushed away from the door. "I'm afraid that time has passed."

"It's never too late to get to know someone."

"I doona know why Fate decided that you and Con wouldna raise Eurwen and me. Maybe it was because both of you were too caught up in the big picture of things to notice the details. Maybe it was to correct the colossal mistake Con made in sending the dragons away."

Rhi's eyes grew frosty with annoyance. "You know as well as I that he didn't make that decision lightly or on his own."

"He decided it. The other Kings merely followed along."

"They could've refused had they believed there was another option."

Brandr shook his head at himself for getting into this debate. "There was another choice. Ulrik made it. The other Kings sided with him until Con changed their minds."

"He reminded them of their true purpose."

"He chose the humans over his dragons!" Brandr jerked back, shocked by his outburst.

Rhi lifted her chin. "If that's what you think, then you don't know your father or the Kings at all."

"I know all I need to know."

The disappointment on her face shook him. She said nothing before teleporting away, leaving him with only the silence of his cottage.

CHAPTER TWENTY-FIVE

"You did what?"

Eurwen winced as Eilish's voice rang with astonishment and exasperation, directed at her mate.

Ulrik lifted his hands, palms out. "Sweetheart, please just listen."

Eurwen looked between them as they stood inside the manor. The other couples and Kings had quickly vanished the moment Ulrik had told them that Vaughn was gone, and Eilish's fury filled the house.

"When did he leave?" Eurwen asked Ulrik.

The King of Silvers turned his gold gaze to her. He studied her for a moment. "Last night."

"Why did you send him to Zora?" Eilish demanded.

Ulrik briefly pressed his lips together. "At first, I thought Eurwen had already left. It wasna until I couldna find you on Dreagan that I realized you two might have gone somewhere together."

"But you didn't tell Vaughn that." Eilish shook her head in agitation.

Ulrik blew out a breath. "All right. I can admit. I didna think this through."

"It's fine," Eurwen said, cutting off Eilish before she could respond.

The Druid's gaze met hers, silently asking if Eurwen were really okay.

Eurwen nodded and returned her attention to Ulrik. "Did Vaughn tell you?"

Thankfully, Ulrik didn't play dumb about the situation. "He told me enough."

"Sending him to my realm won't change anything."

Ulrik reached for Eilish's hand. Their fingers tangled as they smiled at each other, the look full of love. Ulrik's gaze slid back to Eurwen. "As I'm sure my beautiful mate already told you, we're a family here. Vaughn is my brother. He's hurting, and none of us will sit by and no' do something to help."

"There isn't anything for you to do," Eurwen insisted.

Ulrik shrugged. "I disagree. Vaughn believes you're his mate. A dragon willna live long once he's found his mate if he can no' have her."

"I'm aware of that."

Eilish tucked her hair behind her ear. "I think what Ulrik is attempting to say—badly—is that there may have been too much here for either of you to have any time alone together. Perhaps returning to Zora will give you both that. A chance to get to know each other better."

The fact that Eurwen didn't know what to do was a first.

Did she remain at Dreagan and see more of the amazing property? Did she return to her world and Vaughn and the turmoil his arrival brought?

"We'll give you some time," Eilish said and started to turn away with Ulrik.

Eurwen stopped them. "Wait. Vaughn, Con, and Rhi mentioned something to me. Since they aren't here, I thought I'd talk to you about it."

"What's that?" Ulrik asked.

"The Silvers."

He blinked, his expression falling. "I see."

"They've been caged for a long time," she continued. "There is a place for them on Zora. If you so choose."

Ulrik bowed his head in understanding, then walked away with Eilish.

With nothing else to do, Eurwen walked up the stairs and didn't stop until she found herself in front of the door to Vaughn's rooms. She had thought to sleep in his bed with him, to have his arms holding her once more. How could she want to be with someone and yet know that it was the wrong thing?

She put one hand on the wood and the other on the knob. Eurwen closed her eyes and drew in a deep breath. As she released it, she opened the door. She didn't open her eyes until she stepped into the room and softly closed the door behind her. She leaned against it and let her gaze move over the space.

It felt like a lifetime ago that she had stood in this exact spot with Vaughn, though it had only been a day. She remembered his smile, the happiness reflected in his eyes. They could've had a grand time at Dreagan. She would've been free to do whatever she wanted without worrying about what Brandr might say or do.

Why had Vaughn spoken about mates? Why couldn't he have just left things alone?

Because it wouldn't have been fair to him. He wanted his mate. To hold onto what he had found. She would've done the same thing in his place.

Eurwen pushed away from the door and walked to Vaughn's bed. She ran her hand over his comforter. He was charming and gorgeous, and she liked how she felt when she was with him. It was a dangerous combination. If her situation were different, she might even allow herself to believe that he was her mate.

The fact was, she had no idea.

If she returned to her realm, Vaughn would confront her once more. He would want answers. Answers she wasn't prepared to give. Then there was Brandr. He would likely be furious to learn that she had left without telling him. On top of all of that, her parents were there.

Eurwen sat on the bed and curled up on her side. "What did I do?"

How could she know that by creating the doorway for her parents, she would let in a world of apprehension and possibly heartache for all involved? All she had wanted was for Con and Rhi to see that she and Brandr thrived and that the dragons had prospered.

She wanted to remain in Vaughn's room forever, to hide away from everyone. But she couldn't. She pushed up on her arm into a sitting position. Sooner or later, she would have to

return to Zora and face her brother and Vaughn. The longer
she put it off, the worse things would be.

Eurwen got to her feet and turned to smooth out the
comforter before she took one last look at the chamber just in
case she never returned. Then she walked from the room and
down the hall. She didn't meet anyone on the stairs or along
the way as she left the manor to walk to the Dragonwood. She
opted not to teleport so she could savor the last few moments
she had on Dreagan.

She had dreamed of being there for so long. Of
experiencing all that was the dragons and magic and Kings. It
had far exceeded her expectations, and she hoped that she was
able to return and soak up more of it. She longed to shift and
fly over the mountains, looking at them from above.

Once in the trees, she slowed her steps even more. She
meandered through the thick woods, listening to the birds and
the other wildlife. All too soon, she stood before the doorway.
She stared at it for a long time, wondering what awaited her on
the other side.

The snap of a branch yanked her attention to the side and
her gaze collided with Shara's. Eurwen was surprised to see
the Fae. She was one of the few Dark Fae who had turned
Light. Usually, it was Light who turned Dark. So much so, that
many Dark assumed they could never return to being a
Light Fae.

"I didn't mean to startle you," Shara said in the Irish
accent all Fae possessed.

Eurwen smiled in greeting. "I was lost in thought."

"I noticed." Shara tossed aside the stick she had been
holding and straightened from where she reclined against the

tree. The thick silver stripe on the left side of her long, inky hair was all that remained to prove that she had once been Dark. "I'm sure it seems like I was lurking, waiting for you."

Eurwen raised her brows. "Were you?"

"I was," Shara admitted with a smile.

They shared a laugh.

Shara walked towards her. "Are you going back already?"

"Yes."

"That's too bad. I hoped you'd stay longer. And I'm not the only one. Though, I'm sure you want to spend more time with Con and Rhi."

Eurwen inwardly winced. She hadn't thought too much about her parents. Thoughts of Vaughn and the conflicting emotions within her occupied her mind.

"I've heard from some Halflings that it's difficult being from both the Fae and human worlds. I can only imagine it's worse for you, coming from such worlds as you do," Shara said into the silence.

"You could say that."

The Fae's silver eyes were filled with kindness. "You have friends here. Given who you are, Con and Rhi will ensure that you and your brother are always welcome."

"Things are complicated."

Shara shook her head. "No, they aren't. We're the ones who muddle things. Things can be as simple or as complicated as we want them to be. I hope you return soon."

With a wave, the Fae teleported away.

Eurwen considered Shara's words long after she was gone. There was truth to them. If she didn't want a complicated situation, then she shouldn't allow it to become so. She was in charge of her life. She could decide who she spent time with. It was no one's decision but hers.

She felt infinitely better when she stepped through the doorway. However, the minute she returned to her realm, she frowned. Something dark and sinister rushed through her upon entering. It had been only a flash, but she was sure she had felt it. Yet, now that she looked for it, she couldn't sense anything.

Eurwen looked around. Nothing seemed out of place. But she knew what she had felt.

"Brandr," she said, calling for her brother.

The sound of dragons filled her ears. Eurwen sighed, not realizing until that moment how much she had missed their roars. Earth wasn't silent, but its noises were the human kind. The more time passed without Brandr answering, the more concerned Eurwen got.

"*Brandr,*" she said through their mental link.

"*Finally back?*"

There was no denying his irritation. "*I just came through the doorway. I felt something...off.*"

"*I'm aware of it.*"

That made her frown. "*For how long?*"

"*A wee bit.*"

"*Why didn't you tell me?*"

"*I assumed you felt it, as well.*"

She breathed out her anger, trying to stay calm. "*Why didn't you talk to me about it?*"

"*Maybe the same reason you didna tell me about Vaughn. Or about going to Dreagan.*"

"*You're cross with me.*"

"What I am, Eurwen, is doing my duty. Something you might want to remember."

He severed the link before she could reply. Eurwen was just furious enough to immediately reopen it, but it wouldn't serve either of them. This wasn't the first tiff she and Brandr had had, and it wouldn't be the last. They knew when not to push each other. This time, she relented to give him time to calm down.

Hopefully, he would.

Eurwen started to teleport to her cottage before she remembered V and Claire. She didn't want to disturb the couple. She didn't know if the bairn had come yet, but it was better to let them be for the moment.

She didn't want to go to Brandr's, either. Eurwen sighed and began walking in an effort to burn off some anxiety. When that didn't help, she shifted and took to the skies. As she flew among the other dragons, she wanted to tell them how lucky they were. She couldn't stop thinking of the sleeping Silvers at Dreagan, or the Kings themselves, who couldn't be in their true forms until night had fallen.

Of all the things she had expected to learn from her parents and the others at Dreagan, it wasn't how to empathize with the Kings and the decisions they had made. For all she knew, she would've made the same ones had she been in their shoes.

As she flew, she searched for Vaughn. The longer she went without seeing him, the more worried she became that he had left. Her stomach clutched painfully. It was a hollow ache, one born of angst and worry. The more those emotions grew, the more her stomach churned nauseously.

Finally, she saw the loch where she and Vaughn had

spoken. Eurwen landed and returned to human form to sit on
the rocky bank and watch the water lazily lap at the beach.
The sun glittered like diamonds on the water while a soft
breeze teased her hair.

The beat of wings drew her gaze skyward. The instant she
caught sight of teal scales, her heart skipped a beat. This was
the first time she was getting to see Vaughn's dragon form.
She jumped to her feet as Vaughn circled her. She took in the
sight of him, noting how his scales darkened on his back
where a semi-transparent membrane crest ran down his spine.

He landed softly, belying his huge form. Deep-set yellow
eyes stared at her. Bony knobs surrounded his mouth where
his lips covered his large teeth. His wings tucked against his
side and his tail, with its axe–like extension, curled
around him.

There was no denying the pleasure she felt at seeing him in
his true form. His nearness immediately brightened her mood.
A strong woman would look deeper at those emotions. But
Eurwen didn't want to think about any of that right now.

Suddenly, he shifted into human form. Her gaze raked his
naked body. She paused to look at his tat again. A shiver ran
through her as she recalled how his fingers had softly caressed
her spine down her dragon tattoo.

Despite everything she had said to Ulrik and Eilish—and
even herself—all she wanted was to kiss Vaughn. To feel his
arms wrapping around her. To be near him.

CHAPTER TWENTY-SIX

The breath locked in Vaughn's chest. He had spent hours
scouring the realm for Eurwen. With every second he couldn't
find her, he feared that he would spend the rest of eternity
searching for her, only to have her remain just out of reach.

Vaughn hadn't hesitated to go to her the instant he saw her
by the loch. A myriad of emotions swirled chaotically through
him. The entire time he'd searched, he'd made a mental list of
all the things he planned to say to her once he found her. But it
all vanished the instant he spotted her. He wasn't sure whether
to be relieved to find her or angry that she had ignored him
calling for her.

Their attraction was strong. And deep. If that was the only
way he could get through to her, then that's what he would
use. It was why when he took human form, he purposefully
remained naked.

The way her eyes roamed seductively over his body let
him know that she felt their connection. She might attempt to

ignore her heart, but her body was another matter entirely. Vaughn's future was on the line. He wasn't afraid of death. But to have finally found his mate and lose her? There was nothing he wouldn't try to convince Eurwen that she was his, and he was hers.

He had never been at a loss for words before. Yet, as he stood before his mate, he wracked his mind for the perfect thing to say. The problem was, he was still getting to know Eurwen. He knew she was fiercely independent, devoted to her realm, and strong-minded. All traits that made him fall for her even more.

Vaughn usually knew everything about those he faced off against in legal matters. Eurwen kept him spinning, not knowing which way was up. She had shaken up his entire world. And he liked it. It had gotten him out of a rut he hadn't even realized he was in.

He swallowed and parted his lips, hoping the right words would come. Before he got the chance, Eurwen was before him, her lips on his as her arms wrapped around his neck. With his next breath, he enfolded her in his arms and poured all of his longing and love into the kiss.

With her sweet body pressed against his, desire tuned everything else out. Vaughn no longer cared about where she had been, what might be keeping her from wanting a relationship with him, or any other outside factors. All he cared about, all he wanted, was the woman in his arms.

Eurwen slowly ended the kiss. Her silver eyes opened and met his. "I wasn't sure you would want to talk to me after what happened at Dreagan."

"I followed you here. That should tell you everything."

She ducked her head, then looked up at him as her lips twisted. "I arrived a short time ago. When Ulrik sent you here, I was still on your world with Eilish. She took me to an island so we could talk."

"To get away from me?" he asked, praying that wasn't the case.

"I've never had a friend, not like that. Eilish offered to do something, just the two of us, and I accepted."

Vaughn smiled. "And?"

"I had fun," Eurwen replied with a grin. "I swam in the most beautiful water in Thailand, and we talked for hours."

"Eilish is great. All the mates at Dreagan are. You should get to know each of them individually."

Her eyes widened with interest. "You think that would be all right?"

"Aye," he said, seeing for the first time how starved she was for interaction.

As if sensing his thoughts, she said, "I have dragon friends."

"That isna the same as having human or Fae friends. Dragons who can no' shift doona understand the difference. They know their world, and there isna anything wrong with that. The humans and Fae know their world and have no clue about being a dragon."

"How have all of you done it? You've lived in two worlds, just as Brandr and I have."

Vaughn called his clothes to him and took her hand to lead her to a tree with a massive, gnarled trunk and limbs spread wide. Once they were seated against the tree, he turned his head to her. "We must repress our true selves. We hide on Earth. But you already knew that."

"Erith spoke of the sacrifices made to keep your identities secret. I'm sad to admit I didn't realize the extent of it until I visited Dreagan. At least I can be whoever I want to be here."

"You're fortunate."

Her brows drew together. "All of you have survived untold millennia, pretending to be human. You've saved Earth numerous times. You've kept the mortals safe from the Dark Fae and the Others. You're heroes."

"We're merely protecting our home," he explained. "As for the humans, that goes back to the vow we made when they arrived. If we didna kill them so our dragons could remain, we certainly wouldna allow someone else to wipe them out."

"It would've solved one of your problems. At least, you could've been a dragon again."

He smiled as he blew out a breath. "Aye, it would have. The thing is, we're always dragons, first and foremost. We remain in human form out of necessity. It's why so many take to their mountains when things get to be too much. They return to their true forms and shut out everything."

"Erith tried to tell me and Brandr how much everyone at Dreagan suffered."

"You didna believe?"

Eurwen slowly shook her head. "I knew she and Con were friends. She spoke highly of him and Rhi. Brandr and I thought her involvement with them colored her views. When we argued with her, she kept telling us that we'd see our parents for who they really were someday."

"Have you?"

"I'm beginning to," Eurwen admitted. "I'm ashamed that it has taken me this long."

Vaughn twined his fingers with hers. "Look at the path Con and Rhi walked together and then separate before they found each other again. All of us knew they belonged together. They wanted to be together, but the universe has a way of doing things that none of us can even begin to understand."

"All these years, I've only known half the story. Going to Dreagan was fitting the final piece of the puzzle."

"There's one more place you should go."

She cocked her head to the side. "Where?"

"The Light Castle. Even the Dark Palace."

"Why?" she asked with a frown.

Vaughn chuckled. "That is your heritage, too. You need to learn all of it."

"I'm sorry I was partly responsible for keeping you and the other Kings from this realm and the dragons."

He looked into her silver depths, seeing the regret and sorrow there. "You rectified that by opening the doorway."

"I'm not sure how long Brandr will allow it to remain open."

Vaughn shrugged one shoulder. "Since he is responsible for Claire and V's bairn being born alive, maybe there's hope."

She blinked. "What?"

"Rhi told me as soon as I arrived. Claire was in labor for hours. V tried to use his magic. Con tried to use his. Even Rhi attempted to help. All it did was cause Claire more pain."

"What did Brandr do?"

"We'd all like to know."

Eurwen's lips parted. "Does that mean there's hope for the other Kings' mates to have children?"

"I doona have that answer, but I know that everyone at Dreagan will be asking the question."

"We should have something to tell them when they ask."

Vaughn couldn't hold back his smile when he said, "*We?*"

Eurwen dropped her gaze to the ground for a heartbeat. "A slip of the tongue."

"Perhaps. Or maybe you want to be a part of it."

Her expression grew serious. "I know what you want of me, but I don't know what answer to give you."

Hope burst within Vaughn. "I'll accept that for now."

"You make it sound like you aren't giving up."

"I'm no'. Ever. Until you refuse me completely, I'll do everything I can to win your love."

"There's still the problem of our locations."

Vaughn blew out a breath as he looked at the loch. If that were the only thing holding her back, then he would find a way. "There is always a solution to any problem. We just have to find it."

CHAPTER TWENTY-SEVEN

Vaughn surprised Eurwen once more. He was patient, kind, and understanding. He hadn't pushed her, despite what he wanted. He accepted what she could give him right now. It was enough for her to figure things out. Though she knew what little she had given would only last for so long before he would likely force her to make a decision.

And that's what she didn't want. She didn't want to have to choose between her brother, the dragons, Zora, and…the other.

Ugh. She couldn't even say it. Why? What held her back? *You know why.*

Her subconscious knew just where to hit to land the best punch. Eurwen might not want to admit it, but she was afraid. Terrified, actually. The only one who really knew her was Brandr, and he had to like her. They were twins. They were all each other had had for so long. No matter how many times

Eurwen visited Earth and saw others interacting, she couldn't imagine herself in one of their places.

All she knew how to be was the person she was here.

Suddenly, a loud roar split the air, interrupting her thoughts. Both she and Vaughn jumped to their feet. Without a doubt, the sound was a dragon in agony. She didn't say anything to Vaughn, just started running, shifting mid-step before taking to the sky. She was surprised when she looked over and saw the teal dragon next to her.

"That sounded some distance away," Vaughn's voice said in her head.

She nodded as she called Brandr's name through their mental link. When he didn't answer, she flew faster in the direction of the roar. She began to worry that it was Brandr who was hurt.

A peripheral glimpse of gold caught her attention. Eurwen glanced to her other side to see her father coming up alongside her. Vaughn was a big dragon, but Constantine was even larger.

He nodded, and she returned the gesture before saying to both Vaughn and Con, *"Something didn't feel right when I came through the doorway today. It only lasted a second, but that's all it took for me to sense it."*

"I've no' felt anything," Con said. *"Then again, I'm still learning this realm."*

Vaughn's eyes briefly met hers. *"I was too busy looking for you to sense anything, but there are a lot of new sensations here. Like Con said, I'm still learning, too."*

Eurwen had hoped one of them might have felt something as she had. A knot of worry began in her gut.

"Brandr felt it. Apparently, it's something he's experienced before."

"He didna tell you?" Con asked, concern clouding his voice.

Eurwen shook her head.

They flew for several more minutes before the mountains gave way to rolling grassland. Eurwen saw the dragons circling overhead and recognized two as Brandr's generals. She shared the information with Constantine and Vaughn.

"Don't interfere," she warned them.

As they drew closer, the two dropped back, allowing her to approach the dragons first. When she saw the dragon general, Nundro, lying unmoving on the ground with Brandr beside him, the band around Eurwen's chest lessened. At least, her brother wasn't hurt.

The dragons circling moved away as she approached. She tucked her wings and dove from the sky, only to spread them once again to stop her descent and land softly upon the ground before shifting to her human form and rushing to her brother.

"What happened?" she demanded.

Brandr didn't even look her way. When she reached his side, she saw the massive wound that split open Nundro's yellow scales on his side. Her brother tried to stanch the blood.

"Brandr," she urged.

He glanced at her. In that second, she saw his fury, resentment, and apprehension. "I doona know."

She gathered magic in her hands and joined it with his, but it didn't seem to do any good. Nundro moaned in pain, his breathing growing shallow.

"Let me help. Please," Con said from behind them.

Eurwen looked over her shoulder to Con then at Brandr. She could tell her brother wanted to refuse. "This isn't about us. This is about a dragon. Con can save him."

"I wish for nothing in return," Con said before Brandr could allude to such a thing.

Finally, Brandr's lips flattened as he removed his hands and stepped away. "Fine."

Eurwen looked around for Vaughn and saw him circling with the other dragons overhead. That's when she realized that they weren't just there for protection. They were searching for whoever had done this. She glanced about. There were no hiding places in the open fields, and they were far from the border with the humans. So, what could it have been?

When Con lifted his hand, she focused on him. Erith had told her all about Con's magic. Every dragon was born with individual magic, specific to them. Con could heal anything but death. Since Eurwen had never seen him use his power before, she wasn't about to miss it now.

Con didn't make a great show of it. He simply put his hand over the wound and concentrated. Eurwen's gaze slid to Nundro's gaping injury and saw it slowly mending itself until it was gone entirely. Constantine then lowered his hand and took a step back. Nundro lifted his head and looked directly at Con with his purple eyes. Their words were private, but Eurwen knew the general was thanking her father.

The dragon then got to its feet and faced her and Brandr. Eurwen felt a soft nudge in her mind. She opened a channel to hear Nundro say, *"That was closer than I want to admit."*

"What happened?" Brandr asked.

The general shook his great head. *"I didna see or hear*

anything. I was returning from following the mortals when the pain shot through me. My wings wouldna work, and I began falling. I landed here."

Eurwen glanced up at the other dragons. *"Was anyone with you?"*

"I was alone," the general answered.

Brandr glanced at her. *"I wasna far when Nundro cried out. Neither were these dragons."*

"I wish I could tell you what happened and how," Nundro said. *"I doona want this happening to anyone else."*

Brandr smiled at him. *"You've earned some rest. Return to your family."*

Before Nundro left, he paused once more and bowed his head to Con. Eurwen watched a muscle in Brandr's jaw twitch. Con had saved Nundro's life. Brandr should be thankful instead of worrying that their father wanted to take over.

"I take it nothing like this has ever happened before?" Con asked Brandr and her.

Brandr refused to speak. Eurwen gave him a dark look before she faced her father. "No."

Con slowly studied the area. "Does this have anything to do with what you felt when you came through the doorway?"

"Possibly. Brandr knows more about it than I do." She inwardly patted herself on the back when she saw her brother's nostrils flare in anger.

Con looked at Brandr. "You have capable dragons at your disposal. However, I'm offering my, Vaughn's, and V's services while we're here. More eyes can never hurt."

Eurwen was surprised when Brandr didn't immediately

refuse. The fact that he hesitated told her how worried he was. She didn't understand why he had kept it all to himself instead of sharing with her, but now wasn't the time to ask him about it. She would do that when they were alone.

"I'll take you up on that offer," Brandr replied.

The dragons overhead began disbursing until only Vaughn remained. He didn't land, and Eurwen was thankful for that. Brandr had been pushed to his limits today. Sooner or later, he would have to talk to Vaughn, though. Just as he would have to talk to her.

Thank you, she mouthed to Brandr when he looked her way. He shrugged, but it was a step he had refused to take before.

Brandr cleared his throat and turned his head to Con. "Thank you for saving Nundro. He's no' just a good general. He's also my friend."

"I know that feeling well," Con said and raised his gaze to Vaughn.

The hairs on the back of Eurwen's neck prickled with awareness. She whirled around to look behind her, but there was nothing.

"What is it?" Con and Brandr asked at the same time.

She rubbed the back of her neck. "I don't know. I could've sworn someone was there."

A large shadow moved over them as Vaughn swept across the sky and soared about twenty feet above the ground before flapping his wings and darting upward and then turning back to face them.

"*Nothing*," Vaughn told them.

Brandr touched her arm. "Perhaps it's better if we return home and put a plan in place."

"I agree," Con said.

Eurwen gave the area one more look before shifting and jumping into the air. When she saw that Con, Brandr, and Vaughn were flying with her, she could only stare in amazement. This wasn't something she'd ever thought to see.

When they returned to Cairnkeep, they didn't immediately tell Rhi, Claire, or V what had occurred. They all spent time cooing at the newest addition to the Dreagan family. Eurwen had never been this close to a human infant before. She was in awe of the little creature, as well as a bit scared of it.

"Want to hold her?" Claire asked her.

Rhi smiled, nodding. "Go on. I've taken my fair share already."

Eurwen shook her head and stepped back, bumping into Vaughn, who steadied her. "Not now."

"I understand," Claire said with a grin. Then her brown eyes swung to Brandr. "Thank you. I don't know what you did, but I somehow know that you saved Pearl's life."

Everyone turned to her brother. Eurwen had never seen him nervous before. It was like Brandr didn't like the attention, which wasn't like her brother at all. "What did you do?" she asked.

Brandr looked at each of them. "The only way I can explain it is that it was almost as if the bairn called to me. I went to Claire, and that's when I felt it."

"Felt what?" V asked, concern filling his face.

Rhi nodded. "Yes, felt what? We all tried our magic to help, but nothing seemed to work."

"Because that's what she was counting on," Brandr said.

Eurwen shrugged. "Who?"

"Usaeil," he replied.

Con fisted his hands. "Will we never escape that bitch?"

Eurwen noticed the curious way Brandr watched the bairn. "What did you feel?" she pressed.

"Dark Fae magic," Brandr responded. "It was holding the babe in place, refusing to allow her to be born."

"Oh, God," Claire said breathlessly, her eyes clouding with tears as she looked down at her daughter.

Fury rolled off V in waves. "I knew Usaeil would do something like this to us. Brandr, we owe you a debt we can never repay. We can no' thank you enough."

"About that," Con said.

Vaughn added, "Something is going on here. We told Brandr and Eurwen we'd help."

"I'll do whatever is needed," V said.

Rhi nodded. "Me, too."

"Someone has to watch over Claire," V stated.

Rhi grinned. "No one will get near her or your daughter. I promise you that."

"Said like a queen," Con replied with a grin.

Eurwen saw the loving exchange and leaned back against Vaughn. He squeezed her hand, letting her know that he would be there. A flutter of happiness filled her stomach. She wasn't used to such emotions. Sure, she'd dreamed of feeling them someday, but to actually have it? She worried whether it was real. Or did she experience it simply because she wanted it so desperately?

Brandr interrupted her thoughts as he began describing the

attack that had just happened to Nundro. When he reached the part where Con had healed the general, Rhi's face softened into a smile as she looked at her mate.

"Were mortals responsible?" V asked.

Eurwen shook her head. "While the border isn't too far from that area, it wasn't near enough for any humans to attack and run without being seen."

"Unless they had help," Rhi pointed out.

Con shook his head. "The area was grassland as far as the eye could see. If someone had been there, we would've seen movement when we approached. There was nothing."

"There's the crone," Brandr said.

Eurwen blinked. "The one who pulled Varek to our realm? You're still searching for her?"

"I want to know how she did it and why," Brandr replied.

Vaughn scratched his neck. "I would, too. If she did it once, she could do it again. We want to make sure she can no'."

"Did anyone know that someone on this realm could do such magic?" Claire asked.

Eurwen and Brandr looked at each other before shaking their heads in unison.

"Either she's been hiding…" Rhi began.

Con crossed his arms over his chest. "Or biding her time."

"Neither option is good," V said.

Eurwen shrugged. "Perhaps she's running from something. Jeyra said that no one with magic was allowed in Orgate. Maybe the crone was once a part of the human city and had to leave."

"Or she could be a powerful being threatening us," Brandr replied. "That's why I want to find her."

Eurwen threw up her hands in irritation. "You asked Jeyra multiple times. She told you that the crone found her. If you continue hunting the crone as you have, you may never find her."

"We'll find her," V stated.

Brandr raised his brows as he shrugged. "We have to know if she's the one who attacked Nundro."

Eurwen nodded slowly. "If she is, she'll answer for it. But first, we need to find out why. To focus solely on her is foolish. It could've been anyone."

"Especially if there are mortals on this realm with magic," Vaughn added.

Con dropped his arms. "Then we need to start planning how to do this."

CHAPTER TWENTY-EIGHT

Vaughn watched the sunset from atop the mountain near Eurwen's cottage. They had spent hours going over different strategies until a plan formed. His gaze tracked the various dragons as they flew all around him. He noted they liked to stay near Cairnkeep, and he couldn't blame them.

"I wondered where you went," Eurwen said as she walked up.

He glanced at her and smiled. "I didna expect to come to Zora for battle. I hope we didna bring this to your realm."

Eurwen sighed loudly. "No doubt that's exactly what my brother thinks, but I don't believe it. Brandr even admitted that he'd felt something off for a few days, which meant it was before you came."

"As in when Varek was brought here?"

"Maybe," she answered with a shrug.

"Or once he got free of the mortals."

Eurwen's lips twisted. "Possibly."

Vaughn nodded and returned his attention to the dragons. "On Earth, clans stayed together. It wasna that they were no' allowed to mix, they just didna. Mainly because it was hard for any dragon no' of that clan to fit in. Here, all colors mingle."

"This is a different realm. The way things were on your planet was how they needed to be. When Brandr and I first came here, we learned from some of the eldest dragons that they began keeping clans separate because that's how it had always been. Without Kings, however—"

"Things fell apart," he finished.

She twisted her lips in a rueful smile. "Yes. Now, this is what works for them here."

"I'll never grow tired of watching and hearing them."

Eurwen moved closer, her shoulder brushing his. "I'm glad you're here. The generals and the army are good, but they aren't Kings."

"We're going to figure out what's going on," Vaughn promised as he looked down at her.

"Yes, we will."

They stood in silence for some time, watching the dragons. The sun descended behind the mountains, and the colorful sky gave way to a pale blue that finally faded to black. But Vaughn's thoughts weren't on the striking scenery.

"I think you should remove the doorway to Earth," Vaughn said.

Eurwen's head whipped to him. "Why?"

"We need to make sure the evil from our realm isna passing to this one."

"Or can't get from here to yours."

Vaughn nodded once as he looked at her. "Exactly. Another doorway can be constructed later."

"Should we send Claire and the bairn through first?"

"No."

Her eyebrows shot up on her forehead. "If something's here, Earth would be safer for them."

"We doona know what's here. No one has seen the infant, and it needs to stay that way until we can decipher what is going on."

"In case whatever this is, tries to attach itself to the baby. Bloody hell. I didn't even think of that."

Vaughn glanced at the cottage. "Unfortunately, we've come across all kinds of evil. I've learned no' to assume anything."

"Apparently, I have a lot to learn."

He reached for her hand. "I'm glad you've no' had the battles we have. They leave scars that are hidden and never fully heal."

"But when something does come, you know how to handle it. Look at all the battles the Kings have won."

"Because we work together. We move as one cohesive unit."

She grinned. "It also helps that you're all excellent warriors."

"Aye, it does," he said with a chuckle.

"Give me a second," she said before disappearing. A heartbeat later, she was back. "The doorway is gone."

"It's for the best."

Her fingers found his again as her smile dropped. "We've had peace for many, many years. I foolishly believed we would always have it, simply by us not making the same mistakes as…"

Her voice trailed off. Vaughn looked at her and said, "As we did."

"Yes," she replied in a soft voice.

"That isna a bad way to do things. However, new mistakes will inevitably be made. I'm no' saying anyone has made a mistake. I'm merely pointing out facts."

She let out a breath. "You're right. It's something Brandr and I have discussed. We do the best we can."

"That's all anyone can do."

"If we learn that the mortals are responsible for Nundro's attack, we will retaliate."

Vaughn had feared she would say such words. "That isna the answer."

"You think we should stand by and not punish the one who hurt one of us?"

"That isna what I said. You may no' have made the same vows about protecting the humans as we did, but by wiping them out, you'll change something within yourself—and every dragon who helps—forever. You'll never be able to come back from that."

She tucked a strand of hair behind her ear. "We don't have the same magic you do on Earth. Nothing here will remove Brandr and me from our positions."

"Your morality will be compromised. And if you doona think that's a big deal, then it proves that you have no idea of the true consequences of what you're talking about."

"I won't allow humans to jeopardize what we have here," she argued.

Vaughn faced her. "I'm no' asking you to. I'm asking you to find a way to make peace for everyone."

"This is our realm. Why should we compromise?"

He could've given her a million reasons, but they all sounded hollow to him. Being with the dragons again had brought back all the Kings had sacrificed for the mortals to live. Being on Zora made Vaughn wish that things had turned out differently on Earth.

"I know what you're saying," Eurwen continued. "I've thought about it myself. But at the end of the day, I have to look out for the dragons. They shouldn't have to find another home or fight for another one."

Vaughn couldn't argue with that. He nodded and faced forward. Then, he did a double take when he saw a speck of pink in the night sky. To his shock, there was more than one pink dragon. There were over a dozen.

"I can no' believe my eyes," he murmured.

"The Pinks?"

"We thought they were extinct, killed by humans."

Eurwen shook her head. "Eggs were found on their land as the dragons were called across the bridge. The dragons gathered up all they could find and brought them when they left your realm."

Vaughn's throat clogged with emotion as he saw the Pinks fly around the mountain and then disappear. "All this time, we believed they were no more. We mourned them, wishing we could've done something to prevent their slaughter."

"They've thrived here. All the dragons have."

"The Pinks are alive. Varek said as much, but I didna truly

believe him. I thought maybe one had managed to live, but an entire clan? It's more than we could've hoped for."

Eurwen hugged his arm against her. "There will always be dragons. I'm going to make sure of it."

"Me, too," he said as he looked down at her.

"Do you wish to stay out here tonight?"

Vaughn glanced at her cottage. "Your place is taken, and I think Brandr would rather eat glass than allow me inside his place."

"You're growing on him."

He snorted. "I highly doubt that. However, he does know that us helping right now is for everyone's benefit. I'm glad he accepted Con's offer."

"Me, too," she said with a roll of her eyes. "I love my twin, but he can be obstinate at times. I wasn't going to refuse Con. Brandr knew that."

"Maybe us working together will create a bond. I know it will make Con and Rhi happy."

Eurwen looked up at him. "And me."

He swallowed and leaned down to press his lips to hers. "Let's sleep under the stars."

"So you can see the dragons?"

Vaughn shook his head as he grinned. "So I can see the stars shining in your eyes."

"You know just the right things to say."

"I'm saying what's in my heart. The things I've wanted to say since our first night together."

She cupped his cheek with her free hand. "You make me feel special. As if I'm the only woman in the world."

"In the universe," he corrected. "And that's because you are."

Her lips curved into a smile. "Let's find someplace more private."

"The loch?" he suggested.

"You read my mind."

They ran to the edge of the cliff and jumped, shifting and flying toward the loch, side by side.

CHAPTER TWENTY-NINE

The feel of Vaughn's lips on her temple woke Eurwen from her dreams. She smiled to find herself curled tightly against his side. "Not yet," she murmured.

He laughed softly. "I can do many things, but I can no' stop the sun from rising."

All she wanted was to have the day to herself to do whatever she wanted with Vaughn. No interruptions, no battles to fight. Nothing but the two of them. She'd let that slip away from her when they had been at Dreagan.

"We can return," he said.

She rolled onto her back and turned her head to him. It had been a glorious night. Even better than their first on Zora. It made her wonder why she had ever tried to keep him at a distance. No matter how hard she tried, she couldn't stay away from him. "We definitely will. I've found I quite like sleeping beneath the stars with you."

"We didna exactly sleep."

She grinned. "That's what I liked."

Vaughn laughed and rolled on top of her. "Come on. They'll be waiting for us."

Eurwen remained as he jumped to his feet and turned to walk into the loch. He dove beneath the water and surfaced a few minutes later, shaking his head to spray droplets everywhere. She laughed as she sat up to watch.

She wasn't sure when she had stopped fighting the feelings within her, but she was glad that she had. Things with Vaughn had become much simpler. Almost too easy. She liked being with him. She enjoyed how she felt when she was with him.

She liked how *he* made her feel.

Yet, she still couldn't answer if he was her mate or not. Was her Fae side blocking that? Or was she too afraid to look and discover the truth? Sadly, she wouldn't be surprised if the answer was the latter option.

Eurwen knew that love existed. She didn't doubt that. What she questioned was if it was there for *her*. Not once in her long life had she ever had a relationship. She'd had lovers —all from Earth, obviously. Though there had been a few dragons on Zora who'd tried to woo her. If she had felt anything for the dragons, she would've pursued them, but there had been nothing there.

Her lack of relationship experience likely factored into her hesitancy with Vaughn. He knew without a doubt what he wanted. She didn't know which way was up when it came to love and relationships. And none of that even factored into her role on Zora.

The happiness she'd felt upon waking quickly dissipated. Eurwen got to her feet and walked to the loch for a quick swim. Once in the water, large hands wrapped around her and dragged her against a hard body she knew well. His arousal pressed against her stomach. Vaughn's mouth met hers beneath the waves for a kiss unlike anything she'd ever experienced. They surfaced with their lips still locked together.

"Och, lass," he murmured in a husky whisper that made her shiver with desire.

Eurwen closed her eyes for a moment, wishing they could give in to the pleasure they both wanted. Instead, she pushed away from him. "You're the one who said we had to go."

"Doona remind me," he said grumpily.

They swam back to shore. The minute they stepped out of the loch, their magic dried them. Eurwen chose black leather pants and a form-fitting black shirt, and topped it with black armor that looked like dragon scales that covered her upper body and forearms. Black knee-high boots completed her look. She smoothed her hands over her hair, transforming the blond locks into intricate braids like the styles she favored from the Norse.

Vaughn let out a whistle.

She turned to face him to see that he had also chosen dark clothing with a simple black tee, dark jeans, and boots.

"You're every inch a warrior," he said as he walked to her.

"I suppose we'll see."

She took his hand, and with several small jumps, teleported them to Cairnkeep. Just as Vaughn had suspected, Con and V waited for them.

"Ready?" Con asked.

Vaughn nodded and looked at her. Eurwen bowed her

head. It wasn't as if she hadn't been in a battle before, but nothing like what the Kings had been involved in. Eurwen couldn't shake the feeling that her realm was in jeopardy. She hoped she was wrong, but given the way Con, V, and Vaughn acted, she didn't think she was.

"The doorway to Earth is closed," Eurwen told them.

V frowned and started to object.

Vaughn quickly said, "In case whatever is happening here came from Earth."

"Good call," Con said. "That way, we can isolate one variable."

V grunted. "It would be nice to have the other Kings here."

"That might be the verra thing that began all of this," Vaughn stated.

Brandr walked up and said, "We'll know soon enough. My generals have been informed of the plan and are getting the army in place along our border with the humans."

"We should get in place, as well," Con replied.

V was the first to shift, then Con, Eurwen, Vaughn, and finally Brandr. The five of them took to the air. Eurwen noted that the nearby dragons watched, likely wondering what was going on. She looked from V's copper scales, to Con's gold ones as they flew on her left side. To her right was Vaughn and his vibrant teal scales and Brandr with his golden scales that faded to a beige color on his belly.

Whatever was on Zora, be it an entity or magic, would be stopped. Eurwen didn't doubt it for a second. She wouldn't have questioned it even if it had only been her and Brandr facing off against the threat. But she certainly didn't hesitate with three Dragon Kings aiding them.

When they finally reached the border with the humans near where Nundro had been attacked, the five of them met up with the four generals. The army flew high above them, watching for any movement below. The plan was for the generals, Kings, Brandr, and Eurwen to hopefully draw out whatever had come to Zora.

Eurwen and Brandr returned to human form as soon as they landed, each with armor infused with their magic. They had never gone up against enemies like the Dragon Kings had, but she and Brandr were prepared, nonetheless.

She drew in a deep breath as she lowered herself to hide in the tall grass. The generals and Vaughn would stay in the air as Con, V, Brandr, and Eurwen moved about in human form. She glanced to her left to see her father in the distance. To her right, she almost made out Vaughn's shape.

Eurwen scanned the area. They were there as a group, but each of them was also isolated. She was scared as well as anxious to start the battle. "All right. Where are you?" she whispered.

As she waited for someone to strike, she wondered who might have come to their realm. Not knowing who and what brought the infants to their realm opened the possibility that anyone and anything could potentially find them. It was a sobering thought. For so very long, she had assumed that Zora was safe from outside threats. That she and Brandr had things under control. After all, no beings like the Fae or a group like the Others had found them.

That wasn't only foolish, it was also naïve and reckless not to be prepared for anything. Had they merely been lucky all these eons? Eurwen had been so preoccupied with everything the Kings had done wrong on Earth that she hadn't stopped to think about Zora and its vulnerabilities—one of the things the Kings had done correctly on their realm.

But she knew real fear now. The kind that wouldn't ever completely go away. The fact was that the dragons were under attack. It could be humans. They'd been resourceful in the past in capturing and imprisoning dragons to torture. It could also be the crone. Brandr thought it was her, and while Eurwen hadn't ruled her out, she wanted facts.

It could also be another entity they hadn't thought of yet. In fact, it could be several things. And even if they contained it this time, who was to say something else wouldn't get through later?

Eurwen flexed her hands, feeling her magic coursing through her. She scanned the area again, sensing nothing. Not even the tingling on her neck like the day before. That didn't alleviate her worry, though. It was only Brandr and her on Zora. Earth had the Dragon Kings, fighting together whenever something attacked. They needed more than the generals for help here. They needed Kings.

All of them.

Her mind immediately went to Vaughn. She wanted him in Zora. She wanted him with her. He liked it here. But did he like it enough to give up Dreagan and his brethren when she refused to give up her life? She couldn't ask that of him, especially when she wouldn't entertain the notion of him asking it of her.

The wind suddenly shifted. Eurwen was instantly on alert as her senses prickled. But no matter how hard she looked, she didn't see anything or feel anything else.

"*Check-in,*" Brandr called to everyone through the mental link.

One by one, everyone gave the all-clear. Until it was her turn. "*Nothing here,*" she answered.

Thirty minutes went by, still with nothing. Until the wind shifted again. Once more, her nerve endings tingled, alerting her that something was out there. This time, Eurwen felt that same sensation from when she'd walked through the doorway. She frantically scanned the area.

"*The wind,*" she told the others. "*I just felt…something.*"

She waited to hear Vaughn's response. When he didn't immediately reply, she glanced in his direction. That's when she saw a shimmer out of the corner of her eye. She jerked back around, but whatever she'd seen was gone. Yet she knew that something had been there.

"*It's here! It's invisible. I saw a flicker out of the corner of my eye,*" she alerted the others.

Eurwen's heart pounded wildly. She knew that something was coming right for her. She might not be able to see it, but she could sense it. She stood and spread her hands, palms out, ready for battle. Before she could determine where to send a volley of magic, something slammed into her abdomen. She tried to look down to see what it was, but she couldn't move. It was like something had frozen her in place. She tried to call out, to warn the others, but her voice wouldn't work. Eurwen attempted to access the mental link, but words wouldn't form in her head either.

Then she was falling backward. She blinked up at the blue sky before everything went dark.

"Now, you're mine," whispered an eerie voice in her ear.

CHAPTER THIRTY

"*Eurwen?*" Vaughn called as worry filled him.

She kept talking, but her words weren't clear. It was as if something distorted her voice.

"*Eurwen!*"

Soon, the others were calling for her, as well, but she wouldn't answer them either.

"*I'm going to her,*" Vaughn said as he dipped a wing and turned in her direction.

The instant he did, he saw Eurwen stand. Suddenly, she jerked as if something had struck her. In the next instant, she fell backward.

"*Nay!*" Vaughn bellowed and flew faster.

He dove from the sky, tucking into a ball and shifting to his human form so he could land on his feet and run the last few yards to her. As he did, he looked around for an opponent but saw nothing. He slid to his knees and bent over Eurwen as the others rushed to them.

Vaughn stared in shock at the hole through her abdomen, wide enough that he could put his arm through it. Blood coated Eurwen's front and continued pouring out.

"Con!" Vaughn shouted.

The King of Kings was immediately at Eurwen's other side. "I'm here."

Vaughn's heart thumped in his chest as he stared helplessly at his mate. Even though he knew that Con could heal Eurwen, Vaughn couldn't shake the unease rolling violently through him. Someone or something had attacked his mate, and no one had seen anything. Just as with Nundro the day before.

It felt like an eternity before the wound finally mended, and Con dropped his arm to his side. Vaughn looked at him and saw the worry on his friend's face.

"That was different than Nundro's wound," Con said.

Brandr sat at Eurwen's feet, panic and concern etched across his face. "Why hasn't she woken? She's healed."

"Open your eyes, lass," Vaughn urged Eurwen. "We're waiting for you to tell us what you saw."

But she didn't move. Vaughn glanced at Con, Brandr, and V, hoping one of them would have a solution. The three of them looked as helpless as he felt.

"Eurwen," Vaughn called louder. "Open your eyes. Look at me."

V shook his head. "This isna good. None of this is. No' the location, the attack, and no' her lying as if in a coma."

"Whoever did this has to be around here," Brandr declared as he got to his feet. He yelled to his generals, and the dragons took to the sky.

Vaughn smoothed Eurwen's hair from her face. Her

beautiful armor was ruined. Dragon scales were difficult to pierce, but whatever had struck Nundro had managed it then as well as whatever or whoever had done this today. Vaughn looked at his friends. "Did you hear what she said before she fell?"

"It was jumbled," Con answered.

V shook his head. "It was like a radio station that didna come in clearly."

"I couldn't make out anything," Brandr said.

"She felt something yesterday," Con reminded them.

Vaughn stood and backed away as he glanced around. "We need to get her out of here. Now."

"I'll stay with my generals and the army. We'll scour the area. And we'll find who is responsible," Brandr replied.

Vaughn nodded before shifting and gently lifting Eurwen in one of his hands. V and Con flew on either side of him on the way back to Cairnkeep. Halfway there, Vaughn expected her to wake and demand to be put down. He kept hoping he'd hear her voice, but it didn't happen.

Once they reached Cairnkeep, they landed. Vaughn returned to human form and carried her to Brandr's cottage. Con followed close behind. Not much later, Rhi teleported into the house with them.

"What happened?" she demanded.

Con wrapped an arm around his mate as he explained the situation. Vaughn gently lay Eurwen on the bed, still waiting for her to wake.

"Why hasn't she opened her eyes?" Rhi asked frantically.

Con shrugged and shook his head. "None of us knows."

"The general from yesterday? He didn't lose

consciousness," Rhi stated.

Vaughn sat on the edge of the bed and took Eurwen's hand in his. "Everything about today felt different."

"Like a trap," Con said.

Vaughn nodded slowly as he looked at Con. "Exactly."

Rhi's eyes widened. "Then we get back out there and find who did this."

"That's where Brandr and his generals are," Vaughn said.

Rhi's face went slack. "Alone? Are you kidding? After what happened with all of you there, why wouldn't someone remain with Brandr?"

Con kissed her cheek. "I'm heading there now, sweetheart. I wanted to get our daughter here first."

Rhi threw her arms around him. They exchanged soft words before moving apart.

"I'll update you and V often regarding my location," Con told him.

Vaughn bowed his head. "Be careful."

"There's a reason Eurwen was attacked, and we're going to find out what that is," Con promised before he strode out of the cottage.

Vaughn watched his friend go before his gaze slid to Rhi. Unease stamped her face. The last time Vaughn had seen such an expression was when his human lover had been giving birth. He had cared for the mortal, but he hadn't loved her. Not as he did Eurwen. Vaughn returned his attention to his mate.

He couldn't shake the apprehension, the worry that the Kings were somehow responsible for what was taking place on Zora. Whether it'd begun because Varek had been brought here, or whether it'd manifested once Varek arrived was trivial. Something malicious was in the realm. Was it after the dragons? Was it targeting Eurwen and Brandr? Or were the Kings the objective?

"We need to know if the mortals have also experienced such attacks," Vaughn said.

Rhi started to pace. "I need to do something. I can't stand just sitting still. I'll go."

"No," Vaughn stopped her before she left.

Her head whipped to him. "And why not?"

"You're too upset."

She paused for a second. "Perhaps you're right. But if they knew what Varek was, they'll know you, as well."

"That's true."

"There's Claire."

Vaughn snorted. "V willna let her out of his sight, and I doona blame him."

"That leaves only one who can navigate the humans effectively."

"Jeyra."

Rhi nodded. "I'll get her."

"I had Eurwen remove the doorway in case whatever was here came from Earth."

"I'll be quick," Rhi replied. She glanced at her daughter. "Don't let her out of your sight."

Vaughn bowed his head. "I willna."

Once Rhi was gone, he rubbed Eurwen's hand between his. "Wake up, lass. You're healed. There should be nothing keeping you unconscious."

Vaughn let his magic surround her, searching for anything that might stand out. No matter how hard he focused, he was unable to discern anything. He had hoped something would stand out, something they could remove so she would open her eyes and smile at him again.

"I got her," Rhi said as she appeared in the cottage.

Vaughn looked to find Rhi, Jeyra, and Varek.

"What the bloody hell happened?" Varek demanded as he looked at Eurwen on the bed. "Rhi wouldna tell us anything. Just said Jeyra was needed."

Vaughn didn't release Eurwen's hand as he faced the trio. "To summarize, one of the generals was attached yesterday. Con was able to heal him, and we searched the open field but saw no one."

"No one?" Varek asked with a frown.

Vaughn shook his head. "Con offered our help, and Eurwen and Brandr accepted. We came up with a plan and implemented it this morning. Eurwen, Brandr, Con, and V stayed on the ground in human form while the four generals and I stayed in the air, drawing attention to ourselves."

"You were on the border with my people, weren't you?" Jeyra asked.

"The attack yesterday was done far enough from there that we would've seen anyone running away. But, yes, this morning, we were near the border," Vaughn explained.

Rhi pulled her hair back and twisted it into a knot off her neck. "Someone or something attacked Eurwen. Con healed her wound, but she hasn't woken since."

"You know what this reminds me of?" Varek asked.

Vaughn nodded as he looked at Rhi. "That time Ulrik's uncle attacked, and you wouldna wake."

Rhi briefly closed her eyes. "That was Mikkel. This is on

another realm. How could one have to do with the other?"

"It might have something to do with Eurwen's Fae blood," Varek pointed out.

Vaughn rubbed his thumb across the back of her hand. "Rhi eventually woke."

"I didn't want to," Rhi admitted. "If it hadn't been for Con, I wouldn't have."

Jeyra worried her lip. "What does any of this have to do with me?"

Vaughn met Varek's dark eyes. "Brandr and his generals are looking for whoever did this. Once Con saw Eurwen here, he went after Brandr as backup. We need to know if your people are also getting attacked."

"Or if they're doing it," Jeyra surmised with a nod. "I'd want to know the same. All right. I'll do it."

Varek said, "*We'll* do it."

"Is that wise, Varek? After what happened last time?" Rhi asked.

Jeyra looked at Varek and smiled. "Thankfully, we have an ally in Orgate. Sateen will be able to give us the answers we seek."

"And I dare any of them to do anything to us," Varek replied.

Vaughn desperately wanted to go with them, but he didn't want to leave Eurwen. However, someone who had been at the attacks needed to be there.

"Go," Rhi told him. "I'll stay with my daughter."

Vaughn reluctantly released Eurwen's hand and got to his feet. "Let's go. The sooner we get there, the sooner we can get back."

He took one more look at Eurwen and followed Varek and Jeyra out of the cottage.

"Where are V and Claire?" Varek asked.

Vaughn pointed to Eurwen's cottage some distance away as they started down the mountain. "It seems Usaeil used her magic to no' only guarantee that Claire would become pregnant but also make sure the child would never be born. The Dark magic held the baby in Claire's womb. Somehow Brandr figured it out."

"Brandr's mix of Fae and dragon magic seems to have saved the day," Varek said.

"What of the baby?" Jeyra asked.

Vaughn grinned when he thought of the tiny bundle. "She is doing great. Claire and V are beside themselves with joy."

"I can no' believe another dragon–human bairn has been born," Varek said, awe in his voice.

Jeyra frowned. "Wouldn't it have been wise to send Claire and the infant back to Earth with all of this going on?"

Before Vaughn could answer, Varek shook his head and said, "There have been instances where evil has attached itself to a bairn to pass undetected. Everyone is just covering all the bases."

"We need to get to Orgate quickly," Vaughn said, returning the conversation to the matter at hand.

Jeyra shot him a questioning look. "I'm not sure arriving in your true form is the best idea."

"We'll stop at the border," Varek told her.

Vaughn didn't wait on them. He shifted and jumped into the air, flying swift and true to the river.

CHAPTER THIRTY-ONE

Eurwen knew she was in trouble. It felt as if she were bound, but she couldn't figure out with what. No matter how hard she tried to use her limbs, they wouldn't work. She strained, listening for anyone.

Hoping Vaughn was near.

Nothing but silence and darkness surrounded her. Yet, she knew she wasn't alone. *Something* was with her. She recalled the words she'd heard before she fell unconscious. Eurwen didn't know who the entity was. The voice was difficult to pinpoint as either male or female, but it was pure evil. Of that, she had no doubt.

She didn't know how or why the being was on Zora, but she hoped the others would figure it out soon. She wanted to go back with them, to argue with Brandr, to see Vaughn's Persian blue eyes, watching her with desire and longing. To hear Rhi's laughter and talk more with Con.

First, she had to get away from her capture. At least, her

body no longer hurt. Her wound must have healed itself. That would make fighting against whoever held her easier. Because she would fight. She would get free.

And back to Vaughn.

The moment the human-dragon border came into view, Vaughn began his descent. He landed, shifting to his human form. Once Varek alit, and Jeyra slid off his back, the two joined him.

"This way," Jeyra said and began jogging.

Vaughn followed the couple across the stream. The instant they were on the other side, Jeyra started to run. Vaughn and Varek kept pace with her. They could've gone faster, but they wouldn't leave her behind.

Finally, Vaughn spotted the forest giving way to open space. Soon, he heard the sounds of a decent-sized city. Then he spotted the tall barrier and the gate that surrounded the town. Neither Jeyra nor Varek paused when they walked from the trees, simply headed straight for the entrance. Few took notice of them until they drew closer to the opened gates.

Vaughn saw the guards in the tower eyeing them with foreboding. "We've got eyes."

"They'll notify the council that we've arrived," Jeyra said.

Varek met Vaughn's gaze over Jeyra's head. "At least magic can be used in the city now."

Vaughn let his gaze wander around the numerous people walking in and out of the gates. They all wore the same type of clothing as Jeyra. Slim-fitting pants tucked into high boots, sleeveless tops, and armbands on each biceps in an array of yellow to brown tones. He and Varek couldn't have stood out more had they tried.

Conversations halted as they passed while more and more gazes fell upon them. Vaughn noted that not everyone carried weapons, but those who did certainly appeared to know how to use them. Jeyra nodded to a trio of female warriors, but they turned their backs to her. Vaughn couldn't imagine that was easy to bear, but Jeyra kept her chin up and her shoulders squared.

He saw that none of the buildings were higher than three stories. While the architecture wasn't as advanced as the humans' of Earth, there was still skill in the designs and craftsmanship that Vaughn couldn't deny.

The streets began clearing as word of their arrival spread. No longer did they have to weave through the crowds. Instead, the three of them walked shoulder to shoulder down the road as everyone looked on. It wasn't a particularly pleasant feeling. All Vaughn could think about was Varek and how they'd held him in the city's prison for weeks.

And the dragons they'd tortured.

Rage started to build, compounded by the morning's attack and Eurwen, who had yet to wake. It was all Vaughn could do to keep control of it before it erupted, and he took it out on the mortals. It was easy to blame them. After all, they had been responsible for so much on Earth. They could do the same on Zora.

Yet, if his years had taught him anything, it was to get the facts first. And that's exactly what he planned to do in Orgate.

A petite woman bent with age, her white hair pulled into

an intricate bun, walked out onto the road with the help of a cane. She faced them, a smile on her wrinkled face. "I wondered when I would see you two again."

"Sateen," Jeyra said with a bright smile as she hurried to the frail woman.

They embraced before Jeyra stepped aside, and Sateen raised a thin, white brow at Varek, her faded gray eyes watching him. "Are you just going to stand there?"

"I wouldna dream of it," Varek answered with a laugh as he approached and bent to hug the councilwoman. He straightened and stepped to the side, "Sateen, this is my friend, Vaughn."

Sateen's intense eyes slid to him as she looked him up and down. "Another Dragon King. Why do I get the feeling your arrival isn't a social call?"

Vaughn bowed his head. "It's a pleasure to meet you. Jeyra and Varek spoke highly of you."

The elder councilwoman quirked her brow, waiting for him to answer her question.

Vaughn met her gaze, liking her instantly. "Can we go somewhere private?"

"Welcome to Orgate," she said. "The only truly private place is my home. Follow me."

Jeyra walked beside the councilwoman as Vaughn and Varek trailed slightly behind them.

"*The people here doona know what to think of our arrival,*" Varek said.

Vaughn glanced at those lining the road. "*They look to be frightened of what we might do.*"

"We are Dragon Kings. They've been told to fear dragons, and especially Kings."

"How, exactly?" Vaughn asked. *"There are no Kings here. No' like us. I suppose you could call Brandr a King and Eurwen a Queen, but they've kept their distance from the city and mortals in general."*

Varek sighed. *"I've asked Jeyra that many times. All she can remember is being told from an early age to fear us."*

Vaughn met Varek's gaze and nodded. They continued on in silence. He was surprised at how quickly Sateen moved for a woman who appeared as if a gentle breeze might knock her over.

"I should warn you," Varek said. *"Sateen is as sharp as a whip."*

"I gathered that."

Vaughn spotted the entrance to an elite neighborhood in the city and wasn't surprised when they turned down the road. They passed magnificent houses until the road dead-ended in front of an enormous mansion. Sateen didn't even hesitate as she approached the gates. Two men suddenly appeared and opened them for her, waiting to close them after he and Varek had walked through.

Vaughn spotted more warriors stationed in various places outside of the house. Many glared at both Jeyra and Varek. Varek winked at one of the men who bared his teeth as they passed.

"Forgive, Ugar," Sateen said without looking back at them. "His pride is still bruised from the last time you and Jeyra came to my house."

Once inside the stunning manor, Sateen turned to the left

and took them into a sitting room. She sat in a chair that fit her petite frame. Jeyra and Varek sat together on a settee, and Vaughn opted to remain standing.

"Do you fear an attack?" Sateen asked him as servants walked in with a tray of food and what appeared to be tea.

Vaughn waited until the servants had left before he bowed his head to Sateen. "I mean no disrespect. It has been a… trying…morning."

"There was an incident," Jeyra explained.

Sateen set her cane before her and put both hands on it. "I think you'd better explain."

Vaughn spent the next few minutes going into detail of what had transpired that morning and the day before.

The councilwoman's face paled by the time he finished. Her brow furrowed as she swallowed. "That is horrible, but I fail to see why you came to Orgate. Unless you think someone here had something to do with it."

"We're covering all angles," Varek said.

Jeyra glanced at her mate before she asked Sateen, "Has anyone had any such wounds in the city?"

Sateen shook her head. "Not that I've heard about."

"What about other cities?" Jeyra pressed.

Sateen shrugged and shook her head again. "Word of something like that would've spread quickly."

"Is there someone in Orgate you think could be behind the attacks?" Vaughn asked.

The councilwoman pressed her lips together. "I wish I could say no, but the truth is that since Arn's death and the release of the dragons he tortured, the city has been divided.

Some are glad to know the truth. Others... Well, let's just say they would've preferred to go on believing the lies."

"In other words, they could go after the dragons?" Varek asked.

Sateen lifted one shoulder. "If the attack had happened with weapons, I could've told you exactly who we needed to question. But it sounds as if they did it with magic."

"With Arn dead, magic can be used in the city now. Nothing's keeping those with magic from venturing here," Jeyra said.

Sateen winced. "Most aren't willing to give up the old ways. I fear they never will. I'd welcome any and all into the city, but the lines were drawn a very long time ago. I doubt you'd see any of us with magic going to any city."

"Those with magic, where do they go?" Varek asked.

Sateen gave him a sad smile. "I don't have that information. They hide. We're taught from an early age to fear magic."

"And dragons," Vaughn said.

Sateen's gaze briefly lowered to the floor. "The two get blurred, and some are unable to see one without the other."

Vaughn held her gaze. "I still doona understand why."

The elder woman's lips curved into a smile. "After Jeyra and Varek left, I tried to remember how and when I had been made to believe such things about magic and dragons. When I couldn't recall those memories, I went to the younger generation without learning the answers. I went younger and younger, getting the same responses every time."

"I can't remember who told me. It's as if I just knew it," Jeyra replied.

Sateen nodded slowly. "Exactly. I next went to the teachers and asked them. We don't have records of our entire history, but we do have a large chunk of it. When the city was first constructed, one of the first decrees was that magic wouldn't be tolerated."

"All of you are brought to a planet with dragons who have magic." Vaughn blew out a breath. "Why dread magic if you don't know it?"

Varek looked at Vaughn. "Unless they do."

"Of course. Magic brought the bairns here," Vaughn said.

Sateen's brows furrowed. "But why? And who takes us? Do we have families somewhere? Were we thrown away, and someone found us to bring us here? None of it makes sense."

"I want answers, same as you," Jeyra said. "And I intend to find them."

Varek covered her hand with his. "Aye, we will."

Sateen smiled at them before she looked to Vaughn. "What now?"

"Keep an eye and ear out for anything unusual. If you discover someone with magic, see if you can find out where they live. We'll be here until all of this is sorted."

"How do I contact you?" Sateen asked.

Varek said, "Send Ugar with a message to the border."

Instead of walking back through the city, they opted to leave via Sateen's back gate.

"Returning to Orgate was tougher than I thought," Jeyra said when they were out of the city.

Vaughn didn't hear Varek's response since he was deep in thought. He kept going back to those born with magic on Zora. People shunned them because they feared the unknown, but those who hid usually did it together. It was easier that way since everyone watched everyone else's back.

On the flight back to Cairnkeep, Vaughn flew faster, eager to return to Eurwen and see if she had woken. He didn't wait for Varek or Jeyra as he landed before shifting and running to the cottage. When he opened the door, his gaze moved to the bed where Eurwen still lay unmoving.

He walked inside, his eyes sliding to Rhi, who sat on the edge of the bed. "Any change?"

Rhi shook her head. "Did you find out anything?"

"No' as much as we would've liked. None of the mortals at Orgate have been hurt like Nundro or Eurwen. And given it was magic, it isna likely it was a mortal, since those who have the ability are no' welcome within the city. But it could still be a human with magic."

Rhi rolled her eyes. "You and I both know they could be hiding in plain sight."

"Much like we do on our world."

"Precisely."

"Sateen will send word if she hears anything."

Rhi moved so Vaughn could resume his seat. "That's the councilwoman Varek and Jeyra talked about. What did you think of her?"

"I like her. She's shrewd and straightforward. I understand how she got her position. I also believe we can trust her. She understands what's at stake. After what I heard she did for Varek, Jeyra, and the dragons, and then speaking with her myself, I realize she's trying to find a way that everyone can live in peace."

Rhi sat in a chair, tucking her feet to the side of her on the cushion. "I don't think that can happen. Everyone talks about it. It doesn't matter what species you are. Everyone tells everyone else to just get along. Did no one stop and think that sometimes two different species and cultures aren't meant to coexist? That the very thing that distinguishes them might be the very thing that's harmful to someone else?"

"I doona know anymore. It used to be so clear. Zora wasna perfect. Eurwen and Brandr had issues to handle, things with the humans and the dragons, but it was damn near perfect in my eyes. Especially after everything we've been through."

Rhi's lips twisted ruefully. "I'd have to agree with you there."

"*NOOOOOOOOOOOOOO!*" Con's voice suddenly roared in Vaughn's head.

He grabbed his head until the sound vanished. "*Con? Where are you?*"

"What is it?" Rhi demanded.

Vaughn shook his head as he jumped to his feet and headed outside. "I doona know. Con yelled. It was—"

"Anguished," V said as he and Varek strode up, their expressions as worried as Vaughn felt.

Rhi lifted her chin. "Go to your King. Jeyra and I will remain and watch Claire, the bairn, and Eurwen."

The last thing Vaughn wanted was to leave again, but something was seriously wrong. He nodded to Rhi and took off running, following his brethren to Con. In seconds, they were in the sky.

CHAPTER THIRTY-TWO

The longer Eurwen went without being able to control her limbs, the more concerned she became.

And the more certain she was that someone was with her.

She called to her Fae magic without success. She called to her dragon magic and felt a small stirring, but not enough to do anything. But she wouldn't give up. People were out there, searching for her.

Her mind went to Vaughn. She thought of how easy it was to be with him. She'd never get tired of staring into his eyes, the color so unusual and stunning. And his laugh. He had the best laugh. Then there was the way desire took them. There was no ignoring it, no denying it. Even that first night so long ago with the Celts, she had known that what they'd experienced was special.

But she hadn't gone to him. Hadn't allowed herself to even contemplate what *could be*.

Still, Vaughn hadn't given up on her. No doubt he was hurt

that she had let untold lifetimes pass without contacting him. It wasn't as easy as he believed. She'd thought of him every day. In order to not give in to her body—or heart—she didn't go to Earth.

The times she did, she found herself near Dreagan in hopes of seeing him. When she didn't, she was relieved. Because she had known even then that she wouldn't have been able to stay away. With every trip where she didn't see him, she was able to keep her secret from Brandr—and keep lying to herself.

Emotion choked Eurwen. She had been lying. She knew that she wanted to be with Vaughn. Knew she wanted that connection between mates. Not following her heart had led her to centuries of melancholy and unrest, all because she realized that Brandr would fight her about a Dragon King on Zora. And she couldn't live on Earth.

Admitting the truth to herself still didn't work out the problems. Even if she got away from the entity holding her, she didn't want to ask Vaughn to give up his realm. And she didn't want to give up hers. How could they have a relationship if they couldn't even work out where to live?

Then there was Brandr. He might have relented and allowed Con and the others to aid in the hunt for who'd attacked Nundro, but that didn't mean her brother's will had softened when it came to the Kings. Her lying about Vaughn, creating the doorway so their parents could come through, and then going to Dreagan without telling him had created a wedge between them. One she wasn't sure could be mended.

Brandr had never been so cold to her before. For the majority of their lives, they'd only had each other. They were each other's family. It didn't matter that they had parents, because Rhi and Con hadn't been there when they were growing up or when they found Zora. There was even a point where they hadn't wanted anything from Erith. The goddess hadn't pushed them, even though she could have.

Now, Eurwen wondered if Erith *should* have pushed them. But that would be blaming someone else. She and Brandr had made the decisions and taken action. They were the ones to blame for not knowing their parents or the Dragon Kings. At one time, the anger she and Brandr had felt had driven all of their decisions. Now, looking back, Eurwen saw how petty and childish it all was.

Fear clawed at her because she wasn't sure she would get a chance to tell Vaughn or her parents how she really felt, regardless of what her brother thought. She shouldn't worry about admitting what was in her heart just because it might upset Brandr. And he should do the same.

When had everything become so confusing? Eurwen screamed Vaughn's name in her head, anxious to get to him.

That's when she heard the laughter.

The sight of multiple dragons lying dead was all too familiar to Vaughn. There was scorched earth everywhere, the product of dragon fire. Constantine was on the ground in human form, leaning over someone. Varek went one way, and V the other, searching for the culprits.

Vaughn saw a Red struggling to get to its feet. He landed beside it. "*Wait. Con can heal you.*"

The Red turned its white eyes to him and slowly lay on the ground, its breath laborious. *"So much pain,"* said the male.

"Be easy. It willna be long," Vaughn said. Then he shouted, *"Con!"*

When Con didn't reply, Vaughn looked at him to find the King of Kings leaning over Brandr.

No, Vaughn thought. Eurwen and Brandr couldn't both be hurt. He watched Brandr, silently willing him to move. Then Brandr's arm lifted to rub at his brow. Relief surged through Vaughn. Con then rose and hurried to him and the Red.

"Just relax," Con told the Red as he approached and put his hand over one of the many wounds.

Vaughn backed away and shifted to human form while looking for other survivors. Unfortunately, the rest of the dragons were dead. Including all four generals. Vaughn turned his head to Brandr, who sat with his legs bent and his elbows resting on his knees as his hands held his head.

"Shite," V said in Vaughn's head. *"Something terrible happened here."*

Varek circled above Vaughn. *"It's a good thing Con was here."*

"Do either of you see anything?" Vaughn asked.

"No' a bloody thing," V replied.

Con finished with the Red. The dragon got to his feet and bowed his head to Con and then Vaughn before flying away. Con turned to Vaughn as V and Varek landed behind him and shifted.

"What happened?" Vaughn asked.

Con ran a hand down his face, showing his weariness. "I had a difficult time tracking Brandr because he didna want to be found. I heard the dragons' screams of pain. That's what led me here. I saw Brandr and his generals breathing fire in all directions while hovering over these fallen dragons.

"Did you see anyone?" Varek asked Brandr.

Brandr got to his feet and walked to them. "There wasna anyone *to* see. But we were attacked. One by one, my generals fell. I watched them plummet from the sky as I continued looking for the enemy."

The anger and remorse in Brandr's words and on his face was something every King had experienced.

"Many of the dragons were already dead when we arrived," Brandr continued as he ran a hand down his face dejectedly. "A few were still alive, but the instant they moved, another round of magic came at them."

Vaughn caught his gaze. "From which direction?"

"Everywhere," Con answered.

V blinked in surprise. "Everywhere? Like you were surrounded?"

"That's what it seemed like," Brandr said. "I kept telling my generals to move around more. When they started getting hit, I knew I had to find whoever was doing this and stop them before they killed more."

Con briefly closed his eyes. "That's when I saw Brandr get struck."

Now Vaughn understood the bellow Con had let out. "Did you see your attacker?"

"I wish," Brandr said with a snort.

Con raked a hand through his blond hair. "I got to Brandr before he fell unconscious. That might be the difference between him and Eurwen."

"She still isna awake?" Brandr asked, concern clouding his eyes.

Vaughn shook his head. "No' yet. There's a lot we all need to catch up on."

"First, we need to take care of these dragons," V said.

For the next hour, the five of them returned the dragons to their families. It was a somber affair that left all of them drained as the worry of another attack festered. Brandr sent out a message to all dragons to be on the lookout for attacks and to remain in the heart of their territory until the assailants could be found and stopped.

With that finished, they returned to Cairnkeep and gathered together in Brandr's cottage. They spent the evening meal catching everyone up on everything that had occurred.

"Do you think Sateen will come through for us?" Con asked.

Varek shrugged. "I trust her."

"I do, as well," Vaughn added.

Brandr glanced at the bed. "I'm a little more worried about Eurwen."

Vaughn got up from the table and walked to the bed. "I've got an idea. I doona know if it'll work, but it's worth a try."

"Do it," Rhi said.

Brandr jumped to his feet. "Hold on. What are you talking about?"

"My power is dream manipulation. Ever since Eurwen and I first met, I searched for her everywhere. I never found her, but each night during sleep, we were together. I thought they were only dreams until I spoke with her after coming here. It was real. Somehow, the connection we forged so long ago allowed us to find each other in a different way."

Brandr was silent for a moment. "You believe she's your mate."

"I know she is," Vaughn replied.

Brandr looked at his sister and nodded. "Do it."

"Let's leave them to it," Con said.

Everyone filed out of the cottage except for Brandr. Vaughn studied Eurwen's brother. There had been a lot of changes for the twins. Most Eurwen had sought herself. Brandr was trying to keep things the way they were, but unfortunately, that couldn't happen. You couldn't stop change.

"I doona like you," Brandr said.

Vaughn bowed his head. "I know."

"It isna personal. I doona like any Kings."

"You doona know us."

Brandr drew in a breath, his nostrils flaring. "My sister saw something in you. I trust her with my life. She chose you, and while I may no' like it, I'll no' stand in your way. I'm trusting *you* now."

"I would die for her. I'll no' let anything happen to her."

"I'll hold you to that."

"I would expect nothing less."

Brandr's shoulders dropped slightly. He bowed his head to Vaughn before leaving the cottage. Vaughn turned to the bed and looked at Eurwen. He could almost believe that she was sleeping. That all he needed to do was touch her, and she would wake, looking up at him with her beautiful silver eyes.

He walked to the bed and sat before stretching out beside her. Vaughn took her hand in his and turned his head toward her. "We've always found each other in dreams. Find me now."

Vaughn closed his eyes. He didn't wait for sleep. Instead, he released his power and searched for Eurwen's dreams. He was shocked to discover that something was already there. He couldn't tell if it was distorting Eurwen's thoughts or if it was only watching. Regardless, the being was there.

Vaughn moved cautiously. He could manipulate dreams, not search someone's mind. That was Tristan's power, and it was too bad that he wasn't here to help. All Vaughn could do was seek Eurwen's dreams and attempt to talk to her. He wasn't sure how successful he'd be since something had taken up residence in her mind. How, Vaughn didn't know.

Before he went deeper, he wanted to let the others know what he'd found. He connected to Con, Brandr, V, and Varek. *"Something is in Eurwen's mind. I can no' see if it has done anything. I doona know how long it'll be before it notices me."*

"Doona test it, then," V said. *"End this now. We'll wake Eurwen another way."*

Varek made a sound in the back of his throat. *"How? Vaughn may be the only one who can reach her."*

"None of us can tell you what to do," Con told him. *"The decision is ultimately up to you. I doona want to lose my daughter or you."*

Brandr said, *"Perhaps you shouldna be there alone."*

"Even if all of you were here, none of you would be able to do anything to help should something happen," Vaughn told them.

Con sighed. *"You're going ahead with this. It's what I'd do. It's what any of us would do for our mates. Can you give us anything on what you sense is there? Is it a particular kind of magic?"*

Vaughn reached out with his magic, trying to discern anything, only to come up empty. He was frustrated, but he tried not to let the emotion grow because it would only make things more difficult. *"I can only tell that something is there. I can no' perceive if it's a person or magic. Whatever it is could verra well be keeping her unconscious, which would mean only one thing."*

"It wants whatever is in her mind," Brandr said.

V murmured, *"Bloody hell."*

"But Brandr is here," Varek pointed out. *"Whatever Eurwen knows, he does, as well."*

Con blew out a breath. *"We doona know what this being is. We doona know what magic was used. We doona know why it's targeting dragons. How can we begin to determine what it wants from anyone, much less Eurwen?"*

"It's why I have to go in," Vaughn said.

CHAPTER THIRTY-THREE

The fear that rolled through Eurwen was cloying, like tar. The more she felt it, the more it clung to her. She'd known she wasn't alone but hearing the laughter without seeing anything was…terrifying.

It wasn't a reaction she was familiar with. The only thing that had come close was when she and Brandr had first come to Zora and had seen the dragons in such disarray. But this was different. Very different. She feared for her life now.

Being half-Fae and half-dragon meant there was much she didn't know about herself. Dragons and Fae both lived extremely long lives. Dragon Kings were immortal until the magic found someone else to take their position. She didn't consider herself a Dragon Queen, not like Melisse. But… maybe she was.

Eurwen frowned as something dark and malevolent went through her. It was the same sensation she'd had after hearing the laughter and the voice after she'd been struck. She wasn't sure why her thoughts had gone to Melisse, but she didn't like it. She turned her thoughts away, thinking of the feel of the sun on her scales.

That's when she sensed a light near her. She wasn't sure how she knew it was Vaughn, but she did. Excitement rose, choking her as tears stung her eyes. She'd known he would come.

She waited to hear him, feel him, and as each heartbeat passed, she grew concerned. Something was very, very wrong. How had she missed it? She had gotten a touch of it a few times, but now that she took stock of her body, she was able to recognize what she'd missed. Why hadn't she fought to move her limbs more? Why had she accepted that her eyes wouldn't open? Why had she allowed herself to delve deep into her thoughts when she should've been guarding herself?

A tear slipped out of her eye and fell onto her cheek to roll to her temple and then into her hair. She and Brandr had ruled Zora for eons without many hiccups. No other beings had attacked, and they had kept the mortals contained. That had led her—and no doubt, Brandr—to believe that they were powerful beings.

They were getting a taste of what it meant to be attacked now—truly attacked.

And she was failing miserably.

She turned toward the light, instinctively reaching for Vaughn. He had always been there. Even when she hadn't realized it. She had pushed him away, ignoring what her heart told her. How could she have been so stupid? If only she could go back and change things. All those centuries without him.

Without hearing his voice, seeing his smile, feeling his arms around her.

Eurwen released a breath and felt another tear come. She didn't deserve Vaughn. He should be with a woman who recognized his big heart, his gentleness, and his strength. He wasn't showy. His vigor was subtle, and in many ways, more potent because of it.

He used his intelligence and ability to listen to do great things for Dreagan. It was why Con always sent Vaughn to negotiate. Anyone who believed they could take advantage of Vaughn was soon put in their place. He was the type of man who would support her instead of controlling her. He would have her back in all things because he knew that she would have his.

"Vaughn."

As if her thoughts had conjured him, he stepped out of the darkness. "I'm here, lass."

Her shoulders shook as more tears came. "I've been waiting for you."

"You doona have to wait any longer."

Eurwen was surprised to discover that she could move her arm. She reached out to Vaughn, needing his touch.

"Eurwen, no."

She frowned as she saw a second Vaughn. She looked between the two. "What is going on?"

The first Vaughn caught her eyes. "You *know* me, Eurwen."

"Lass," the second Vaughn said. "Look at me. *See* me."

As she looked between them, she realized that she wasn't seeing them with her eyes. They were in her mind. It caught her so off guard that she didn't know what to think. She had felt trapped, so she believed she was. To the extent that she hadn't thought to use her magic. Worse, she was afraid to try now.

Her gaze moved between the two Vaughns. She shook her head, unable to tell one from the other. Then a third appeared. And a fourth. More and more emerged as if from thin air. All identical to the first in every way. She lost count of how many Vaughns there were. Each of them asking her to choose him.

Eurwen subtly called to her magic. It moved through her, answering her immediately. Nothing felt amiss, but at the moment, she didn't trust anything. Eurwen surrounded herself with a shield of magic to protect herself from attacks. Or, she should have. She still didn't understand how she had been wounded. Nothing should've gotten through her armor. Regardless, she was going to use magic now. She had no other choice.

She tuned the numerous Vaughns out. It was obvious that whatever was with her used her thoughts against her. Well, she wouldn't let it happen anymore. Whatever this was might hinder her movements, but she didn't need her body or her voice to command her magic. She just needed her mind.

The Vaughns were incessant. She wanted to scream at them to shut up, but she knew it wouldn't do any good. They kept talking while trying to get her attention. It was maddening and frustrating. As she turned away, she saw something. She moved back a step and caught the sight of him through the others.

Their gazes locked. He was dressed differently, and he wasn't talking. This Vaughn winked at her. That's when she knew it was the real Vaughn. He stayed back, letting her find him on her own. It was exactly something he would do. She wondered why he hadn't tried to come to her. So far, the Vaughns didn't seem to notice him. She debated going to him but ultimately decided against it. It was possible the Vaughns might attack.

Eurwen had thought she was in her head, but if Vaughn were here, that meant this was a dream. Erith had told her how Usaeil had trapped her nephew, Xaneth, in his mind. Was that what had happened here? More troubling was that she didn't know if her magic actually worked since this was a dream. Or where her body was in reality.

Her stomach tightened. Vaughn could manipulate dreams. Was he responsible for this? Surely, not. He cared for her. He would never hurt her. Would he?

Strong arms came around her from behind. Warm breath fanned her neck as his lips pressed against her skin. "You'll never be lost to me if I can find you here."

She looked to the Vaughn behind the others. He was gone. Was this him now? Eurwen turned in his arms and searched his face.

"It's me," he said as he held her gaze.

She wanted to believe him, but she had been wrong before. What if she was wrong again? It was as if she were in a maze that she couldn't get out of.

"I spent lifetimes scouring my world for you," he said.

"Anyone in my mind would know that."

A small frown formed, but he hastily smoothed it away. "You doubt it's me?"

"Look around," she retorted.

His lips curved in a smile. "They're gone, lass."

A quick look confirmed that he was right, but she still didn't trust him. "This could be a ruse like the others."

"Nothing's holding you here. You can wake up. Con healed you."

She shook her head and stepped out of his arms. "I've tried. I've tried to move. I've tried to call out to you."

"I've been by your side the entire time," he said solemnly. "I came here, hoping to find you. The only place I've held you until recently was in my dreams."

Eurwen shook her head. "Stop."

"You're going to have to trust someone if you're going to get free."

She hated that he was right. So much of her yearned for this to be the real Vaughn, but she couldn't take that chance. If she were wrong, she didn't want to think about what could happen. She didn't even know all that had transpired since being attacked. All she knew was that something held her, and she wanted free.

Eurwen squared her shoulders and lifted her chin. "You're right. I do have to trust someone. And that someone is me."

Vaughn grinned and nodded. "Exactly. What are you waiting for then?"

She couldn't stop the smile his words brought.

"You're a product of one of the most powerful Dragon Kings to ever be born, as well as a formidable Light Fae who never lets anything stand in her way. With the blood of those two flowing through your veins, nothing should hold you. No' now. No' ever," he said, his words and gaze intense.

Eurwen realized the truth of what he said. She hadn't used

her magic because something had told her she couldn't. She hadn't been able to move because someone had put something in her mind that convinced her of that. She hadn't been able to open her eyes or call out for help because the entity had made her believe that it was impossible.

The more those thoughts occurred, the stronger her magic coursed through her veins. She drew in a breath, feeling her magic take over every inch of her body. Her eyes closed as she thought about breaking free, of eradicating whatever had trapped her. She saw a bright light through her eyelids. When she opened her eyes again, she realized that the light was her. She was glowing.

And it felt amazing.

With a shout, she shattered the bonds holding her.

Eurwen came awake, gasping for air as she sat up, ready to fight. There was movement beside her. She turned, trying to see through the glow of her body. Through the bright light, she saw Persian blue eyes filled with pride and love staring back at her.

"You did it," Vaughn said with a smile.

She swallowed as the light dimmed and then faded completely. "Am I really free?"

"Oh, aye," he said.

She threw her arms around him and held on tight. Everything felt real. She sank her hands into his hair, feeling the cool strands sliding through her fingers. She breathed in the scent of sunlight and pine from his skin and clothes. His arms held her firmly against him.

The door of the cottage flew open, and people spilled into

the house. Eurwen and Vaughn released each other as
surprised smiles greeted her.

"You did it," Brandr told Vaughn.

Vaughn looked at her and shook his head. "Your sister did
it herself. I simply reminded her who she was."

Eurwen reached for his hand, needing to feel him.

"What happened?" Rhi asked.

Con added, "We saw glowing."

"That was Eurwen," Vaughn told them.

Eurwen knew that everyone wanted details. They needed
it. But right now, she just wanted some time with her thoughts.
"I'll tell all of you everything, but I need a wee bit."

"Of course," Rhi said as they began walking out.

Vaughn rose to his feet, but she stopped him with her hand.
"Not you."

Surprise flashed in his eyes. "Oh?"

"We need to talk. There are some things I've not told you.
It's time you know everything."

CHAPTER THIRTY-FOUR

Vaughn's heart pounded rapidly. He tried not to read anything into Eurwen wanting him to stay behind, but it was impossible not to. Her face and voice gave nothing away—nothing that would allow his poor heart to stop worrying.

Vaughn glanced at the door to see Brandr bow his head to him slightly before closing it behind him. In all his years, Vaughn had never been so nervous. Had never been so anxious to hear news. He remained standing. Eurwen gracefully rose from the bed and moved around the cottage.

He didn't take his eyes off her. She moved fluidly as if she contained all the elements—embodied them. Despite her ordeal—or perhaps because of it—she seemed to have a radiance from within. Vaughn still couldn't believe that she had glowed as much as her mother did when Rhi became angry.

It also brought to mind seeing multiple versions of himself in her dream. They had looked just like him. Sounded like him, too. It had been disconcerting and unnerving to see so many copies of himself. It was no wonder Eurwen hadn't believed that it was him when he arrived. He had no idea how long she had been tormented so, but it was a testament to her strength of mind and will that she was able to find a way out of such deception.

For the first time, Vaughn noticed the two halves that Eurwen embodied. For her dragon side, she had the patience and discipline that dragons were known for. Now, however, she also had the same light within her that Rhi had. It had always been there, but now, it was brighter, stronger. Her battle had given her that. To Vaughn, it looked as if the two halves within her had finally come together, uniting into one powerful being.

Eurwen turned to him. As she did, her black battle attire faded away. A flowing silk dress of deep mauve that cascaded elegantly to the floor at the sides and to mid-calf at the front and back replaced it. Spaghetti straps connected a bodice with a scoop neck at the front. She turned slightly, and he saw the sexy racerback of the gown. Her golden hair was free and hung to her waist in soft waves. She was barefoot with only a slim, gold ankle bracelet around her left ankle. Her silver eyes were steady as she gazed at him.

"Thank you," she said.

He shook his head. "For what?"

"You helped me break free."

"You did that all on your own."

Her lips softened. "It was you who urged me to see what was within. I was too trapped to know what to do."

"You would've figured it out on your own eventually."

"Maybe," she said with a shrug of one shoulder. "Or maybe we work well as a team."

Hope leapt in his heart. "I agree with that."

"Was I here the entire time?"

Vaughn nodded once. "After you fell and Con healed you, I brought you here. Nothing we did revived you. You were unconscious for a full day."

"I thought I was being held somewhere else. I couldn't move, couldn't open my eyes or talk."

"Whatever it was, it was in your mind."

Her head turned slightly as she looked out a window. "Did you find who attacked me?"

"We searched. There was nothing."

Her eyes snapped back to him. "Did you not get my warning?"

He frowned as he shook his head. "What warning?"

"Before it struck me, I said that it was invisible. I only saw a shimmer out of the corner of my eye."

"We never heard that. Whatever you said before it attacked was distorted. As if something intentionally prevented your words from reaching us."

Her eyebrows shot up in shock. "They were able to interfere with our telepathic conversation?"

"It appears so."

"And they're invisible." Her shoulders lifted as she drew in a deep breath. "I've never been so scared."

Vaughn took a step toward her. "None of us was going to allow anything to take you from us. I was prepared to do whatever it took."

"I knew you would find me. There was never any doubt."

"Good." He wanted her to know that he would've stopped time to free her.

She licked her lips and walked to him, closing the distance between them. "I realized a few things while being held."

"Is that so?"

Eurwen pressed her lips together, a hesitant expression crossing her face. "I've never been in such a situation before. I'm not too proud to admit that I believed myself too powerful to be put in harm's way or captured. I now know that isn't true."

"All of us have been in similar situations. When you have the power we do and the abilities we possess, we sometimes forget there are ways that others can get to us. No one is infallible. No' even a Dragon King."

A hint of a smile pulled at her lips. "Thank you for attempting to make me feel better. The thing is, I'm thankful for what happened. I was shown that I need to strengthen certain aspects of my magic. But I also learned that I'm able to access power I never knew I had. I could feel it running through me."

Vaughn nodded slowly. "I see the changes in you. It's in the way you hold yourself, how you speak. You were already powerful. Now, you are more so."

Her eyes dropped to the floor for a heartbeat. "As wonderous as all of that was, it wasn't what really changed me."

"Then what did?"

"Realizing that I might never see you again."

Vaughn's heart skipped a beat. He searched her face, too afraid to speak for fear she might stop talking.

"All I could think about was you," she admitted. "I realized how many centuries I lost with you. More than anything, I realized I've been a fool."

He shook his head, his lips parting to speak when she held up a hand.

"Please. Let me finish."

It was the hardest thing Vaughn had ever done, but he remained silent.

"I put this realm, my brother, and the duties I have before my heart. I stopped hearing what my soul needed. Stopped listening to what my heart cried out for. I deadened myself to all of it because I thought I had to choose between my life here and…you," she finished with a whisper.

Vaughn yearned to reach for her. The need was so great that he fisted his hands to keep them by his sides.

Tears filled her eyes as she blinked rapidly. Her body was stiff with emotion, her pulse erratic at her throat. "What I'm trying to say—badly—is that I love you."

"I love you," he whispered as he gently cupped her face and pressed his lips to hers. "I love you. I've always loved you."

Her arms came around his neck as she returned his kiss. He lowered his arms and snaked them around her, tightening his hold as the kiss deepened. As much as he wanted to finish what he had begun, now wasn't the time. Vaughn slowly ended the kiss and lifted his head.

"Forgive me," she said.

He frowned as he shook his head. "For what?"

"For not returning to you all these years. For putting you off once you found me again. For causing us to miss so many lifetimes together."

Vaughn gazed down at her, wondering how he'd ended up with someone as beautiful and special as Eurwen. "There's nothing to forgive."

"I disagree."

He smiled and tucked her hair behind her ear. "If you need an example that the universe brings people together when it's time, look at your parents. Same goes for us. We may never know why we spent so many centuries apart, and I doona care. What matters now is that you're in my arms."

"I never want to leave them," she said with a smile.

"Just what I wanted to hear."

Eurwen's smile dropped. "We're going to have to work out something regarding our living arrangements."

"Whatever you want. I doona care."

"Of course, you do."

"I doona," he insisted.

She gave him a flat look. "Vaughn, Dreagan is your home. Your family is there."

"They are. But the one who holds my heart is here."

Her smile was radiant as it spread across her face. "Please don't ever stop talking about me like that."

"It willna happen," he promised.

"As much as I want to celebrate this, we still have business to take care of."

"Trust me. I'm aware. So is everyone outside."

"How do we fight something we can't see?" she asked.

Vaughn gave her a quick kiss. "With an army."

"Brandr will balk."

"He was struck, same as you. Con got to him before he fell unconscious. That may be the only reason he wasna affected as you were. But the generals are dead. As well as about fifty dragons."

Shock made her face pale as her lips went slack. "No."

"I'm sorry."

Eurwen swallowed and lifted her chin. "You're right. We need an army. An army of Dragon Kings."

"We'll be a united family. It might no' hurt to consider using some of the mates, as well."

She nodded excitedly. "I hadn't thought about the Druids and the Fae, but you're right. We can't allow whatever is here to stay. Let's go tell the others."

As she turned to walk to the door, Vaughn held her hand and pulled her back to him. He smiled as their gazes held.

"What?" she asked softly.

He shook his head. "Nothing. I just wanted to tell you again that I love you."

"And I love you."

After another lingering kiss, they walked from the cottage together.

The group was upon them the minute they emerged. As Eurwen fielded questions from others about her experience, Vaughn listened with half an ear since she had already told him everything. He noted Brandr watching him. Vaughn wanted to talk to him. Brandr might have been civil when it came to helping his sister, but Vaughn wasn't sure how far that would extend. Especially once Brandr discovered that they were to be mated.

"Invisible?" Varek asked.

V crossed his arms over his chest. "Shite."

Vaughn looked at the other Kings, each of them likely thinking the same thing—it would take the Dragon Kings.

"And nothing like this has ever happened on Zora before?" Rhi asked.

Brandr shook his head. "No' since Eurwen and I have been here anyway."

"I've never heard of it either," Jeyra added.

Rhi turned her head to Con. "We might need to speak with Erith. If she created this realm, she might have an idea what this is."

"Good idea," Con replied.

Eurwen got Vaughn's attention before she looked at her brother. He nodded to her. She took Brandr's hand and moved away.

Once they were out of earshot, Claire asked, "What is that about?"

With all eyes on him, Vaughn looked at Con and Rhi. "She's talking to her brother about her and I being mates."

"She finally admitted it?" Rhi asked with a brilliant smile.

Con's lips turned up in a grin as he and Vaughn clasped forearms and slapped each other on the back with their free hands. "I never had any doubt."

"Congratulations," Varek said.

V chuckled. "How long before Con warns you no' to hurt his daughter?"

"No' long at all," Con replied.

The group erupted in laughter.

Vaughn took a deep breath. Despite the threat that still hung in the air, he felt lighter than he had in a long time. He had his mate. At one time, he'd feared never finding her. Now, she was his. No dragon or man in the entire universe could be as happy as he was.

CHAPTER THIRTY-FIVE

"I know what you're going to say," Brandr said before she could speak.

Eurwen faced him and looked into his black eyes. "Do you now?"

"You're Vaughn's mate."

"Or you could've said, he's *my* mate. I am half-dragon."

"I'm happy for you."

Brandr said the right words, but Eurwen wasn't sure he meant them. "Are you?"

"I am," he said with a nod. "You deserve to be happy."

"So do you."

He glanced away. "One day, perhaps. Are you living on Earth?"

"I don't know what we're going to do. My home is here. Vaughn's is there. But there has to be a way to work it out. That is if you aren't going to banish me."

Her brother smiled at her. "I was never going to banish you. I was angry when I said that. As for where to live, split time between the realms. I can cover things here while you're gone."

Eurwen was so surprised that she couldn't speak for a moment. "You're all right with a Dragon King living here?"

"He's your mate, Eurwen. If I refuse him, I refuse you. Mates are as one. And you're my sister. I willna sever that bond."

Emotion choked her. She quickly blinked back tears. "Thank you."

"I'm the one who should be apologizing for putting you in a position where you thought you had to choose. This is your home. You have as much right to make decisions as I do."

She swallowed past the lump in her throat and quickly wiped away the few tears that had escaped. "I'm glad you see that."

"Sadly, I didna until you were injured. It all quickly came into perspective. I didna realize how I had been acting, but the real factor was Vaughn. He was willing to die for you, and I know he would've. There isna a doubt in my heart that he doesna truly love you."

"And I love him."

"I have one request," Brandr said.

Eurwen shrugged. "Anything."

"Have the mating ceremony here."

She hadn't even thought that far ahead. "Here? You know that means the Kings will come to Zora."

"As they should. We have no right to keep them away from the dragons. They should witness their brethren's mating. As the dragons here should bear witness for one of theirs."

Eurwen threw her arms around him and held him tightly. "You're the best brother."

"I'm your only brother," he said as he returned her embrace.

"Which makes you special." She leaned back and gave him a kiss on the cheek. "You will be at the ceremony, right?"

"I wouldna miss it."

Eurwen gave him one last hug before she stepped back. "As far as this new threat—"

"I agree," he said over her.

She blinked. "What?"

"We're going to need help. You and I have done well on our own all these years, but we've no' dealt with a threat like this before. I'm no' going to allow my pride to stand in the way as more dragons are slaughtered. Or worse, you get killed."

"Or you," she interjected.

"We need help. Be that from Erith and the Reapers, the Dragon Kings and their mates, or whoever else, I'm no' going to deny anyone who wants to aid us."

Eurwen flashed him a smile. "We'll find whatever this is and eradicate it from Zora forever." She frowned then. "Vaughn told me about the generals and the other dragons."

Brandr's grim expression returned. "We need to attend the funeral."

"All of us should," she said.

He nodded in agreement. The two of them returned to the group and readied for the funeral, explaining how they worked

here. Rhi would teleport Claire and the bairn to their
destination while Jeyra rode atop Varek as the rest of them
flew. There had never been anything like this on Zora. Even
when Eurwen and Brandr had first come, the dragons who had
died hadn't been killed as these had. It was like a dagger to her
heart.

She wasn't surprised to see the families bringing the
deceased to what had long been called Dragon Valley. The
mystical place was extraordinary. Steep, flower-covered
mountains ridged like draped cloth made a near-perfect
circle full of lime green moss, forests of rhododendron,
majestic flowers of all colors and sizes, and stunning
waterfalls.

Soulful mourning roars filled the air as the families laid
out their dead on the valley's floor. Eurwen was the first to
land atop the mountain and shift. Vaughn alit on her right,
while Brandr took her left. Rhi arrived with Claire and the
baby. Varek, with Jeyra on his back, Con, and V each set
down.

They stood silently, solemnly as their group watched the
families say their final farewells. The chorus of roars was
deafening, anger in every syllable. Eurwen glanced at Vaughn.

"You and Brandr should go," he said. "We'll follow
behind."

Eurwen looked to her brother. He nodded. Together, they
stepped off the cliff and shifted, their wings catching the
current. They soared over the dead dragons and joined the
roars of anguish.

As they turned to fly back, Eurwen saw Vaughn and then V
with Claire and the bairn on his back, Varek with Jeyra on his,

and Con with Rhi atop him. At the sight of the Kings, the dragons halted their roars.

Con met Brandr's gaze and then hers before letting out a thunderous roar. Vaughn, Varek, and V joined him. She and Brandr let out roars of their own. Soon, the other dragons echoed. The six of them flew back and forth over the valley, waiting for the families to alert them that it was time. When the first family did, Brandr and Eurwen released dragon fire on the body, incinerating it.

One by one, they burned the dead dragons, leaving behind charred earth.

Once the funeral was finished, they all returned to Cairnkeep. Everyone went their separate ways. Eurwen and Vaughn once more found themselves without a place to go. No words were needed as they flew to the loch, their favorite place.

They lay beneath the sky as she leaned against his chest, his arms holding her as he rested against a tree. She told him about her conversation with Brandr. They spoke about the funeral and the future between long stretches of silence as they enjoyed just being together.

When the moon hung in the sky, she said, "I'd like to have the mating ceremony soon."

"I think that would be a good idea," Vaughn said.

She turned her head to meet his lips. Eurwen looked deep into his Persian blue eyes. She knew their life wouldn't be perfect. There would be difficult times, but she also knew that he would be there for her as she would be for him. Knowing that no matter what came, they had each other. It was a wonderous, remarkable feeling.

They shared a smile before looking back at the silvery moon reflecting on the loch. She had believed that she would have a lonely life. How wrong she had been. Not only did she have the love she'd never thought would be hers, but she had it with one of the most incredible Dragon Kings.

EPILOGUE

Two days later…

It was happening. Vaughn couldn't stop smiling. Even with the threat hanging over Zora, and the dragons' deaths, he was too happy for Eurwen to become his mate to let any of that dampen his spirits.

Rhi created another doorway to Earth so those at Dreagan could come for the mating ceremony. But before that, the Silvers were to be moved to Zora and woken so they could live out their lives as they should. It was the right decision, but everyone at Dreagan would miss the Silvers. Fortunately, it looked as if Brandr had come around somewhat since he had not only agreed that they needed the Kings to fight this new foe but also that the Kings needed to see the dragons.

Vaughn had opted not to be at Dreagan when they removed the bars from around the Silvers. None of them had

liked the idea of imprisoning them, but it had been necessary
in case they somehow managed to wake from the magic.

Now, he stood with Brandr, Con, and the other Kings as
Ulrik carried the Silvers one by one from Earth to Zora. When
all four were on their new world, the Kings used their
combined magic to wake them. As the dragons woke, Ulrik
was there before them. Then, he shifted to his human form.

"A verra long time has passed since we last spoke," Ulrik
told the four Silvers. "The Kings captured you and banished
me from Dreagan. I carried hatred and anger with me for too
many lifetimes. My story is long, and if any of you wish to
hear it, I will tell it. Suffice it to say, I caused most of my
suffering before I found my way back to Dreagan and my
brethren."

The Silvers slid their gazes from Ulrik to the Kings.
Vaughn saw the confusion in their eyes, and he understood it.

Ulrik took a deep breath and released it. "I found my mate.
And the dragons were located. I've brought you to their realm,
Zora, where they live free. It's time all of you do the same.
There are humans here, but they remain on their side of the
barrier, which you willna cross. I'll return, and you will see
other Kings. However, Brandr and Eurwen, Constantine's
children, rule Zora. I wish I could say that things will be easy,
but they willna. Everyone you knew is gone. There are no
longer clans as you once knew them, but you are the best of
my Silvers. You will find your footing."

Ulrik then motioned to Eilish. The Druid walked to his
side and held his hand. She smiled up at the Silvers before
moving to each and speaking softly, continuing from one to
the next. When she finished, Ulrik nodded. The four Silvers

bowed their heads to Ulrik and Eilish and turned to look at their new home.

Vaughn wondered what was going through the Silvers' minds. A war had raged in the time they'd been contained at Dreagan. Now, eons later, they woke in another realm with everything they knew and loved gone. It would be hard for anyone to adjust to.

Minutes ticked by without the Silvers moving. They were clearly uncertain and wary. Ulrik was the first to shift and take to the sky. Then, one by one, the Kings joined him. Con was the last. They circled Cairnkeep, the mates, and the Silvers. Ulrik and Con flew side by side. Vaughn didn't know what gave the Silvers the courage to embrace their new home, but something did. It took one of them spreading its wings and taking to the skies for the others to follow.

The Kings flew with the Silvers for several minutes before leaving Ulrik with the last of his clan. The Kings watched the five of them, all wishing they had been able to have one last flight with their clan, as well. It was a heartbreaking and poignant moment. One that would be burned into their memories.

Vaughn returned to Cairnkeep as Ulrik and the Silvers disappeared into the distance. Back in human form, Vaughn looked over his shoulder for one more glimpse of the Silvers and the last connection the Kings had to their former lives. The other dragons on Zora were curious about the new arrivals. It wouldn't take long for the Silvers to find their place among the other dragons.

"It's for the best," Con said.

Vaughn nodded. "It is."

"That doesna mean we doona feel the loss."

Vaughn met Con's eyes and smiled sadly. "Dreagan will be different."

"A lot of changes are coming, but I doona think that's something we should mind."

"All the Kings have been mated at Dreagan. It's a big change."

Con made a sound as he smiled. "Scores of Kings were mated on Dreagan, aye, but no' in the cavern. Are you worried it willna mean the same if you do the ceremony here?"

Vaughn thought about that for a moment and then shook his head. "Zora was a new start for the dragons. It's different from Earth, aye, but still verra much a part of us. The two realms will forever be connected. As for the ceremony, it doesna matter where it's performed. What matters is who performs it and the mate by my side."

"I couldna agree more."

Vaughn looked toward Eurwen's cottage. It wouldn't be long before they stood together and pledged their love. He couldn't wait to see the dragon eye tat on her arm. Suddenly, he frowned. Would she have one?

"What is it?" Con asked.

Vaughn's gaze swung to him. "Is Eurwen a Dragon Queen? She has a tattoo like ours."

"I thought she was able to shift because she's half-Fae, but perhaps she *is* a Queen."

"She's no' a solid color like us or even Melisse in dragon form."

Con grinned. "There are many differences on Zora. Perhaps this is another one."

Vaughn spotted Brandr. "Your son seems fine with what's happening. At least, that's what he told Eurwen."

"My children have a bond that goes deeper than ours as Kings. I have no doubt Eurwen will make sure Brandr finds his way if he stumbles."

Vaughn nodded slowly. "The last thing I want to think about on my mating day is the battle, but Kings will be coming and going from Zora to fight this unknown foe."

"I've been thinking about that. I know you and Eurwen plan to split your time between the two realms. And Jeyra is from here, so she'll have an easier time. However, I'm reluctant to send mated Kings."

"Because their mates would travel with them, splitting their attention," Vaughn said with a nod. "I thought about that earlier."

Con's lips twisted as he glanced toward a group of Kings. "That's no' to say that a mated King willna come, but there's a lot of upheaval, and I'd like to minimize things."

Vaughn followed Con's gaze to a group of unmated Kings. He looked between Cullen, Merrill, Kendrick, Evander, Hector, Ranulf, and Shaw. "I agree."

"Enough of such talk," Con said as he slapped Vaughn on the back of the shoulder. "You need to prepare. And I have things I must take care of."

Vaughn smiled as Con walked away. However, his eyes slid back to Brandr. Vaughn made his way to his mate's twin brother, who stood off by himself, looking over the valley from the edge of the mountain.

"This must be a lot for you," Vaughn said as he walked up.

Brandr released a sigh without looking at Vaughn. "I willna lie and say it isna."

"I know how much this realm means to you and Eurwen. I vowed to her, and I'll do the same to you, that I willna allow anyone or anything to take it from either of you. That includes my brethren."

Brandr turned his head and met his gaze. "You would fight the Kings?"

"If they attempted to take over this realm solely because they wished to, aye."

"You'd go against Con?"

Vaughn nodded. "I would."

"That's...unexpected."

"It shouldna be. I love Eurwen. This realm is important to every King. None would dare take it from you or your sister. For one, Con wouldna allow it. And neither would I."

Brandr glanced at the ground. "Things were so peaceful that they became almost mundane."

"We've done nothing but battle one foe after another. We long for peace and a mundane life. Though, anything kept constant becomes constrictive at times."

"Aye," Brandr replied with a chuckle. "It can get constrictive."

"None of us expects your trust immediately. We're going to earn it."

Brandr's lips curved into a smile. "The last thing I wanted was for Eurwen's mate to be a King, but I'll admit, you're a good man."

"Thanks," Vaughn replied with a grin.

Brandr moved closer and lowered his voice. "I doona

have to tell you to treat her right. If you doona, it willna be me who kicks your arse. It'll be her. But I'll be laughing."

"I can no' promise we willna argue, but I vow I'll never do her wrong."

"That's all I can ask for."

They clasped forearms, smiling.

Eurwen looked at herself in the mirror of her vanity before her gaze lifted to meet Rhi's. Her mother's silver eyes crinkled at the corners as she stood over her.

"You are breathtaking," Rhi said.

Eurwen laughed softly. "I would've never found this gown without you."

"We have many, many more shopping trips coming. I promise."

"I'm going to hold you to it."

Rhi squeezed Eurwen's shoulders with her hands. "The few hours we had went by entirely too quickly. We've got centuries to make up for. Which means, you might need to get a bigger place with a bigger closet."

Eurwen laughed louder, nodding. "I was thinking of that yesterday while we were shopping."

"Don't rub it in," Lily replied.

Eilish rolled her eyes. "I agree. We all wanted to be there, but I think it was good that it was just the two of you. Unfortunately, Eurwen, we'll all be asking you to come shopping with us."

"No, a girls' weekend," Bernadette said wistfully in her Scots brogue.

Jane nodded her auburn head and replied, "Absolutely."

Rhi winked at Eurwen in the mirror. They shared a smile. Eurwen had never thought she would find a mate, much less have Rhi there to share the day with.

"Thank you," Eurwen said.

Rhi shot her a watery smile. "Thank you for allowing us to be here."

A knock sounded on the door, silencing everyone instantly. Eurwen watched in amazement as the mates rose from their places and filed out of the cottage. When they were gone, Con entered. Eurwen turned on the stool and looked her father over from head to toe. He wore a tux jacket and a formal shirt along with a kilt in a tartan she had never seen before.

"You look dashing," she said as she got to her feet.

Her father stood staring at her for a long moment.

"I know," Rhi said as she walked to her mate and kissed his cheek. She turned her head to Eurwen. "We have a gorgeous daughter."

"Aye," Con said as a slow smile pulled at his lips.

Eurwen got to her feet and fidgeted with her gown. "Is the gown too much?"

Rhi made a sound in the back of her throat. "Not even close. Wait until you see Vaughn's face."

Eurwen moved her gaze to Con and raised her brows in silent question.

"It's perfection," her father said.

Con then looked at Rhi, who nodded and patted his arm. "Right. Well, then, I'll see you both outside."

"Wait," Eurwen said as she took a step forward. "Don't forget."

"Heading there now," Rhi said before teleporting out.

Con quirked a brow. "Everything all right?"

"Perfect. I just have a wee surprise," Eurwen said with a smile.

Con cleared his throat. "We have a couple of traditions. I always gift my King's mate with a piece of jewelry."

Eurwen had learned of this tradition from Rhi when they had gone shopping the day before, but she was still excited to see what her father presented her with. When he held out a small gold velvet box, she eagerly took it.

Anticipation fluttered in her stomach as she slowly opened the lid. The instant she saw the Montana sapphire with its teal color that perfectly matched Vaughn, her mouth fell open. The stones themselves were stunning, but it was the ring that took her breath away.

"If you doona like it—"

"It's perfect," Eurwen interrupted him before he could finish.

She drew out the full finger ring and slipped it onto her right index finger. The teal stones wound in a delicate, beautiful pattern from the base of her finger to her nail. She held out her hand and gazed at it, struck by its simplicity and splendor.

"It's me," she said after a moment and looked up at Con.

Her father was beaming. "I've never been so worried about handing a piece of jewelry to someone as I was you."

"You did great," she said and wrapped her arms around him for a hug.

For a heartbeat, he didn't move. Then he wrapped his arms around her. "You'll never know how happy your mother and I are to be here."

"I have an idea." Eurwen leaned back and smiled at him. "Now, if we don't stop this talk, I'll start crying."

Con took her hands and stepped back as he shook his head with a proud smile. "It's a good thing you and Vaughn found each other. Otherwise, every eligible King out there would be after you."

Eurwen laughed, her heart full. She, Con, and Rhi had a long way to go, but they had already crossed the most significant hurdles.

"Shall we?" Con asked as he held out his bent arm for her to take.

She looped her hand around the crook of his arm. "Let's."

Vaughn shifted his shoulders, the jacket feeling tight. The sun was setting, the sky streaking in the most amazing colors, but he didn't see any of it. His eyes were locked on Eurwen's cottage as he waited for her to appear.

He stood at the outcropping of the mountain at Cairnkeep. Dragons had begun pouring in hours ago. The sheer number of them kept most of the Kings in awe. Vaughn popped his knuckles and adjusted the sleeves of his dress shirt beneath his tux jacket. Other Kings, also dressed in their finest, surrounded him.

Suddenly, voices quieted. Vaughn turned to find Rhi making her way toward him. Her long, black hair was pulled away from her face to cascade down her back. She wore a black sleeveless tulle gown with a plunging neckline and a fitted waist. Gold metallic leaves grouped tightly together at the top and spread apart the farther down the dress they went.

"I don't think I've ever seen you fidget so much," Rhi told him.

Vaughn swallowed hard. "I'm worried she willna come."

Rhi flashed him a wide smile. "She'll be here. Now, I wanted to do this privately, but you were already out here."

"What?" he asked worriedly.

Rhi held out her palm to reveal a black velvet box.

Vaughn blinked at the unexpected gift.

"Kings have never been gifted anything for their matings before, but that's because a King has never married a Dragon Queen before."

Vaughn reached for the box, his hand shaking. He opened the hinged lid to find a gold dragon head torc bracelet with Celtic knotwork.

"Eurwen told me how the two of you met. I felt it fitting that a nod should be given to the Celts."

Vaughn put the bracelet on and bowed his head to Rhi as he placed his right hand over his heart. "I'm honored and touched by such a gift. Thank you."

"Get ready," she said with a knowing grin. "You're about to get your socks knocked off."

No sooner were those words out of her mouth than the dragons surrounding them went silent. It was so quiet, a leaf falling could have been heard. Vaughn didn't need to ask what had caused it. He knew.

He spotted the top of Con's head. Thankfully, Vaughn

didn't have long to wait until he got to see his mate. When he did, his lungs seized at the exquisite woman making her way to him through the throng of people and flowers.

Eurwen's golden hair was pulled back in a messy style with wavy locks framing her face. The teal gown was a masterpiece of lace and tulle. The upper bodice dipped into a low V in the front and back with wide floral lace edged in beaded teal fringe four inches long that brushed against her arms. The waist was cinched tight before the polka dot tulle and floral lace fell gently to her feet. A three-foot skirt train trailed behind her. The dress was feminine and unique, just like his mate.

It wasn't until she reached him that he saw the gold multi-strand head chain that adorned her hair along her center part before draping into two separating parts across her forehead to meet at the back of her head.

Vaughn didn't wait for Con to bring Eurwen to him. He met her halfway and gazed into her silver eyes with wonder and joy. When she put her hand in his, he felt something on her finger and looked down to see the full finger ring of Montana sapphires, a gift from Con.

"Wow," she said as she looked him over. "Can you please wear that more often? I like you in kilts."

He grinned and tightened his fingers around hers. "You are exquisite. And, aye, I'll wear it anytime you want."

"Everyone is watching us."

"I only see you."

Her smile widened.

They walked to the outcropping together where Con awaited them. Vaughn glanced out over the mountains to see the dragons watching them. Before, only Kings were allowed to witness ceremonies, but it seemed fitting that the dragons were present.

Con drew in a breath. "It wasna that long ago that Rhi and I learned we had children. I'm happy to be at a binding ceremony with my daughter and Vaughn, King of Teals. I couldna imagine two people more worthy of each other than you."

Vaughn faced Eurwen and took her hands in his. They stared into each other's eyes, smiles upon their lips.

"Vaughn, do you bind yourself to the Dragon Queen, Eurwen?" Con asked. "Do you vow to love her, protect her, and cherish her above all others?"

"Absolutely," Vaughn replied in a clear voice.

Con turned his attention to his daughter. "Eurwen, do you bind yourself to the Dragon King Vaughn? Do you swear to love him, care for him, and cherish him above all others?"

"Oh, yes."

Vaughn glanced at her left arm, but no dragon eye tattoo appeared, which proved that Eurwen was, indeed, a Dragon Queen. A King and Queen mating, which was a first for all of them.

Con raised his voice for all to hear as he said, "I present our first mated Dragon King and a Dragon Queen!"

Vaughn vaguely heard the Kings' cheers and the dragons' roars as he pulled Eurwen into his arms to seal their union with a kiss. When he pulled back to gaze down at his mate, she was smiling brightly.

"You are being heralded," she said.

Vaughn frowned, then turned when she pointed over his

shoulder. All the Teals flew in a circle, their roars louder than any others.

"Go," Eurwen urged him.

Vaughn linked his hand with hers. "We go together."

Her smile proved that he had said the right thing. Together, they moved to the edge of the cliff and stepped off, shifting into dragon form and going out to meet the Teals. As they flew, the tips of their wings brushed.

Vaughn had never thought to see his Teals again, much less fly with them. The dragons welcomed him, their voices congratulating him and filling his head. He was with his dragons and his mate. Life couldn't get any better.

Thank you for reading DRAGON MINE! I hope you loved Vaughn and Eurwen's story as much as I loved writing it. Next up in the Dark World is the Reaper book, DARK ALPHA'S NEED.

Buy DARK ALPHA'S NEED now at https://dgrant.co/34Sjhv5

To find out when new books release SIGN UP FOR MY NEWSLETTER today at http://www.tinyurl.com/DonnaGrantNews.

Join my Facebook group, Donna Grant Groupies, for

exclusive giveaways and sneak peeks of future books. If you loved the Dragon King series, you'll be thrilled to know Cullen gets his HEA in the next book, DRAGON UNBOUND...

He's never been tempted.. until her.

Buy DRAGON UNBOUND now at
https://dgrant.co/3dlCkmr

Keep reading for an excerpt from DARK ALPHA'S NEED and a sneak peek at DRAGON UNBOUND...

EXCERPT OF DARK ALPHA'S NEED

REAPERS, BOOK 12

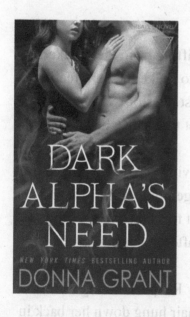

New York Times bestselling author Donna Grant returns to the Reaper world with a passionate new installment in the thrilling Reaper series.

There is no escaping a Reaper. I am an elite assassin, part of a brotherhood that only answers to Death. And when Death says your time is up, I'm coming for you…

The latest threat uncovered, it is my honor and duty to oust those responsible for the slaughter of so many and make the Fae Others pay for their crimes. However, nothing could have prepared me for the stunning and curious female that crosses my path. She's an enigma: equal parts strength and vulnerability. She quiets the rage I've carried within me for so long and makes me question Death's directives for the first time ever. Her tragic, emotional story touches something deep within me, and her bravery is awe-inspiring—which makes it doubly hard to let her return to the enemy and the dangers that await. I never expected her, but I *need* her. She is everything to me, and I will do whatever it takes to make sure she's safe and by my side. Forever.

Sly Stag Pub
Dublin

Nothing about the mellow music drifting from the speakers calmed Torin. He hadn't been able to shake the dark feeling hanging over him since Rordan's last mission. Something wicked was coming, and for the first time since becoming a Reaper, he was worried.

Torin sat at the bar, his gaze moving across every face in the tavern. The Fae Others were targeting Reapers. He and his brethren wouldn't stand by and wait for the Others to find them. No, the Reapers were going after the bastards—on Death's orders.

His gaze met those of his fellow Reaper, Aisling, across the bar. Her long, black and silver hair hung down her back in dozens of small plaits. She wrapped her fingers with their long, red nails around her glass. Her disinterest in those around her had males and females alike doing everything they could to get her attention. Aisling lifted the glass of whisky to her lips and took a long drink before winking at him, even as a female Light rubbed her breasts against Aisling's arm.

Torin hid his smile and gave a slight shake of his head. They weren't here for fun. They were at the Sly Stag to find someone. Being out among so many Fae—both Dark and Light—was dangerous for them now. Once, the Reapers had been dismissed as monsters that Fae children's parents used to keep them in line.

The Reapers had hidden in plain sight for centuries, walking among Fae and humans alike without anyone the wiser. When they became Reapers, they left their lives, families, and friends behind, allowing everyone to believe they had died. Secrecy was imperative. Death made sure of that because she had foreseen that some might take advantage of knowing a Reaper.

Torin finished off the last of his ale and leaned his arm on the bar as he shifted sideways to look at those behind him. This wasn't the only Fae pub in Dublin. There were others in the heart of the tourist area where mortals walked in without realizing just what type of establishment it was.

Fae had mingled with humans since first coming to the realm. Some Fae—as well as a few Druids—had created certain places that were deemed neutral ground so the Dark and Light Fae, as well as *drough* and *mie* Druids, could mingle without fear of being attacked. The Sly Stag was such an establishment. Torin had visited it before becoming a Reaper. He hadn't liked it then.

He didn't like it now.

If the Fae Council came to fruition, they wouldn't need places like the Sly Stag. Light and Dark had been getting along fine in neutrally defined pubs for eons. They could get along outside of them, too.

Well. Most could.

The bartender caught Torin's eye and jerked his chin toward the door. Torin's gaze fell on the Dark female as she came to a halt just after entering. Her gaze darted around quickly as if searching for someone.

Or hiding.

When she ducked into one of the back hallways, Torin knew she was hiding. From what, was the question. He slid his gaze to Aisling to find that his fellow Reaper had seen their target, as well. Torin tossed money onto the bar to pay for his drink and walked to where the Dark had gone. Aisling untangled the Light Fae from her arm and made her way toward the other hallway.

This wasn't the first tip they had tracked down in an effort to find the Others. Fae everywhere were talking about the group, many touting that they were involved when, in fact, they weren't.

The original Others had been comprised of a *drough* and *mie* Druid from another realm, a *mie* and *drough* Druid from Earth, and a Light and Dark Fae. The six had combined their powers to wipe out the Dragon Kings and take over Earth to claim the magic. Ultimately, the Dragon Kings had triumphed, though it had been close. The Reapers had joined in to help the Kings defeat the Others. When the Others were all gone, everyone believed the threat was over. Unfortunately, the Fae, as well as a group of Druids, were attempting to form their own factions.

Torin was ready to find the Dark female and get whatever

information she had—if she had any at all. He wasn't optimistic after so many failed missions. On top of it all, they had to keep an eye out for the Fae Others, who were most likely trying to track the Reapers and do away with them.

The hallway made a U, complete with private rooms. Light and Dark lovers often met there for dalliances they didn't want their kind to learn about. The rooms were locked with magic, preventing anyone but those renting them from entering. Thankfully, that didn't stop Torin and Aisling from finding their target.

Death, whose real name was Erith, was a goddess. She only had two requirements for someone to become a Reaper: they had to be skilled warriors, and each of them had to have been betrayed—the betrayals leading to their deaths or murders. Erith would come to them right before their last breath and offer them a second chance as a Reaper to do her bidding without question or fail.

Upon acceptance, Death gave a tiny portion of her power to enhance what each already had. A Fae could veil themselves for seconds at a time. A Reaper could veil themselves indefinitely. Their magic also exceeded that of any other individual Fae. The Others combined their magic, which was why the Reapers were concerned.

Erith was the judge and jury for all Fae. She decided when it was time to reap a soul, and that's when she sent the Reapers. It was Death who kept the balance within the Fae. Disrupting that in any way could have dire consequences.

Torin waited until he was in the hallway alone before veiling himself. The Fae could teleport into the pub but not into the rooms. It was done to guarantee the privacy of those renting the spaces. However, that didn't stop a Reaper.

He jumped into each room, searching for the target until he finally found her in the back corner. To his surprise, she was alone on the bed with her back pressed against the headboard, staring at the door as if she expected someone to come through it at any second. Her black and silver hair hung past her shoulders and draped over one side to show that the lower half was shaved. To his amusement, he spotted silver stud earrings in the shape of mushrooms. She wore a white tank top beneath an oversized dark gray sweatshirt that hung off one shoulder. The sleeves were rolled at the cuff and pushed haphazardly up both arms to reveal several bracelets on each wrist, varying from beads to silver and gold. Black jeans were tucked into knee-high biker boots, complete with silver buckles at the ankles.

She had a classic, delicate beauty that unnerved him. Her large eyes were framed with thick lashes and gently arching eyebrows. Her high cheekbones seemed to have a sheen that made them stand out even more. Her full lips were a deep mauve color. She was unbelievably stunning.

The longer Torin watched her, the deeper his frown grew, and the more rattled he became—though he couldn't discern why. He stayed until Aisling appeared. As another added benefit of Erith's powers, Reapers could see each other while veiled. They couldn't, however, speak, or they would be heard.

Aisling jerked her head to the side, motioning for Torin to jump back into the hallway so they could talk. He found himself hesitating after Aisling left. Something about this

Dark female didn't sit right with him. It could be her fear. It was so obvious, he could almost reach out and touch it.

"About damn time," Aisling said when he met her in the hallway with their veils dropped.

Torin glanced at the door that led to the room. "What do you think of her?"

"I think I'm tired of spying on people."

Torin jerked his head to Aisling, her quip not what he'd expected. "What?"

"Nothing," she said with a shake of her head. "She looks petrified."

"Aye."

"Want me to talk to her?"

Torin thought about that for a moment. "She might respond better to you."

"But?" Aisling asked, her brows raised.

"I don't know. There's just something...off...about her."

Aisling rolled her eyes. "Here we go again."

"I know what you're thinking, but it isn't going to happen."

She snorted. "You, Balladyn, and I are the only Reapers who haven't found our mates. The last time I went on a mission with Cathal, he found Sorcha. He also kept saying there was something about her."

"I'm not Cathal, and I'm not looking for anything."

"Yeah, well, it doesn't matter if you're looking or not. When love comes, it'll knock you off your feet whether you're prepared or not."

Torin studied Aisling. They all had pasts. Once they became Reapers, they were no longer Light or Dark. They did, however, keep the coloring of their former lives. Aisling had been a Dark Fae. She never spoke of her past. Hell, none of them did. But if the nightmares she had meant anything, then she had one hell of a former life that hadn't loosened its hold.

Yet, he didn't think her comment about love had anything to do with her past. In fact, he suspected it had something to do with Xaneth, though Aisling would probably never admit to it. She, even more than Death, was intent on finding the royal Light Fae who had been tortured by his aunt and Queen of the Light, Usaeil.

Aisling put her hands on her hips and sighed as she looked around. "Stop it."

"Stop what?" Torin asked, frowning.

"Looking at me like I might fall to pieces any second," she answered as she glared at him with her red eyes.

Torin bowed his head in acknowledgement. "We might not be blood, but we're family. We look out for each other. Always."

"You think I don't know that?" she asked, a tinge of anger in her voice.

"I think we all need to be reminded that we aren't in this alone. That we have others to lean on."

"I've always been alone, Torin. I've only ever been able to depend on myself—until Erith offered me a position as a Reaper. Death may have found us, but it was Eoghan who brought us together."

Torin smiled, thinking of that day. "We've survived so much. We'll get through this."

"First, we need to see what information, if any, our target has."

"I've a feeling she won't open the door."

Aisling twisted her lips. "We can't wait for her to come out."

"She's hiding."

"Then we need to find out who she's running from. Or… we can jump into the room and alert her to who we are."

Torin ran a hand down his face. "We don't have time to wait."

"Nope."

"Fek," he murmured.

Aisling shrugged and knocked on the door.

Torin glared at her.

She smiled, shooting him a sassy look.

Time stretched as the target within didn't utter a sound.

Aisling knocked again. Then, in her best helpless voice, she said, "Hello? Is this room open? I'm trying to get away from someone. All the others are occupied."

Torin turned to lean against the wall, crossing his arms over his chest when the target still didn't reply.

Aisling threw up her hands in defeat.

Torin really didn't want to teleport into the room. He didn't want anyone to know about the Reapers, not to mention, the female could start screaming. Or she could attack them. Neither option was viable. But neither could they wait her out. If she had information, they needed it.

Immediately.

And if she knew who the Reapers were, then she was already dead. Death didn't let anyone who wasn't part of the Reapers know of them and live—unless there were special circumstances and very good reasons.

Torin dropped his arms and turned to Aisling.

"I tried," she whispered.

That only left one choice.

Buy DARK ALPHA'S NEED now at
https://dgrant.co/34Sjhv5

NEXT IN THE DRAGON KINGS SERIES...

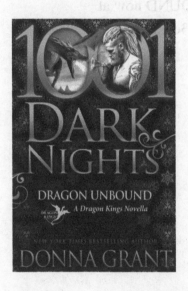

In a new story brimming with sizzling heat and untold mysteries, *New York Times* **bestselling author Donna Grant brings together a devilishly handsome Dragon King and a woman who dares to challenge him.**

He's never been tempted...until her.

Sexy. Mysterious. Dangerous. He's an immortal Dragon King bound by ancient rules and eternal magic. Cullen has one objective: find and destroy the evil that threatens the new home of the dragons. Just when he's closing in, he's ambushed and finds a stunning warrior woman fighting alongside him.

No amount of magic could prepare him for the beguiling lass who spurns his advances and defies him.

From the moment Tamlyn takes a stand against her kind, she's had to fight one perilous battle after another. Staying alive is an endless struggle, and the lines between good and evil are blurred with every encounter. She's always stood alone—until she comes to the aid of an irresistibly handsome stranger. Cullen will force her to face truths she's been running from...even as enemies plot to destroy them both.

Buy DRAGON UNBOUND now at
https://dgrant.co/3dlCkmr

ABOUT THE AUTHOR

New York Times and *USA Today* bestselling author Donna Grant® has been praised for her "totally addictive" and "unique and sensual" stories.

She's written more than one hundred novels spanning multiple genres of romance including the bestselling Dark King series that features a thrilling combination of Dragon Kings®, Druids, Fae, and immortal Highlanders who are dark, dangerous, and irresistible. She lives in Texas with her dog and a cat.

www.DonnaGrant.com
www.MotherofDragonsBooks.com

facebook.com/AuthorDonnaGrant
instagram.com/dgauthor
bookbub.com/authors/donna-grant
amazon.com/Donna-Grant/e/B00279DJGE
pinterest.com/donnagrant1